Trial by Fire

Kelly Cheek

ISBN: 978-0-9909982-8-0

Fiery Muse Publishing
Littleton, Colorado 80129

Printed in the United States of America

Also by Kelly Cheek

All We Hold Dear

The Lost Colony

JackSimile and the Phantom Fury

Profile

Private Messages

Poked

And I will bring the third part through the fire, and will refine them as silver is refined, and will try them as gold is tried.

- Zechariah 13:9

Gold is tried by fire, brave men by adversity.

- Seneca

A wispy tendril of white smoke twisted upward through the trees. Writhing and dancing sinuously during its unhurried ascension, the blowing pine needles sliced and dispersed it a little, before it finally emerged above the top of the trees, where the wind caught it and blew it away.

Down on the ground, and unseen at first, the flame was fanned by the hot dry winds, and it rapidly began to flow along the tinder-dry forest floor with all the unimpeded ease of a wave on the surface of the ocean. Within just a few minutes, a shapeless cloud could be seen beginning to hover over the area known as Black Forest, near Colorado Springs, and northeast of the picturesque little town of Manitou Springs, Colorado.

A 911 call was received and firefighters were dispatched, but the weather was working against them. A 'perfect storm' combination of high temperatures, low humidity and gusty winds over the course of the next few days would thwart the combined efforts of multiple fire departments, the Colorado Air National Guard and even the United States Air Force Academy, situated just north of Colorado Springs.

In a matter of days, the "Black Forest Fire" would become the state's most destructive fire in history.

§

Dora Baskin was resting her head on her hand, holding the phone with the other, trying not to sigh audibly.

"I've seen the news, Ms. Baskin," the caller said, with an irritated 'I don't believe you' tone in her voice. "Colorado is on fire, and I saw on the map how close that Black Forest Fire is to Manitou Springs."

"I understand, Mrs. Rutherford," Dora said, forcing a calm tone of voice. "I'm just letting you know that the media does tend to sensationalize things a bit."

"You're saying that the Black Forest fire is not a big deal? Shepard Smith did a whole segment about it. You're saying he's lying?"

"No, ma'am, I'm not saying that at all. I'm just saying that, here in Manitou Springs, the fire is not currently a threat. It's on the other side of the interstate and blowing north, away from here. We can't even smell any smoke here."

"Well, my husband and I have decided that we're not going to Colorado. We don't want to take the chance. We're going someplace else for our vacation this year, so I want to cancel our reservation."

"Yes, ma'am. I'll cancel your reservation and refund your deposit right away."

"Okay, then. Thank you." Mrs. Rutherford sounded relieved before disconnecting.

Dora had the reservation software up on the computer in front of her. She clicked the "Cancel" button and issued the refund.

Now she gave in to a sigh. The Rutherfords had reserved the Atsila Suite, the largest and most expensive one in the inn. Now, it was open, with no immediate prospects for filling it anytime soon.

Dora's assistant, Robin Murphy, heard the sigh and looked up from where she was cleaning nearby in the kitchen.

"Another cancellation?" she asked with a sympathetic tone. Dora just nodded. She minimized the reservation program and stood up, coming out of the little cubbyhole office that she had made, just off the kitchen. She rotated her head, trying to stretch and loosen her neck muscles.

"July's less than three weeks away," Dora said, "and we don't have any week-day reservations, and only a couple of weekend reservations. And those are locals who know what it's really like here. The media coverage of the fire is killing us. Looks like the tourist season is going to be pretty slow this year."

Dora was a beautiful, vivacious young woman, with golden hair and naturally tanned skin, which she acquired, to varying degrees, from both of her parents.

Robin, on the other hand, was a slight woman, kind of mousy and quiet, with fair skin and black hair. Dora had found her to be shy and reserved when she first met her almost a year ago, but now she knew her to be friendly and witty.

"It'll pick up," Robin said, trying to be encouraging. "They'll get the fire put out and people will come."

"I know." Dora forced a smile. "And it doesn't help that my B&B is still less than a year old. I guess I should expect some setbacks early on."

Dora walked out of the kitchen, toward the front of the house. She remembered what the place had looked like when she first inherited it. The interior of the enormous log house had been covered with fingerprint dust from the investigation following the murder of Dora's grandmother upstairs.

Coming through the front door that first time, the large foyer, where Dora was now standing, had been quite bare, with just a small table and chair arrangement and a combination coat rack and bench. Dora had gotten more furniture, to create a welcoming entryway for the guests, with a large antique desk for check-in.

Most of the other rooms had been furnished in old but comfortable furniture. Many of the pieces were valuable antiques. Aside from updating the arrangement of the furniture, Dora had kept the rooms pretty much as they had been.

She went out the front door and onto the massive wrap-around porch. She couldn't see the fire from here – she could barely see the distant smoke over the top of the trees in front of the house. Just looking around the property, despite the loss of business, still made her feel better.

It was an almost idyllic setting. Beyond the gravel parking areas in front was the road, one which, fortunately, didn't have much traffic, making Isadora's Bed and Breakfast a quiet and tranquil destination. Contributing to this tranquility was what used to be a river back in the time of her ancestor, Isadora Byrnes. Now it was more like a creek, but it still gurgled peacefully down the southern side of the property, on Dora's right. It passed under the road in front of the inn, and then continued north and east, down toward town.

Dora heard footsteps and looked up as Robin joined her on the porch. She had her purse over her shoulder. They sat down in two of the many welcoming Adirondack chairs that dotted the porch.

"I don't mean to be a lazy bum," Dora said. "I feel like I should be doing something."

Robin shook her head. "Breakfast is over now and the kitchen's clean. We only have two guests, and all the vacant rooms are clean. There's nothing that really needs to be done. Looks like you're off the hook."

"I guess so," Dora sighed as she leaned back in her chair.

"I guess that means I am too, right boss?"

"Sure, you're done for the day."

"Good," Robin said. "Today's our anniversary, and we're going out tonight. I want to have some time to get ready before Colin gets home."

"Oh, absolutely! Go," Dora smiled. "Happy anniversary!"

"Thanks. I'll see you tomorrow." Robin stood up and walked down the steps, then got into her car. She waved through the windshield at Dora as she backed out of the space. Dora smiled at her and waved back as Robin drove away.

Dora's life had changed drastically a year ago. She had been a social worker in Denver, working at placing underprivileged and homeless people into government programs that could help them get back on their feet and be self-sufficient. Her daily exposure to the dark underbelly of society was often depressing, and while her efforts were sometimes rewarding, the job took its toll.

When her grandmother was murdered, Dora inherited this house, along with a sizable portfolio of stocks and bonds. She could hardly believe that she had survived the following week, which included finding a valuable coin collection in the house, and the evasion of Irish mobsters who were after the treasure.

After auctioning the treasure for nearly thirty million dollars, Dora used the money to establish a trust fund for Cherokee Indians, her own distant relatives, living in a poor community in New Mexico. She quit her job and moved to Manitou Springs to turn the house into a bed and breakfast, but she still felt the need to give. So she volunteered some time, usually once or twice a week, at a Colorado Springs orphanage and adoption agency.

Robin was barely out of sight when a rusty old Datsun, leaving a trail of blue smoke, pulled up in front of Dora and parked. She didn't recognize the car. In fact, it didn't look like anything that her usual clientele would drive.

She watched curiously as a man looked at her through the glare of the windshield. There was something oddly familiar about him. He pulled himself out of the car, his white hair and beard catching the sun. He slammed the car door and looked up at Dora, and Dora's breath caught in her throat.

"Hello, Dorie," he said.

"Daddy?"

§

Dora and her father were sitting in the living room. When he first arrived, she thought that he had made a move to hug her, but she wasn't sure she was ready for that. She purposely chose a chair, instead of the sofa or love seat.

"I thought you were dead!" Dora said with tears shimmering on her eyelids.

"Why did you think that?"

"Why?" Dora scoffed. "You were a mess. You disappeared eight years ago, just walked away from your family who desperately needed you. You never made any contact in all that time, not even a card to just let us know you're alive. Mom was severely depressed to the point of finally cutting her wrists, and still no word from you."

"I know, honey," he said sadly. "I'm sorry. I just couldn't take it any longer myself. Like you said, your mother was depressed, which made me depressed. I wasn't doing her any good. I just thought the best thing for everybody was for me to go away."

"And leave *me* to deal with mother by myself."

"That wasn't right, Dorie. I know that. I'm not making any excuses for my actions. And I know I don't deserve your forgiveness."

He left the thought hanging there, as if he was hoping that she would pick up on it and happily bestow forgiveness upon him. Dora looked at him, not knowing whether to forgive him or hate him.

"Even when your own mother was murdered here in this house," she said, her voice hardening a little, "still not a word from you."

He looked down at his hands, folded in his lap, as if he were ashamed to meet her eyes.

"So, why now?" Dora asked.

"I'm an old man," he replied with a sigh. He dragged his eyes back up to Dora's. "I decided I didn't want to die with this between us."

"Are you dying?"

"You never know." He smiled a tired smile, but when he got no reaction from Dora, he decided that the time was apparently not right for flippancy. "I'm not sick, if that's what you mean, but there *is* that old saying about spring chickens. The end is getting closer every day."

He gazed out the window for a few moments, lost in thought.

"We had you late in life, honey. I was forty years old when you were born. I'm seventy-three now. I'm definitely on the back stretch, and I just decided it was time to make up with my baby."

"That's kind of a tall order, don't you think?"

"Yes," he said looking back at her face. "Yes, I do. Dorie, I know I can't make up for all the shit I put you and your mother through. You didn't deserve that, and neither did she. But I'm hoping you'll let me do whatever I can now to prove that I really am sorry."

Dora looked at him with mixed feelings. She looked at his face, lined with age and regret. She looked at his clothes which had also seen better days.

"Where are you staying?" she asked.

"I haven't gotten a place yet."

"You look tired."

"Yeah, I am. I've been driving for a while. I slept in the car for a couple of hours, just west of Strasburg, but that's about it."

She studied his haggard face for a few more seconds before responding.

"You can stay in the Danny O'Riordan Room," she said, her voice lacking emotion.

She stood up, again without making contact. After going to her cubbyhole office in the kitchen to retrieve a key, she led him upstairs. He pulled himself up the steps slowly and Dora already had the door to a room open by the time he caught up with her.

"Thank you, honey," he said as she dropped the key in his hand. "Looks like you've done very well. I'm proud of you."

"Thanks," Dora replied, still conflicted. "Why don't you lie down and get a little rest. We can talk more later."

He nodded as she closed the door. He looked around the room – the Danny O'Riordan Room as she had called it. He remembered somebody in the family history named Danny O'Riordan.

Having grown up in this house, he was familiar with the room, but it had never looked like this. Dora obviously had a flair for decorating. The room was comfortable, with numerous pieces of artwork and fabric prints depicting bobcats in the wild. Something like that could easily have been overdone, but the room was tasteful.

Clark Baskin eased himself down onto the bed, feeling all seventy-three of his years. He hadn't realized how tired he was until he lay back on the bed.

He was so fatigued, his body almost ached. The stress had been wearing on him, and he just didn't have the stamina he used to have when he was younger. He took a deep breath and slowly blew it out, feeling himself relax a little, for the first time in several days.

Seeing Dora again conjured up the past in his mind. But as he lay there, his mind kept going back, remembering his own younger days. In fact, it went beyond that, for his story, and what led him to this point in his life, all the lessons unlearned, actually began with his father.

Colorado City, just east of Manitou Springs, was founded as a supply hub, via Ute Pass, between Denver and the new gold mines in central Colorado. After only a year, though, a more direct road was built from Denver to the mines, leaving Colorado City out of the equation. After this, the town became an agricultural community.

Colorado City served as the capitol of the new Colorado Territory, for about five days in 1861. The legislative body met there only once, in a tiny log cabin. They very quickly decided that the accommodations, and the decidedly questionable reputation of the town, were not suited to their needs and promptly moved to Denver.

With the discovery of gold in Cripple Creek on the southwest side of Pikes Peak, Colorado City became a bustling community, now serving the mining industry. Gold mills and smelters were kept busy refining the ore coming in from the rich gold fields.

To support the booming mining industry, other industries of varied reputes also thrived. Some of those businesses were not ones that the higher class residents of nearby Manitou and Colorado Springs cared to be seen frequenting, but Colorado City's discreet network of underground tunnels allowed people to come and go without sullying their reputations.

It was in this town that Silas Baskin was born in 1886, the same year that Grover Cleveland became the only president to get married in the White House. The year the Statue of Liberty was assembled on Bedloe's Island in New York Harbor. The Civil War was twenty-one years in the past, while Colorado had been a state for only ten years.

Born to Cheri Baskin, a poor prostitute, Silas never knew who his father was, although if he was a regular, it's likely that Silas may have seen him a few times.

Goldie's was not a terribly prosperous saloon, being on a side street, and on the eastern outskirts of Colorado City. But it did have a small, loyal following. And it had one advantage of being one of the first saloons to greet visitors arriving from Colorado Springs.

Goldie herself, a woman who had seen her prime a couple of decades before, was usually upstairs with the rest of the ladies, and she always tried to treat her people well. This included allowing Cheri to bring Silas to work with her.

Sometimes, between customers, Cheri would take the time to play with Silas and nurse him. When she was occupied, the other ladies would watch him and dote on him, so some of his earliest and fondest memories were of the brothel, and of Goldie and the other ladies who worked there.

When she was not at work, Cheri tried to teach him right from wrong. Silas never thought about the incongruity of a prostitute teaching him about God and morals, about honesty and hard work. He didn't think of her occupation in terms of being right or wrong, it was just what she had to do to live and to support her little family.

As he grew, he enjoyed greater freedom, indeed more than most children of his age. He roamed about the dusty streets of Colorado City, learning whatever tricks were necessary for a poor child to survive.

Especially was this true after his mother died.

§

"Big man of fourteen, huh?" Odin, the bartender at Goldie's was a big man himself. His big, round, ruddy face was covered with a big, bushy blonde mustache and topped by a big head of blonde hair. He was leaning with one elbow on the bar. As usual, he had his long barreled Colt 45 revolver stuck through his belt.

"Yes, sir," Silas said with a broad smile. It was March of 1900, and it was Silas' fourteenth birthday. He was big for his age, a tall, powerful-looking young man. And this evening, he was wearing his best clothes, dressed for a night out.

"What are your plans for tonight?" Odin asked.

"My mother's taking me out to Tucker's Restaurant for dinner."

"Tucker's Restaurant?"

21

"Yes, sir. It's a nice restaurant in Colorado Springs. She's taking the night off work, to spend it with me." Silas had eaten meals in saloons, like Goldie's, but never in a nice restaurant, and he was anxiously looking forward to it.

Their conversation was interrupted by the din of whistles and cheers. At the sound, Silas and Odin turned to see Cheri coming down the stairs. She was wearing a nice dress and had toned down the makeup she was wearing. Silas thought she looked beautiful, and Cheri, smiling to her applauding audience, curtsied in response to the attention.

Silas got up from his stool and went to her as she reached the landing three steps up from the floor. The whistles had quieted down now, as the people in the saloon looked at Cheri and Silas. They smiled as they heard hushed expressions of "beautiful," "isn't she pretty?" and "what a charming couple."

At that moment, just below them, four men, armed with revolvers, made their way quietly through the tunnel under the street, hoping to make a surprise appearance in the little den of iniquity. A radical temperance group from dry Colorado Springs had taken it upon themselves to clean up their rowdy next door neighbor, Colorado City. They were going to cut their teeth on the little saloon on the outskirts of town. Their desire was to force them to stop the flow of alcohol, and the immorality that took place upstairs.

It did not go quite as they had planned.

Coming up the stairs from the tunnel, they had hoped to slip quietly into the saloon, unnoticed, until they had positioned themselves to their advantage. They had not expected someone to be leaning against the door. The element of surprise now taken from them, all eyes were on them as the door was opened, and they slowly, nervously came into the bar. The patrons were suspicious, to say the least.

That the four men were tensely fingering their guns didn't help.

One of the intruders pulled his gun and pointed it at the first threat he saw, the big bartender. Odin, still behind the bar, had already pulled his Colt 45 from his belt at the first sign of trouble. The intruder did not have time to fire a shot before he fell dead with a bullet in his brain.

Other customers had guns with them as well. Shots were fired from both sides, but in less than a minute, the four men lay dead, barely ten feet inside the door from the tunnel.

The danger past, the smoke hanging thick in the air, the guests were beginning to return to their drinks. It was then that Justine, Cheri's best friend, noticed Silas crouched on the landing of the stairs, crying.

At his feet was Cheri, a bullet through her chest.

§

Silas, stepping up onto the front porch of the boarding house where he had lived with his mother, was approached by the landlord, a hefty man of about fifty.

"I heard about your mother," he said quietly. "I'm sorry, son."

"Thank you, Mr. Wilcox." Silas' face was streaked from the tears he had cried.

"Will you be able to pay the rent?"

Silas looked at him, trying to hold back the tears again. With all that had happened that evening, he hadn't thought about rent, or the cost of food, or any other expenses for that matter, but he knew that he had no income.

"I don't know, sir," he replied, hesitant to give a definitive answer to the negative.

"Do you have any money?"

"No, sir."

Wilcox looked out onto the street, at the scattered people passing by in the twilight, and he sighed.

"I see. Well, I'm afraid you're going to have to move out."

"Where am I supposed to go?" the boy asked, tears quivering on his lower eyelids.

"I don't know, son. But I need the room for paying tenants."

Silas looked away as the tears fell again, his shoulders shaking with his silent sobs.

"Alright, son," Wilcox said, overcome by a sudden surge of benevolence. "You can stay overnight, but you'll have to clear out in the morning."

Silas nodded, unable to speak, and he went upstairs into the room and closed the door. The only family he had ever known was gone. Throwing himself down on the lumpy bed, he cried harder than he ever had in his life.

He finally fell asleep in the early morning hours and had managed to snatch a couple of fitful hours of sleep. Morning arrived with Wilcox pounding on the door. He already had someone interested in occupying the room and was now in a hurry for Silas to vacate it.

Under the watchful eye of his former landlord, and presumably the new tenant standing beside him, the boy gathered his few articles of clothing and put them in a worn satchel. He found a tin of biscuits, and a tarnished silver frame containing a photograph of his mother, taken years before when she was young, pretty and still relatively unused. He placed them in the satchel as well. He cast a quick glance around the room, then turned toward the door.

"Good bye, Mr. Wilcox," Silas said softly as he walked out.

"Good bye, son. Good luck."

Silas plodded down the stairs and out the front door, squinting into the cool and bright early spring sunshine. The air was frosty, but the brilliant golden light reflecting off the new leaves of the trees just seemed contradictory to the way he felt.

At first, he just wandered the streets, unexpectedly frightened by them. They were familiar to him, of course, but at the same time, they were now different. Before, when he was out on his own, he had a home and a mother to come back to. Now, he was all by himself in the world.

That evening, Silas curled up on the ground in an alleyway, wrapped in only his dirty coat. After a fitful and uncomfortable night, Silas knew he had to do something.

He tried panhandling – he had done it a few times when he was younger. But he found that people just didn't respond with as much generosity to a fourteen-year-old boy who was big for his age as they did to a cute little child.

His second day on his own, he was hungry. He had eaten the few biscuits that had been left in the tin the day before. Now he had nothing. As the day progressed, his stomach began complaining loudly, and the boy was feeling weak.

On the third day, after having nothing at all to eat the day before, Silas felt desperate. He hadn't planned on it, the thought hadn't even occurred to him, but as he passed a display of apples in front of a store, he took one. He waited until the busy storekeeper was distracted by someone else and his back was turned, then Silas snatched up the apple and quickly stuffed it in his coat pocket.

Walking hastily away, at the edge of town, he turned a corner and sat on a fence. He ate the apple as he cried and prayed for forgiveness. He knew he had to find a way to get some money. He didn't want to be looked down on as a sinner and a thief by God, or worse, by his mother.

The thought of his mother brought tears to his eyes again. He knew that, while she hadn't seemed to feel guilty about what she had done for a living, she hadn't really liked it either. But she had needed to make money.

Knowing what their life had been like, Silas knew that her job really hadn't paid that much. They had lived in poverty his whole life, barely having what they needed to survive. They always had food and a place to sleep, but not much more than that.

Now that she was gone, he had even less, and was now reduced to stealing apples to fill his stomach. He knew he couldn't keep that up.

He vowed that he would find a way to not be poor any longer. He didn't know how, but he would do whatever he had to do to never experience poverty again.

Silas wiped the tears from his eyes as he finished the apple, and he looked up. A large stone building stood across the street, with a constant muffled din emanating from it. Silas had been too distracted by his stolen apple, and his thoughts of his mother, to even notice it until now.

Under a sign that said "Hodges' Mill," there was a "Help Wanted" sign in a window of the front office. He had never had a job before, and he wasn't sure how to get one. He decided that it wouldn't hurt to ask.

He picked up his satchel and walked across the street, careful to avoid the scattered piles of horse manure. He stepped up onto the sidewalk, looking up at the imposing edifice.

He opened the door which made a bell ring over his head, and two men looked up. One was a handsome young man with blonde hair, dressed in a brown suit, leaning over a desk. The other man was older and was in his shirt sleeves, sitting at the desk. The man in the suit smiled. The older man looked impatient and grumpy.

"What do you need, boy?" the older man asked.

Silas cleared his throat and suddenly realized how dirty and unkempt he must look. He looked down at his clothes, wrinkled and soiled from his night in the alley, and he felt a sudden wave of embarrassment wash over him.

"Well?" the man asked impatiently. Silas took a deep breath.

"I would like a job, sir," he said.

"I'm sorry, boy, we got nothing for you."

"But that sign," Silas said, pointing to the window.

"Are you a bookkeeper?"

"No, sir."

"Then we got nothing for you."

"Yes, sir," Silas said with a disappointed tone, and he turned to leave. "Thank you, sir."

He opened the door, ringing the bell again.

"Hold on, son," the other man said. "What's your name?" He was walking away from the other man's desk, coming toward the counter. He seemed to be looking intently at Silas. Silas closed the door and turned back toward him.

"Silas, sir. Silas Baskin."

"How old are you, Silas?"

"Seventeen, sir." Silas felt another twinge of guilt. If the man knew he was lying, he gave no indication of it. He looked Silas over for a few moments before replying.

"Do you have any work experience with gold extraction or refining?"

"No, sir." Silas noticed that the older man sneered and shook his head, looking back down at the papers on his desk. Silas looked back at the younger man.

"Well, what can you do?"

"Anything you show me, sir."

The young man smiled again. It looked to Silas as if there might have been a trace of admiration in the man's eyes.

"Why don't you come with me, Silas. Let me show you around."

Silas looked back and forth between the two men. The older man looked unhappy and irritated, and he focused his attention again on his work. But the well-dressed younger man was lifting a hinged section of the counter and beckoning him through.

He held his hand out toward Silas. "I'm John Hodges," he said. Silas shook his hand.

"How do you do, sir?"

§

Hodges showed Silas around the mill. The immense building was even larger than it looked in front. Just behind the front offices, the structure cascaded in steps or terraces down the hillside. It was a noisy operation, with the steam engines on one end, powering the grinders that chewed the ore into sand.

Silas was a little mystified by the huge vats where the ground up ore was soaking in a cyanide solution, and being agitated to extract the gold from it.

The workers generally seemed to be somewhat welcoming toward Silas, and they displayed a certain deference or respect to Hodges.

Hodges put Silas to work right away, doing various odd jobs around the mill. It was mainly cleaning up, manual labor, but Silas didn't mind. He got to know his broom and his shovel very well.

Having a job that he had to go to every day took some getting used to, but receiving income certainly helped. And he learned that hard work attracted the notice of management, and reaped greater rewards.

Here at Hodges' Mill, management was primarily the owner, John Hodges himself, who did indeed take notice of Silas' hard work.

A couple of days after he started, Silas was standing on the sidewalk in front of the building, trying to decide where to go. He heard the bell on the door ring as Hodges came out from the front office. He was wearing a long duster but was still holding his hat in his hands.

"How do you like it here, son?" he asked Silas.

"I like it just fine, sir."

"Good." Hodges paused, looking around. He seemed to know a lot of people. Men and women alike would smile and greet him by name as they passed, and he always smiled and greeted them in return.

"Where are you from, Silas?" he asked, turning back to the boy. "Your family around here?"

"No, sir," Silas replied nervously.

Hodges looked at him for a moment, then leaned closer to him in something of a conspiratorial posture, speaking quietly. "Do you have a family, Silas?"

Tears started forming in Silas' eyes, but he fought them back. "No, sir," he said, looking up at Hodges. "My mother died a few days ago."

An expression of sympathy washed over Hodges' face, and he put a hand on Silas' shoulder. "Oh, I'm so sorry. What about your father?"

"I don't know him."

Hodges looked at Silas' clothing, the same clothing he had been wearing for the last few days, and at the satchel that he always carried with him.

"Where are you staying, son?"

The combination of the questions and the physical contact was making it difficult for Silas to hold back his emotions, and he took a moment before he responded.

"Wherever I can find, sir."

"All right," Hodges said with a nod. Putting his hat on, he guided Silas to the side of the building, away from the street. "Come with me."

Silas thought he was in trouble, that perhaps somehow he had gotten caught in a lie and was being sacked for it. He followed Hodges apprehensively, and they rounded the northern corner of the building and came around to a small stable and corral. Hodges approached a brown and white paint mare, untied her and climbed up into the saddle.

"Up you go," he said, offering Silas his hand.

"I don't understand, sir," Silas said.

"You're coming home with me. I can give you a hot meal and a warm bed. You're already a good worker, Silas. But you'll be even better, and of more use to me, if you're well-rested and well-fed."

"I don't know what to say, sir."

"You don't have to say anything, son." Silas just stood there, still undecided. He looked around, trying to make up his mind. "It is a bit of a walk, though," Hodges continued, "so you might want to get up on the horse." He smiled and slipped his foot out of the stirrup, still holding his hand out to the boy. Silas stepped into the stirrup, took his hand and swung up onto the horse behind him.

"Thank you, sir."

Hodges turned his horse and they came out of the stable into the sunshine. It had been a beautiful day, almost spring, and the sinking sun still shone brightly ahead of them. They rode at a leisurely pace through Colorado City, west up Colorado Avenue and eventually past the red rock hogbacks outside of town.

After a few minutes' ride, they entered Manitou. Silas had been here a couple of times before, a few years ago, when his mother brought him to sample the legendary waters. He remembered that the water tasted a little odd, but he liked the town.

Now, though, Silas was captivated by the grand homes, hotels and boarding houses lining Manitou Avenue, the main street through town. A riotous tangle of wires, supported by tall poles lining the street, passed overhead, supplying electricity to many of the buildings in the bustling resort town. To Silas, the buildings appeared almost as imposing and majestic as palaces.

About the time they reached the twin conical-roofed shelters over the Navajo and Cheyenne Springs, with the sprawling Cliff House Hotel in the background, Silas heard a bell sound behind them. Turning around to find the source of the sound, he saw a trolley car trundling toward them, drawing its power through an arm on top, from one of those overhead wires.

Silas watched, fascinated, as the trolley car passed by them on its track, magically pulled along without the need of a horse. A few people were sitting down inside the trolley, probably on their way home from work, some reading newspapers, while others jumped on or off while it was moving.

The car reached its station at Ruxton Avenue where the tracks formed a loop, and the trolley turned around, ready for its return trip down to Colorado Springs.

Hodges and Silas had ridden all the way through Manitou, and yet they kept going, ascending the mountain roughly westward. A river appeared on their left, with a well-worn path alongside it, and they followed the path, into the deepening shadows of a forested area.

Dusk was falling, and there was a chill in the air. They emerged into a clearing, and an immense log house, larger than any Silas had ever seen, appeared in front of them. The windows glowed with a welcoming warmth.

"My great grandmother, Isadora, and her family built this house," Hodges explained as he pointed at the big house. "She's an Englishwoman who settled here before there was even a town. Now this place is an inn. Isadora and her daughter Clara, my grandmother, still run it."

They didn't stop there, though. They continued riding up the trail, past a couple of stone houses. Then they arrived at another log house. Though it had been enlarged over the years, it still was not nearly as large as the one they had passed.

But it looked just as warm and welcoming.

"This is where my wife and I live," Hodges said. "During the busy season, if the inn is full, we take on guests here, too. My wife helps out at the inn, unless we have guests staying with us."

As they approached, a young man trotted toward them from the barn, meeting them at the front porch.

"Good evening, Mr. Hodges," he said as he took the reins. Hodges helped Silas down from the horse, then climbed down himself.

"Good evening, Ethan," Hodges replied. He motioned toward Silas. "Meet Silas Baskin."

"Hello, Silas," Ethan said with a friendly smile. "Welcome."

"Thank you, sir."

Ethan began leading the horse away, toward the barn. Hodges guided Silas, with a hand on his shoulder, up a couple of steps to the front door. The door was opened by a woman who seemed to be about Hodges' age. Unlike him, though, she had darker skin and shiny black hair.

"Hello, Abbie," Hodges said, as they entered the house, and he gave her a quick kiss on the cheek.

"Welcome home, dear," she said, and she cast a curious glance toward Silas. Silas was hesitant, still standing in the doorway, but Hodges again placed a hand on his shoulder and conducted him in, closing the door behind them.

"Abbie, say hello to Silas Baskin," Hodges said. "Silas, I'd like you to meet my wife, Abigail." Hodges had taken off his hat and duster and hung them on a hook on the wall, and was helping Silas out of the ragged and dirty coat he was wearing.

"How do you do, ma'am," Silas said quietly, with a slight head bow.

"Hello, Silas." Abigail smiled at him, then looked back at Hodges. "Dinner is almost ready."

"Good," he said. "Abbie, Silas is going to stay with us for a while."

"Wonderful," she said without a moment's hesitation. "Come with me and I'll show you to your room where you can get cleaned up." She started up the staircase to their right, and when Silas hesitated again, she held a hand out, motioning for him to follow her.

At the top of the stairs, Abbie opened a door and conducted him into one of the guest rooms. The bedroom was larger than the room he and his mother had lived in.

Against one wall there was a comfortable looking bed, covered in blankets and quilts. On the other side of the room was a lowboy and a tall wardrobe, both constructed of mahogany. On top of the lowboy was a pitcher and bowl.

"I hope you'll be comfortable here," Abbie said. "If there's anything you need, please let us know."

"Thank you, ma'am," Silas said, and Abbie quietly left, closing the door behind her.

Silas looked around the room. There was a window looking toward the east, in the general direction from which he and Hodges had come. In the deepening dusk, he could just make out the trail they had ridden in on, and flashes of moonlight sparkling on the river.

He went to the lowboy and poured water from the pitcher into the bowl and washed his hands and face. Just as he was feeling embarrassed about his dirty clothes, there was a knock on his door. Silas opened it and saw John Hodges standing in the hallway, holding some folded clothing.

"These belonged to my little brother," he said quietly. "He died a couple of years ago. I think they might fit you. You're welcome to them."

Feeling a flood of emotion, the boy took the clothes from him with a quiet 'thank you.' Hodges took his leave with another smile, leaving Silas to change.

A few minutes later, he went downstairs, washed and wearing clean clothes which were only a little too large for him. He could hear silverware clinking against dishes, and the voices of people near the back of the house, but Abbie greeted him at the bottom of the stairs.

"John just told me you lost your mother," she said quietly, her face filled with sympathy. Her eyes were even glazed with tears. "I am so very sorry."

She put her arms around him and held him close, and Silas couldn't hold back his emotions any longer. Holding Abbie tightly, desperately, he cried racking sobs against her shoulder.

§

On his second evening with the Hodges, they had gone down the road to the inn for dinner so that John Hodges could introduce Silas to his relatives. The great grandmother took a bit of an interest in him.

The old woman was short, several inches shorter than Silas, and was bent over a little besides. Due to her age and her infirmity, she was living in a room on the main floor at the back of the house. The room, Silas learned, had originally been used as a medical clinic when the house was first built decades before, treating Indians and trappers in the area. More recently, though, they had turned it into a bedroom so the elderly woman would not have to climb the stairs.

Her hair was silver, but rather than piling it on top of her head as older women usually did, she pulled it back, secured with a strip of rawhide and a mother-of-pearl comb, and allowed it to hang down loose behind her shoulders.

Her clothing was unusual, too. She wore a dress made of deerskin, decorated with beads and ribbons. There were several jewelry items around her wrists and throat, made with beads, stones and feathers. She also had what appeared to be a bobcat tail on a leather thong around her neck.

Aside from her facial features, her fair skin, and her very light blue eyes, Silas thought she might be an Indian. But when she spoke, he was sure she wasn't.

"Hello, dear boy," she said with a smile and an English accent. "Welcome to my home. It's so very nice to meet you."

"Thank you, Mrs. O'Riordan," Silas said.

"Please, call me Isadora," she said, and she extended her hand.

Silas took her hand, and was surprised. He had never shaken an old person's hand before. Hers was thin. He could easily feel all the bones through her delicate skin, and he was afraid to hold it too tightly. But it was very soft, and she squeezed his hand with an unexpected strength.

Her daughter Clara, Hodges' grandmother, was quite nice too, but she didn't have an accent. Her hair was part blonde and part silver, and was arranged in an elegant coiffure. She was attired nicely, wearing a dress more in keeping with the style of white women in the area.

Silas had little experience at judging a person's age. He knew Clara was old, but she was still a very pretty woman, really elegant looking.

"Please come in, Silas," she said with a sweet and becoming smile. "We're just about to sit down to dinner."

"Thank you, ma'am."

There were four other guests staying there at that time, and Silas was introduced to them and promptly forgot their names. The food which Isadora and Clara prepared together was delicious, and the atmosphere very friendly. Everyone sat comfortably around a yellow pine table that nearly filled the spacious dining room.

During the lively discussion during dinner, Silas learned that Isadora's husband, Danny, had died after being gored by an elk almost twenty years before. Her first husband was a Cherokee Indian, so Clara was part Cherokee herself.

Clara's husband, Peter, a doctor like his father had been, was also there. His father had been the one who had designed and built the house, and who had practiced in the medical clinic that was now Isadora's bedroom. Peter was nearly seventy years old and was looking forward to retiring.

Silas also learned that John and Abbie had lost their young son to tuberculosis a few months before. Abbie, whose father was an Arapaho Indian, was very attentive to Silas, making sure he had everything he needed.

By the time the evening was over and Silas and the Hodges returned to their home up the trail, Silas felt warm and well-fed.

And loved.

ora was back in her chair on the front porch, pondering the sudden unexpected appearance of her father. She felt something akin to disorientation. So many years had passed without hearing from her father or knowing anything about him. Remembering what she knew about him, what he had been like before he disappeared, Dora had gradually come to believe that he was most likely dead. Now he had unceremoniously plummeted back into her life.

Her thoughts meandered backwards into the past. Dora saw her life as if through a sort of gloomy filter, as her mother had been prone to frequent bouts of depression for as long as she could remember. Thinking back on it now, it seemed to her that her father *did* seem to have been influenced or affected by it too.

He had often been in a bad mood, sometimes giving in to fits of temper. Dora was not usually the focus of his anger, but she did feel his wrath on occasion. As far as Dora could tell, it began, or at least she started to notice it, about the time of his father's death.

Dora was only about six years old when Grampa died. She remembered traveling as a family to Manitou Springs to attend his funeral. She was mainly curious since she had never been to a funeral before.

Dora remembered not really being that sad. She had not been that close to Grampa. He was extremely old. Not just as a young child thinks of old, but *really* old. Thinking back, Dora knew, from hearing the tale related later on, that he had always been in good physical condition. But he had suddenly begun to deteriorate very quickly and had started having unusual symptoms.

At first, he had started experiencing joint pain. Gramma called the doctor about it, who wrote it off as arthritis. The doctor said that Grampa should consider himself lucky that it had not bothered him until so late in life. Grampa soon became easily fatigued and couldn't get enough sleep. The doctor said that that was not at all uncommon with elderly people, and that he should just listen to his body and sleep when he needed to.

When Grampa's arms and legs became paralyzed, the doctor decided that it was time to do some tests. Grampa was checked into the hospital where his liver and kidneys shut down almost immediately. He died within a day.

The minister who spoke at the funeral said that Grampa had lived a very long and productive life. But Dora's father had been deeply affected by his death. He had made numerous trips to Manitou, to visit him when he was sick, and now that Grampa had died, he sank into a deep depression.

Mother, of course, was little help, and others said that her father was simply mourning. Indeed, in time, he did seem to come out of it.

But he was different. He was short-tempered, and would get angry with little provocation. Dora quickly learned to keep her distance when she saw the signs.

§

A shift in the wind carried a faint, brief scent of smoke to Dora's nostrils, bringing her back to the present. But the scent was gone just as quickly.

She took a deep breath and sighed, looking at her surroundings. The forest, the creek, the vast sky overhead. It always calmed her.

Today, there was something else, though. A tense feeling just below the surface that she couldn't quite pinpoint.

She heard a familiar, gradually amplifying hum, and she looked at the road to the left, where it emerged from the forest. Within a few seconds, a royal blue Malibu convertible pulled into the parking area. Seeing Dora on the porch, Shawn waved as he killed the motor, but he took a minute to put the top back up.

Shawn Murphy was part owner of an estate appraisal and liquidation business called Estate of Mind, along with his brother Colin, Robin's husband. Dora had met him the year before, after her grandmother was killed. Thinking that this house was too much for her to handle, Dora was considering selling it and had called Shawn, who then proceeded to talk her out of selling it. In fact, he was the one who had introduced the idea of turning it into a bed and breakfast.

He looked briefly at the rusty old Datsun, then came bounding up the steps toward Dora. She stood up to greet him.

"Hi baby," Shawn said.

"Hi," Dora replied as she practically fell into his arms. She hadn't realized until this moment how much she needed some companionship.

"Well, that's some welcome!" Shawn held her tightly for a few moments. "Another guest?" he asked, gesturing toward the ancient Datsun.

"Yeah, you could say that." Dora uttered a deep sigh, then looked up into Shawn's face. "My dad showed up." Shawn pushed her away by the shoulders to see her face better.

"Your father? He's alive?"

"It would seem so."

"That's great! So you're not an orphan anymore."

Dora shrugged and raised her eyebrows in an expression that Shawn took as being noncommittal, or perhaps unimpressed.

"You don't seem to be that happy about it, though," he said.

"Well, I'm not sure how to feel about it. I mean, how do you just welcome someone back into your life, when you obviously didn't mean enough to them for them to stick around in the first place? And especially after they just left you to deal with your morbidly depressed and suicidal mother all by yourself?"

"Yeah, I guess that would be tough."

"I've just got such mixed feelings about seeing him again."

"So, he's here now?"

"He's upstairs," Dora nodded. "He was tired, so he's resting in the Danny O'Riordan room." She sat back down in her chair and Shawn sat in the one next to her. She seemed lost in her thoughts. "He seems so old. I didn't realize how old he was until he showed up here."

"Do you want some time alone with him, or would you like for me to stick around?" Shawn asked. He had a house in town and, though he spent the greater amount of his time here with Dora, he still sometimes spent the night at his house, depending on what his work schedule was like.

"I'd like to have you around," she said, touching his hand. "I could use the moral support tonight."

"You got it, babe," he said, taking her hand in his.

Silas very quickly settled into his new home with John and Abbie Hodges. While Silas couldn't replace their offspring any more than they could replace his mother, they each had a cavity in their hearts that the other was uniquely able to occupy.

While Abbie helped Isadora and Clara with their busy inn, Hodges took Silas under his wing and helped him to learn the gold business. Silas, staying true to his vow to himself to never be poor again, worked hard and applied himself to doing the very best job he could do.

During his first year at the mill, while his usual duties still involved sweeping up, shoveling ore, or running errands, he also became adept at performing various other duties at the mill whenever necessary.

He learned how to start up and maintain the steam engines. He learned to operate the big crushers with their cone-shaped grinders that converted the rock into smaller particles, from which the gold could more easily be extracted. He even learned how to mix the cyanide solution that went into the enormous vats where the sludge was agitated, causing the gold to almost magically separate from the other materials.

In May of 1901, Isadora O'Riordan passed away in her sleep. Her death was mourned by all in the household, and by many down in Manitou. A few months later, since Clara was no longer bound to taking care of her mother, Peter Hodges retired from his medical practice, and he and Clara left to travel in Europe.

At that time, John, Abbie and Silas moved a few doors down, taking up permanent residence at the inn. Abbie, with the help of Gwenn, a young woman they hired, managed the inn from that time on.

In August of 1902, the Western Federation of Miners organized the workers in Colorado City mills, including those in John Hodges' mill. As a worker, Silas himself joined the union, which caused no little conflict between himself and Hodges. Silas quickly became a staunch supporter of the union. At this time, they were engaged in a battle with mine and smelter owners over the length of a work day.

The Western Federation of Miners made the case that working ten or twelve hours underground, or in the fumes of a smelter, was hazardous. Pushing for a reduction to eight hours per day, an amendment to the state constitution was proposed and put to a vote in 1902.

The amendment was passed by more than seventy-two percent of the state's voters. However, under pressure from mine and smelter owners, and from the Republican Party, the state actively ignored the results of the vote and allowed the amendment to die. Journalist Ray Stannard Baker wrote that, "Rarely has there been in this country a more brazen, conscienceless defeat of the will of the people."

In response, miners in Idaho Springs and Telluride decided to go on strike. This resulted in the strikers being rounded up at gunpoint by vigilante groups and run out of their towns. Warrants were sworn out for the arrest of the vigilantes, but it was mainly for show, since no arrests were ever made.

In 1903, when Silas really was seventeen years old, two new women entered his life. In April, amid the ongoing union turmoil, Abigail Hodges gave birth to a baby girl named Emily. The other woman, however, gave a little less advance notice.

§

In late September, the days were still warm but the sunlight had a slightly different quality to it. It was a little sharper and cooler, with just a bit more contrast due to its steeper angle. A warm fire was welcome in the evenings as the nights were just beginning to chill in the shadow of Pikes Peak.

Silas climbed the steps to the front door of the inn as Ethan led his horse to the barn. Silas still looked older than his years, his face hard, his body large and strong. He was a handsome young man, always soft-spoken and polite.

In the years since he had moved in with the Hodges, Silas had become accustomed to the house being full of people. The inn was quite successful and the Hodges were well-known for their kind hospitality.

This evening, he was greeted at the door by John and Abbie, along with a pretty young lady with dark eyes and rich auburn hair. She looked to be about nineteen or twenty. Silas took his hat off and hung it on the hook by the door. As he slipped off his duster, John made the introductions.

"Victoria, let me introduce Silas Baskin. Silas, this is Victoria Stewart. We've hired her to be Emily's nurse."

"How do you do?" Silas said.

"It's very nice to meet you, Mr. Baskin," Victoria said with a sweet voice.

"I'll show her to her room," Abbie said, as John guided Silas into the parlor. John opened a cabinet and took out a couple of glasses. Pouring whiskey from a decanter, he handed one glass to Silas.

They stood there silently for a few moments, sipping their drinks.

"The United Mine Workers called a strike," John finally said.

"I heard," Silas replied.

John took a drink and looked at Silas with narrowed eyes over his glass.

"That's all?" he said, trying to keep the anger from his voice. "You heard? This is going to affect your job too, and everybody else in the mill. Without men working the mines, there won't be ore coming in."

"Without good working conditions," Silas calmly fired back, "there will be fewer men to work the mines. Men can't make a living if their living is killing them."

"Silas, I don't want the miners, or anybody else for that matter, to work in dangerous conditions any more than you do. But don't you see that conditions can be improved without taking these drastic steps?"

"Sure, maybe some. You treat your people well. I know that. And that's definitely a credit to you. But there are too many mine and mill owners who are willing to let conditions go to hell, without taking the necessary precautions, and their workers be damned."

Hodges sighed and shook his head.

"Those workers sign up with your beloved unions and they suddenly get soft and lazy. The flow of commerce in Colorado is inextricably linked to gold. But your unions are interfering with that."

"Well, I don't think you'll have to worry about it for too long. I also heard that the Colorado National Guard has been called out, and they're taking the side of the mine owners." Silas tossed the rest of his drink back.

"That's enough, you two," Abbie said in her quiet, firm voice as she came back down and entered the parlor. She looked back and forth at both of them. "We all know your respective views on the labor unions. But please let our home be a haven from your work squabbles."

"These aren't just little squabbles, Abbie," John said. "This is about our livelihood."

Abbie looked at him with one eyebrow raised, apparently unmoved by his argument. Having seen that expression before, John knew not to continue. He smiled sideways at Silas and finished his drink.

"Agreed," he said.

§

Silas woke during the night to the sound of Emily crying. He usually didn't hear her since the nursery was at the back end of the house, near John and Abbie's room. Silas occupied a room at the front of the house. The baby's crying was coming from the sitting room next door to his.

As the minutes passed, the crying continued, and Silas was unable to go back to sleep. Sighing, he got out of bed and went to see what the problem was.

He knocked softly on the door of the sitting room, and a moment later, from inside, he heard a nervous "come in." He opened the door and saw Victoria in her nightclothes and a robe, her hair fallen about her shoulders, as she rocked Emily in her arms. At the click of the door opening, Emily quieted briefly. She turned her head to see the source of the sound, but then she started crying again.

Silas, wearing only his nightshirt, quickly came in and closed the door behind him, hoping the baby's crying would not disturb the guests staying there.

"What's the matter?" he asked.

"She's just a little fussy," Victoria said.

Knowing now that there was nothing seriously wrong, Silas felt a bit of anger at having been woken.

"What are you doing in here?"

"I didn't want to wake John or Abbie," she said with a defensive edge.

"So you decided to wake me instead?"

"It was not my intention. I apologize."

"Well, why don't you put her to sleep?"

"How would you suggest I do that, sir?" Victoria asked with some ire of her own.

"You're the nurse," Silas sputtered. "Do your job."

Victoria's eyes chilled as she looked at him.

"Mr. Baskin," she said, her voice equally chilled, "you are neither my employer, nor the son of my employer. In fact, I'm somewhat at a loss as to who you are. Your position here in this household is not as a family member, but – well, tell me, what is it exactly?"

Silas, rather than becoming angry, was instead amused by Victoria's tirade, and he smiled a little. The whole time she was still rocking Emily, trying to calm her.

"What are you smirking about?" she asked, now with a tone of growing irritation in her voice. That just made him smile all the more, and he shook his head, looking at the fireplace. It was dark.

"It's cold in here," he said, ignoring her question. "Maybe a fire will help."

He knelt down at the hearth and began arranging wood for a fire. Victoria, somewhat taken aback by his odd manner, turned her attention back to the baby. But she stole several glances at Silas while he worked at arranging the wood. She couldn't help but notice how his thin nightshirt clung to his muscular back.

In a few minutes, the fire was blazing, chasing the chill out of the room. Emily, as much by the warmth of the fire as by the dancing shadows on the ceiling, calmed down and started getting drowsy.

"Well, it looks like that may have done the job," Silas said with a quiet note of self-satisfaction in his voice, still kneeling beside the fire.

"Thank you," Victoria replied reluctantly. Feeling more comfortable, warmed by the fire, she looked down at the baby falling asleep in her arms, and her annoyance melted away. She looked up at Silas and seemed embarrassed. "I'm sorry I snapped at you the way I did."

"You were a little wildcat," he said with a chuckle.

"I've been called worse."

When she actually smiled at Silas, he was instantly smitten. He watched for a few moments as Victoria continued gently rocking Emily in her arms.

"Despite the awful display I saw when I first came in here," he finally said, "you seem to be pretty good with babies."

She shook her head but smiled good-naturedly.

"I've had some experience with them," she said. "I raised my sister and my brother. My mother died when I was just seven years old."

"I'm sorry. My mother died too, about three and a half years ago. But I was an only child."

They passed a few more quiet moments until Victoria looked at Silas and his nightshirt.

"I hope word does not get out about this."

"About what?" Silas asked with a half smile.

"I worry about the impropriety of the two of us in our nightclothes, alone with each other in here in the middle of the night. News of that sort could prove devastating to our families if anyone hears about it."

"I have no family."

"Well, I do. My father would be positively scandalized!"

"Who is your father?"

"William Stewart."

Silas was momentarily shocked and his face expressed the surprise he felt.

"William Stewart? The regional vice-president of the Western Federation of Miners?"

"Yes, that's him."

"Is John aware of this?"

Victoria looked up at Silas curiously. "I don't know. I don't think so. Why?"

"John is the owner of Hodges Mill in Colorado City. He's not very fond of unions in general, or the WFM in particular."

"Father and his friends do seem to have a knack for making enemies. The WFM is not very subtle, is it?"

"Well, no," Silas conceded. "But I don't really think it should be, either."

"What do you mean?"

"The things they're fighting for — fair pay, reasonable hours, safe working conditions — they're important issues. Given the amount of opposition they face, I think force might sometimes be called for."

"Hmm," Victoria said, casting a sidelong glance at Silas, "I think Father's going to love you."

§

Early the next Sunday afternoon, Silas and Victoria drove into Manitou. It was a sunny day, with an impossibly blue sky. But the weather was somewhat lost on Silas. Instead, he was filled with wonder by the tawny sheen of the early autumn sunlight on   Victoria's auburn hair. She played it to great advantage by wearing a dark green dress and hat.

During the drive, Silas was repeatedly drawn to her fine porcelain features, contrasted by the rich colors of her hair and clothing. Silas blushed after she caught him looking at her the third time, and Victoria smiled.

As they entered Manitou from the west, Victoria directed him to veer the carriage to the left onto Park Avenue, and after a few blocks, left again onto Canon Avenue. They went uphill, past the Cliff House Hotel on their right, and stopped at the corner of Grand Avenue and Canon Avenue.

Silas climbed down from the carriage and tied the horse to the hitching post. Going around to Victoria's side of the carriage, he reached his hands up to her waist and helped her down, and she kept her hand on his arm as he guided her up out of the street and toward the stone steps that led up to the house.

Standing in front of Victoria's house, Silas looked up at the imposing structure. Dominated by a four-story turret, the house made of rough-hewn stone stood tall, and seemed even taller atop the grassy hill.

"Father's not too extravagant," Victoria said, but the look on her face told Silas that she was being sarcastic. They walked up a few steps that took them past the stone retaining wall at the edge of the property, then they started up another flight of steps that finally placed them on the porch.

"Alright," Silas said when they reached the top, "you win. Your front porch is three times higher than ours. Your father built this?"

"Oh, no. He just bought it. Interestingly, it was built by a wealthy lumber baron from Colorado Springs. To this day, I'm still not entirely sure why a lumber man made his house entirely out of stone."

Before Silas could respond, the front door opened, and the doorway was suddenly filled by a big man. He was not only large in stature, but his personality was almost overwhelming to Silas. The man stood over six feet tall, with a substantial frame and a ruddy complexion.

But when he saw Victoria, he smiled and immediately softened the effect.

"There's my little girl," he bellowed, and he opened his arms wide and enveloped Victoria in an almost crushing embrace. She seemed a little overwhelmed by him too, and held on to her hat to keep it from being pushed back off her head. After a few seconds, she pulled away, attempting to hide her embarrassment at his public display.

"Father," she said, "this is Silas Baskin."

"Hello, Silas," he said, thrusting a big, meaty hand toward him. "I'm William Stewart. Victoria tells me you're a fan of the WFM."

"A fan, sir?" Silas asked confused, his hand nearly crushed in William's grip. "I don't understand."

"A fan is an enthusiast or a supporter of something. I heard somebody use that word a few days ago." He lowered his voice conspiratorially. "I think it might be short for 'fanatic,' but I think it's still a good word."

"Father is quite a 'fan' of words," Victoria said. "He's always going on about some new word he's learned, what it means, where it came from."

"Well, words are powerful tools," Silas said, as Stewart ushered them into the stately house. "I've never been a very fluent speaker myself, but I've always admired those who can use words well to influence people." Stewart smiled at the indirect compliment.

"Well, Silas, admirers are good, but we also need people who can take action, too."

"What kind of action do you mean, sir?"

"Action that gets peoples' attention when words don't. It's an unfortunate fact that, with some people, nothing short of a board smacking them between the eyes will make them take notice of what's completely obvious to others."

"Can we, please, not spend my Sunday talking about your WFM issues?" Victoria asked a little impatiently.

"Of course, my dear," Stewart said in a conciliatory tone. Turning to Silas, he winked and continued, "My daughter is not much of a partisan to the cause."

Silas smiled and looked toward Victoria, who seemed aloof and unmoved, but she looked up when she heard the pounding of footsteps coming down the stairs. The landslide they heard turned out to be a boy and girl coming down to meet them.

"Ah, there they are," Victoria said with a smile. She gave each of them a hug and a kiss on the cheek. Then she turned to Silas.

"This is my sister Elizabeth, and my brother George."

"How do you do?" Silas said.

George was about fourteen years old and had his father's ruddy complexion but not his height or girth. Elizabeth seemed to be about twelve years old, and she looked like what Silas imagined Victoria would have looked like a few years earlier. They were both very polite, but then they each took one of Victoria's hands and led her toward the parlor, hoping to catch up on what was happening with her after being apart for a week. Victoria looked back at Silas with a helpless smile.

"George, Elizabeth and Victoria," Stewart said to Silas with a smile, hooking a thumb toward his retreating offspring. "My wife, God rest her soul, was an admirer of English royalty."

He clapped a big hand on Silas' shoulder and guided him toward a different room, one filled with cabinets, book shelves and a large desk.

"Have a seat," he said, motioning to a leather armchair. Silas sat down as Stewart poured two snifters of brandy. "I don't think it's too early for one of these, do you?"

"No, sir," Silas said as he accepted one of the snifters. "Thank you."

Stewart lowered himself down into a large chair behind his desk, and Silas had the rather uncomfortable feeling that he was about to be interviewed.

"Silas, I understand you work at Hodges' Mill down in Colorado City."

"Yes, sir, that's correct."

"The Western Federation of Miners has been trying to organize a strike with all the mill workers in Colorado City, but we haven't been able to get Hodges' onboard with us."

"Yes, sir. I know. John Hodges treats his workers quite well, and most of them are hesitant to strike. They feel it would be disloyal to him."

"Hmm." Stewart looked at Silas for a moment, then he swirled the brandy in his glass, inhaled the aroma and took a sip. "And what about you?"

"Well, sir, I can see their point. It's awkward to endanger a good existing relationship." He puckered his brows in thought. "But I do think that being united with others in the profession can certainly be a good thing."

"You're absolutely right, son," Stewart said with a satisfied smile. "I agree, solidarity is certainly a necessity. So, what do you think can be done to win Hodges' Mill over to our way of thinking?"

"I'm afraid I don't know, sir," Silas said. "I have to say that I'm hesitant, too, since I live with John Hodges."

"Yes, that is a delicate situation. But you have to see how vitally important this is."

"Yes, sir. I do."

"We have people here who are wage slaves of mining corporations." Stewart banged his glass down on the desk, and Silas flinched. "We have mines and mining companies that are owned by hoity-toity absentee landlords back east who have no idea about what life is like out here, and who likely wouldn't give a shit about it if they did."

"But John Hodges lives here," Silas said.

"Yes, John Hodges lives up there in his frontier mansion on the mountain that he inherited from his rich family. He doesn't know what it's like to scrape and save for what you need, or to have to decide which necessity to do without because you can't afford it this week.

"Awkward or not, son, the only salvation of the working classes is a complete revolution of the current social and economic system."

"A revolution, sir?"

"That's right!" Stewart thumped the desk with his knuckles. "History is full of instances where the only acceptable option was a revolution.

"Just look at our own history. America was settled by a hearty breed of colonists. They crossed the Atlantic, farmed the land, did all the hard work, but England was still trying to control everything. Being absentee landlords. That damned tyranny was the reason the colonists left England in the first place.

"The colonists tried protesting, but that didn't do any good. It just fell on deaf ears. England didn't care how the colonists felt, as long as they were able to rake in their taxes. Finally, the colonists' only viable option was a revolution.

"Do you think it was awkward? Some of them probably still had friends and family back in England. Or daily dealings with the English here in America. Do you think it was uncomfortable? They knew that there was no guarantee that they would survive. Hell, there was no guarantee that the revolution would even be successful.

"But they knew it was their only viable choice. They had to do it. They fought for their freedom, and they won. It was successful. They established a country where people were free to carry on their lives without having to pay exorbitant taxes to a king who knows nothing about them or who doesn't give a shit about the conditions in which they live.

"But now, these mine and mill owners are doing the same damn thing as the king of England back then. Trying to control the lives of their workers, working them hard, in dangerous conditions, while paying them a pittance. Meanwhile, they sit back and get rich without having to lift a finger.

"These mine and mill workers are living in poverty, son, going to sleep with empty stomachs, sending their little ones to bed hungry, while the owners and managers get fat and throw away their leftovers."

Silas was entranced. Stewart was an emotional speaker, forceful and convincing, and Silas was reminded again of his vow that he would not be poor. He himself had stumbled into a good thing, but he knew that most of the workers didn't have that kind of luck.

"Protesting is useless," Stewart continued. "Even strikes have only limited success. The owners just bring in scabs to do the work."

"Well, if strikes aren't the answer, then what do you suggest?" Silas asked.

"A revolution, son," Stewart said calmly but firmly. "Before the American Revolution started in earnest, the colonists made numerous attacks against the British on a small scale. Guerilla warfare. Scattered attacks that confused and divided, but definitely got their attention.

"We're organizing deliberate and carefully prepared attacks against mines and mills to get the attention of the owners. And we need people like you, Silas. People who are trusted by the owners, but who sympathize with our cause. We especially need them over in Cripple Creek, where it's practically a war zone already."

"I know several people at some of the mines in Cripple Creek," Silas said. "I've heard about the conflicts that workers have had with the Colorado National Guard there."

"These people shouldn't have to work their lives away and have nothing to show for it," Stewart continued, indignant. "Or end up scarred or with lung diseases for the rest of their lives, not being able to support their families. Their children shouldn't be sent to bed hungry, or worse, orphaned. Not when there are things that others can do to help."

"I want to help, sir," Silas said with conviction in his voice. "What can I do?"

§

Silas stealthily approached the entrance of the Odysseus mine in Cripple Creek. It was after midnight and, while there were widely-spaced lanterns, there was no moon. Numerous soldiers patrolled the area, but Silas, dressed all in black, had been watching them from concealment. He had learned their movements, and when he came to be able to predict the gaps in their patrol, he made his move.

William Stewart had overseen his brief but thorough training. The emphasis had been on negotiation with the owners, capitalizing on Silas' acquaintance and good relationship with them. But if diplomatic efforts failed, they had more forceful methods at their disposal.

Of course, John Hodges knew only about the arbitration efforts. Silas had tendered his resignation, and told Hodges that he was going to work for the Western Federation of Miners, to help the workers. Hodges was disappointed, naturally, but Silas was sure he would be even more so if he knew the nature of Silas' new responsibilities.

Stephen Porter, the owner of the Odysseus, had been friendly at first, having met Silas before in his dealings with Hodges' Mill. But when he learned the reason Silas was calling, to try to negotiate on the eight-hour work day issue, he turned cold and aloof, even becoming belligerent at times.

In the end, he asked Silas not to come back.

Now inside the entrance to the mine, Silas pulled two sticks of dynamite from his coat pocket. He slipped one into each of the diagonal braces on the upper part of the support timbers, about fifty feet inside the shaft. Each stick had a long fuse, to allow him plenty of time to get out.

He drew in a deep breath to calm his nerves.

With a glance in each direction, Silas lit a match and touched it to each fuse, tossing them farther back in the shaft. Then he ran back toward the entrance to the mine, waiting for a moment until the soldiers provided an opportunity for him to slip out unseen. Then he calmly walked away, back toward the inn where he was staying.

He heard the explosion and felt the shock, but nobody saw him again until he emerged from his room the next morning.

ora, still feeling nervous and conflicted about the presence of her father, carried a plate out the back door to where Shawn was heating the grill. Shawn looked up as he heard the door close, and he smiled when he saw the food. Dora had seasoned and skewered chunks of chicken and alternating slices of red, green and yellow bell pepper and onions.

There were three skewers.

She sighed as she put the plate down, and Shawn, seeing the expression on her face, gently put his arm around her. Dora leaned into him and turned her face toward his. Looking at him from two inches away, Shawn thought she looked cross-eyed, and he smiled again, kissing her nose.

"Have I told you I love you?" he asked.

"Not in the last half hour."

"Hmm. I've obviously become remiss in my duties. Please allow me to remedy that situation right now. I love you, baby."

Dora smiled now, putting her head on Shawn's shoulder, her face snuggled against his neck. She sighed as she pressed her body against his, and he held her tightly, kissing the top of her head.

"I love you, too," she sighed again.

"Do you really?"

Dora looked up at him again, this time with an expression of confusion.

"You know I do."

"Prove it."

Dora narrowed her eyes a bit and looked at him slyly.

"My dad's in the house," she said. "I mean, he's up in his room and wouldn't hear us downstairs. But still, we don't have time for that. We have to make dinner."

"Oh, get your mind out of the gutter, woman," Shawn said. "Marry me."

Dora gasped. At first, she thought that she had heard wrong, but the thought quickly left her mind as she saw Shawn lower himself to one knee and withdraw a box from his pocket. He opened the box and held it up to Dora, displaying a gold ring with a fine Celtic knot design around it, topped by a sparkling solitaire diamond.

"Isadora Baskin, will you marry me?" he asked.

Dora looked from Shawn's face to the ring and back again, tears perched on her lower eyelids. When she rapidly nodded her head, smiling, the tears rolled down her cheeks.

"Yes!" she said as she lowered herself to her knees and kissed Shawn. He wrapped his arms around her, holding her tightly, seemingly oblivious to the summer heat.

After about a minute, though, Shawn spoke up.

"Well, honey, I'm sorry to spoil this romantic moment, but my knees are starting to ache on this deck."

Dora chuckled.

"Mine too."

They both stood up as they heard the phone ringing inside.

"Hold on," Shawn said. "Don't go just yet." He took the ring out of the box and slipped it on Dora's finger. Her eyes filled again as she looked at it. With her hand still in his, she leaned forward and kissed Shawn.

Then she reluctantly pulled away to go inside, while Shawn opened the grill to cook their dinner.

§

Bridget Lindstrom stood naked, looking at herself in the full-length mirror on her bedroom door. She turned, alternately to each side to get a good angle. At forty-nine, she thought she still looked good. Her chestnut-colored hair had a few silver hairs mixed with it, but that actually provided a bit of a shimmering effect, which she decided that she liked.

Her torso was not bad. She had put on a little weight in recent years, but not excessively. She hadn't been happy about it at first, but now, as she looked at the whole package, she concluded that her curvy figure was actually kind of sexy, also something that she liked.

Bridget's dark eyes still had a sparkle in them, giving her face a mischievous air, which was enhanced even more when she smiled. Considering how often she noticed men looking at her, she knew that she wasn't just deluding herself and seeing what she wanted to see in the mirror. She was still a good-looking woman.

She was happy, not only about the way she looked, but even more about what she had done with her life. Many women who had been through what she had endured years ago might have crumbled and gone running back home.

But not Bridget. She had decided back then, in 1986, after enduring the 'hard lesson' as she referred to it, to stay in Colorado Springs. To that end, she did a search for scholarships. She hadn't been able to find one that paid her full tuition, so she worked and scraped to pay the balance herself, finally emerging from the two-year course with her teaching certificate.

She knew back then that she wasn't going to get rich being a history teacher, but that wasn't the point. She loved it, and she was able to pay the bills. And eventually, it allowed her to buy her house. It wasn't a big house, but it was nice, situated in a decent neighborhood, and she had added her own touches to it. Many of those touches were often reminiscent of a by-gone era, reflecting Bridget's love of history, and of her homeland.

In fact, it was history that had tempted Bridget to come to America in the first place.

Her family lore included stories of an adventurous young woman named Isadora Byrnes. Several generations back in their history, Isadora had left England and come to America, and her emigration was surrounded by some kind of dark mystery. Isadora's parents and younger sister had been brutally murdered shortly after she left, and that branch of the family tree seemed to have gotten lopped off at that point.

Bridget, fascinated by tracing her family's history, and by the enigma of Isadora Byrnes, had made the trip herself in 1986. Having saved for several months for the undertaking, her funds were further reinforced by a handsome gift from her parents upon her graduation from college in Liverpool.

Ever since she had first heard the stories, Bridget had thought that Isadora Byrnes must have been very brave, making such a long sea voyage alone, to a new country where she didn't know anyone.

And now, she was proud of herself, of her own bravery and initiative, for making such a pilgrimage all by herself. The undertaking had certainly been much easier than in Isadora's day, but still, it was scary for a young woman to travel to another country alone.

In those days before the internet, tracing a family tree was not so easy. But the trip had been fruitful as she followed what clues she could find.

Isadora Byrnes had originally sailed to Charleston, South Carolina, then eventually settled in Gainesville, Georgia. Bridget had found a few references to Isadora Byrnes in various public records in Gainesville, as well as in the name of a charitable organization which provided medical treatment to underprivileged people. It had started out long ago as an organization dedicated to helping Native Americans, particularly the Cherokee, but now catered to everyone.

From Gainesville, Bridget then went to Tahlequah, Oklahoma, the final destination of the Trail of Tears. There, the trail seemed to go cold for a time. But after some persistent digging, and with the aid of some helpful people at Fort Gibson, Oklahoma, she found a remark in a historic army record that pointed her toward Colorado.

Eventually, Bridget found the huge log house just outside of Manitou Springs, near the base of Pikes Peak. The woman who lived there then was also named Isadora. She had been very kind but guarded. When Bridget learned that this Isadora was caring for her husband who lay inside, ill, she expressed her sympathy and quickly excused herself.

After that, she had gone back into Manitou Springs for dinner and drinks. Bridget had been attracted to the historical reference in the name of The Ancient Mariner, a bar and restaurant on Manitou Avenue, the main street through town.

And that's where all her trouble had started.

She never did get back to the big log house, or to her family history. She was so distracted by the fiasco that the genealogy just didn't seem that important anymore.

Bridget's phone rang, interrupting her reverie, and she fished it out of her purse. The name on the display was one she hadn't seen in a while.

"Hello, Jack," she said.

"Bridget," the man responded, "I just wanted to let you know. I was doing a few follow-up checks today, and an interesting name showed up. He's in town."

Silas Baskin rapidly became quite adept at his new responsibilities with the Western Federation of Miners. Due to his close association with John Hodges, Silas was trusted by miners and mine owners alike. Even though he was a great champion of workers' rights, he was also able to negotiate freely with those in charge.

Negotiations were not always effective, though. When that was the case, Silas was easily able to slip into his more aggressive role as militant bomber, remarkably without raising the suspicions of the owners. And he had an uncanny ability to sneak in and out without a trace, leaving not a single clue to point back to William Stewart, or to the Western Federation of Miners in general.

For that, Silas quickly became Stewart's most effective secret weapon.

Silas spent the remainder of 1903 being an outspoken proponent of workers' rights, mainly in the hotbed town of Cripple Creek. But he always returned to Manitou, to his room in the Hodges' inn.

And to Victoria.

Victoria spent most of her time taking care of her little charge, Emily Hodges. Then, every Sunday, Silas drove Victoria down into town, either to visit her family, or to just spend the day together.

But they managed to find other opportunities to be together, as well.

During the week, whenever Silas was in Manitou, the little sitting room adjacent to Silas' room became their clandestine night-time meeting place. Thus, late one night in early 1904, there was a small fire burning in the fireplace, while Silas and Victoria, each in their nightclothes, were sitting together on the divan. Their initial concern about the lack of propriety had been trumped by their mutual attraction.

"I sure wish you didn't have to spend so much time in Cripple Creek," Victoria said, snuggling under Silas' arm. "I worry about you. I've heard about what's going on there."

"Oh, don't worry, puss," Silas said softly, pulling her close. "I'm in clover."

"I wish you wouldn't make light of such a bad situation."

"It's not so bad."

"But what about General Bell?"

Silas, with a sneer on his face, scoffed at the name.

"Sherman Bell is an arrogant, egotistical imbecile."

"A dangerous combination," Victoria said.

General Sherman Bell was the leader of the Colorado National Guard. While perhaps not an imbecile, he was indeed enormously egotistical. He usually made it a point to be seen in full dress uniform, which included gold lace, cords and tassels. The cost of this custom-made uniform was estimated to have been about a thousand dollars.

Besides his salary from the state of Colorado, he also supplemented his income with pay from the mine owners. Therefore, he was single-mindedly against the unions and union workers.

"I'm not worried about Bell, or his squad of ruffians," Silas said. "Bell's just hungry for praise as a dashing hero. He's nothing but a dandy who's too concerned with dressing up and showing off his finery."

"That's not all he does, Silas," Victoria protested. "I've heard about riots, about people being arrested and beaten, some even killed."

Bell many times sanctioned arrests and beatings, regardless of the legality, and he justified his reign of terror as a "military necessity, which recognizes no laws, either civil or social." The fact that his force was usually the instigator of the violence did not faze him in the least. Thomas McClelland, one of Bell's junior officers in charge of beating striking miners, was quoted as saying, "To hell with the constitution. We aren't going by the constitution."

"Well," Silas responded with an easy tone, "your father is a good teacher, and I do my job very well. You don't have to worry about me."

Victoria's face still expressed concern, though. She was certain that Silas was simply downplaying Bell's nature and activities to keep her from worrying. She tried to put it out of her mind and enjoy their quiet time together. Silas held her tightly, caressing her arm.

They sat for a while, watching the hypnotic dance of the flames, feeling the warm closeness of their bodies through their thin nightclothes. Silas looked down at the curve of Victoria's leg pressed against his, and he gently placed his hand on her knee. His breaths accelerating, he felt the heat of her skin through the fabric. Moving his hand upwards a bit, the hardness of her knee turned into the soft flesh of her thigh.

Victoria turned to Silas, the uneasiness of their conversation now dissipated as she felt his hand inching higher. Her first inclination was to push his hand away, but she felt almost helpless in the heat and longing that was growing deep inside her.

Silas felt Victoria's gaze and he looked up, again taken by her beautiful face, the flames clearly reflected in her dark eyes, almost like an inner phosphorescence. He felt spellbound by her luminous skin and her auburn hair, now ablaze in the firelight.

Victoria's lips parted slightly, as did her legs, and Silas leaned toward her and kissed her.

He held her in his arms now, feeling the warmth of her body through her nightclothes, wanting to feel more.

Victoria seemed to read his thoughts.

Wrapping her arms tightly around Silas, she lay back on the divan, taking him with her. Leaning on his elbow, and pressing against Victoria's body, his other hand caressing her side and her hip, Silas pressed his lips hungrily against hers. His heart was pounding in his ears as he reached up and untied the laces on the front of her nightdress. Victoria let go of him only long enough for him to open it up, and to help him draw his nightshirt off over his head.

Silas watched, mesmerized for a few moments, as the firelight cast dancing shadows across Victoria's breasts and belly. Then she pulled him back down on her, pressing his body hard against hers. She looked deeply into his eyes, wondering if his attraction, his passion, was as strong as her own.

It was.

By June of 1904, despite his previous flippant responses to Victoria, Silas had begun having serious doubts about his role in the labor war. He still believed strongly in the WFM's creed, in the things they were fighting for.

But he hadn't wanted to kill anyone.

He had a long time to think about it as he rode back toward Manitou from Independence, Colorado, where William Stewart had sent him to help out with a particular operation.

While the annual convention of the Western Federation of Miners was going on in Victor, Stewart and a few others wanted to shake things up a bit. They likely figured that no WFM officials would be implicated if they were at the convention. And they wanted something bigger, something that would get more attention.

There had been much wrangling within the union of late, with little being accomplished. They wanted to hasten constructive dialogue and unify the people.

They decided that they needed an explosion at the train depot in Independence, Colorado.

Though Silas was not privy to the discussions and reasoning behind it, the idea was apparently to strike the train that carried the night shift of scabs, the non-union workers, to and from the mines.

Silas had misgivings about it from the start.

"I've become accustomed to doing small jobs," he had told Stewart, "working by myself."

"And you've done a very good job," Stewart had replied.

"Thank you, sir. And I don't mean to sound unappreciative for what you've done for me. But now, you're asking me to work with a group of men, led by this man named Harry Orchard?"

"That's right."

"I don't trust the guy. I'm not even sure Harry Orchard is his real name."

Stewart had smiled at that.

"I'm not entirely sure either."

"I just don't like the idea of doing this kind of work with others, especially with some who seem to ooze malice."

"I understand, son. But this is a bigger job, one which requires the cooperation of more people to pull off. I need my best people working together in one location."

"Well, the location is another thing," Silas continued. "In the past, I've always been protected by the fact that I had acquaintances at the locations I visited. In fact, I would meet with them and negotiate with them directly before taking any action. That was always my cover – meeting with people I knew from my past dealings.

"But I'm not familiar with Independence. I don't know anybody there. Hodges' Mill doesn't have any contacts there, so I have no alibi."

"Which is partly why I have you working with these other men. They're experienced with this sort of thing, Silas. Follow them and you won't need an alibi."

Silas still hesitated.

"Is there something else?" Stewart asked.

"Yes," Silas said. "The target. It's not a mine. I mean the fact that the train is transporting non-union workers – that seems like a pretty shaky connection to my usual mine targets."

"I know you're unaccustomed to this kind of job, son. Again, that's why you'll be working with other experienced men."

"But it's not just the kind of job," Silas argued. "It's also the target itself, and the scope. And the potential for injuries. I have a bad feeling about this. I've been bombing mine shafts, and nobody has gotten hurt. Why can't I just keep doing what I've been doing?"

"Times are changing, Silas. We have to change with them. Bombing mine shafts gets the attention of the owner of the mine, but it doesn't seem to do much beyond that anymore. Not enough people are paying attention. We need to be able to get people's attention better. To shake them up."

Silas still wasn't sure about it. He didn't like it, but after much consolation and many assurances, he finally agreed.

Damaging the depot, and a train, should be easy enough, though it was more exposed and out in the open than Silas was accustomed to. That's where it became necessary for him to rely on the other men who were more experienced.

The exposure turned out to not be as much of a problem as he thought. If anything, for at least part of the operation, the problem was that there was too little light. Silas was under the train platform a little past midnight. But he became particularly concerned when he saw the explosives.

He was helping Harry Orchard put the explosives in place – two full boxes of dynamite with giant blasting caps.

Silas tried to very quietly protest the amount of dynamite being used, but Harry shushed him, reinforcing it by grasping Silas' arm in a painful grip. Silas was quiet after that, but he couldn't bring himself to help Harry any further.

The bomb was to be detonated remotely, by pulling a long wire, which Harry was going to do himself. He was planning to wait until the train arrived and people were crowded on the platform for maximum effect.

Silas had left by that time. He wanted nothing more to do with it, and in fact had decided at the last minute to ride toward the depot, to try to warn people of the impending danger.

But he was too late.

The explosion shook the ground at about 2:30 in the morning, as Silas was just coming in sight of the depot. Rocks and debris rained down around him as he shielded himself from it and steered his panicking horse for cover.

He later learned that thirteen people were killed, and many more maimed and crippled for life.

Silas watched for a few moments from his place of cover, trying to decide what to do. He wanted to assist in some way if he could. But he knew that, having no other business in town, not having the benefit of a cover story, if he showed himself in public, he ran the risk of being suspected in the bombing.

In the end, as he saw lights coming on in various houses and buildings, and people heading toward the depot carrying lanterns, he decided to take his leave.

That's when he saw Tom Gardner, the owner of the Golden Eagle mine in Cripple Creek, running toward the depot. What business Gardner had here in Independence, Silas didn't know. But Silas had been in union negotiations with him a few months before, and it did not end well. Silas followed up the failed discussion by blowing up a shaft in his mine. He wanted to get away before Gardner saw him.

But again, he was too late.

Gardner stopped in his tracks as Silas wheeled his horse around and rode swiftly away. He thought he had heard Gardner call after him, but he didn't stop or turn around to find out.

§

The Hodges' inn looked especially welcoming when Silas finally arrived. It was a warm Tuesday afternoon, the day after the bombing. Silas knew that William Stewart would still be at the convention in Victor, so he had just headed for home. The knowledge that Victoria would be there made the destination even more appealing.

As his horse was being led toward the barn by Ethan, Silas laboriously climbed the steps to the front door and went inside. His long ride home had not gotten any easier as he bore on his shoulders the guilt of the injuries and fatalities resulting from his latest job.

Abbie was in the kitchen preparing dinner. She heard Silas come in and leaned around the kitchen door. Silas waved at her and she smiled and went back to work as he climbed the stairs.

Once he reached the second floor, he saw that Victoria was in the nursery with Emily. The door was open and, though Victoria was already happily engaged with the baby, her face utterly glowed when she saw Silas.

That alone lifted his heart immensely.

Emily gurgled as she watched him kiss Victoria. Then Silas eased himself down in the rocking chair.

Victoria noticed his weary demeanor.

"Is everything alright?" she asked.

Silas shook his head.

"What's wrong?" she asked when he offered no further explanation.

"I don't want to talk about it in front of her," he replied, nodding toward Emily.

"Oh, she doesn't understand." Victoria turned toward Emily. "Do you?" she asked, using the voice that people universally use to talk to babies. "No, you don't. You don't understand anything, do you?"

Emily smiled and drooled in response. Victoria looked back up at Silas as Silas blew out a heavy sigh.

"I don't think I want to work for the WFM any longer," he finally said.

"Why?"

Silas couldn't tell from her face if she was happy to hear that or apprehensive. Probably both.

"I've decided I don't agree with their methods of motivating changes." Victoria's face still showed confusion as she waited for a more comprehensive response. Silas allowed a few moments to pass before he spoke again. "I helped them kill and wound a lot of innocent people."

He related briefly about the bombing in Independence, and his role in it.

"My father instigated that?" Victoria asked, trying to keep her anger in check for the sake of Emily.

"He was one of several," Silas replied. He shook his head and tried to think of how to soften the news. There wasn't much that came to mind. "I don't know how many people were behind it, or how the idea came about."

A few moments of silence passed between them. Victoria was visibly angry but, for the sake of the baby, she seemed to be struggling to keep it in. Emily looked from one to the other, smiling obliviously.

"What will you do?" Victoria finally asked.

"I think John will take me back on at the mill. I don't think I've burned that bridge. But on the ride back home, I was thinking that a regular job sounds pretty good."

"Definitely safer," Victoria added, and Silas could see the relief on her face for certain now.

"And better for my conscience."

Victoria smiled sympathetically.

§

Hodges did indeed take Silas back on at the mill. He seemed genuinely happy that Silas was not working for the Western Federation of Miners any longer.

Stewart was not so happy.

"You are throwing away your opportunity to make a difference, son," he said, thumping his desk with his beefy knuckles for emphasis as he often did. Silas sat in the chair in front of his desk, while Victoria was visiting with her brother and sister in another room.

"Well, sir, I don't think I want to make that kind of difference any more. I mean we certainly made a difference for those people in Independence, didn't we?"

"I understand, Silas," Stewart said with a conciliatory tone. He was smoking a cigar and looked relaxed behind his desk, only partly facing Silas. He took a long pull on his cigar and blew a thick cloud of smoke over his head. "It's natural to feel that way at first. But you need to expect some civilian casualties when you're at war. It's a necessary evil. I don't like it either, but sometimes, it can't be avoided.

"It happened in Victor, too, while our convention was still going on. It was just shortly after your bombing took place. Riots broke out and two people were killed. The National Guard showed up and they surrounded the union hall and several of our people were arrested.

"But," he took a dramatic pause and looked straight at Silas. "People took notice!" He thumped the desk again, once with each word.

"Oh, I'm sure people noticed," Silas said. "But don't we want more than just notoriety? How are we ever going to make people agree with our cause and change their thinking when innocent people get killed because of what we do? What kind of example is that?"

"Like I said, son, we're at war! Besides, the people killed in Independence were not innocent. They were strike breakers. They're our enemies, enemies of our cause."

"Not my cause, sir," Silas said. "I don't want to have anything to do with it anymore."

"Damn it, boy!" Stewart said as he turned fully toward Silas and pounded his fist on the desk. A half inch of ash fell from his cigar onto his wrist, and his face turned red as he angrily brushed it off. "You're in shit up to your neck! You think you can just turn around and walk away?"

Silas suddenly saw the position he was in. He worried now that Stewart was going to hold this over his head, the threat of revealing Silas' violent actions. Would he do that, knowing that Silas could implicate him? But Stewart quickly softened his stance. He took a deep breath and the redness in his face gradually faded.

"What happened to your beliefs? Your desire for better working conditions?"

"Nothing, sir, they're still there. I just don't want to fight for them this way anymore."

"You think it's easy to change things? You think you can just make it magically happen without anybody getting hurt?"

"No, sir, I don't think it's easy. I know it takes a lot of hard work. And I'm willing to do it. But I don't like the way the WFM is doing it. And I don't want to be a part of it anymore."

"Then just get the hell out of my house!" Stewart bellowed, his face reddening all over again. He stabbed a chunky finger toward the door in case Silas wasn't sure what he meant. "I don't want to see your face!"

Silas looked at Stewart for a moment, wanting to say more, but not knowing what to say. He had already defended his own viewpoint and could see that Stewart, his face still red, his eyes bulging in anger, was not open to hearing any more. With a sigh, Silas stood up and turned, and when he opened the door, he saw Victoria standing there, her face registering surprise at the outburst she had overheard through the door.

"And you can just stay away from my Victoria, too," Stewart spat.

Victoria gaped at Stewart, shocked at his display.

"I will not be a pawn in your little union game," she said.

"No namby-pamby little sissy is going to spend time with my daughter."

"Whoever spends time with me is not for you to determine, Father," she said, her own anger rising now.

"As long as you're under my roof, little lady, it is for me to determine!"

"Then I suppose we should go," she responded. Taking Silas' hand, she cast one last look toward her father as she pulled Silas toward the front door. "Whatever things I still have here, I shall retrieve later."

Stewart, suddenly at a loss for words, sputtered something after them, but they were already gone.

§

Silas was driving Victoria away from her father's house. They were going northwest on Park Avenue, though they did not have a destination. Victoria just wanted to be away.

"I'm sorry I've come between you and your father," Silas said.

"It's not your fault," Victoria replied with an impatient shake of her head. "This has been building for a while now. If it wasn't you, it would have been someone or something else."

"Well, I'm sorry it was me."

"My father doesn't seem to care about anything but his precious union."

"I know that's not true, Victoria."

"Oh really?" she said with a derisive laugh.

"Even his forbidding me to see you was, in his crooked way, an expression of his love for you."

Victoria looked up at Silas, a look of disbelief on her face.

"How can you be so good and kind?"

"I'm not good or kind," Silas scoffed with a pained expression. "I've done terrible things."

"You haven't done anything so terrible."

"Victoria, I'm partly responsible for thirteen people being dead and a lot more being wounded and crippled."

"No, you're not, Silas. You didn't do that last job, and you tried to stop it.

"But I couldn't. It still happened."

Victoria sighed and shook her head. She put a hand on his arm, as Silas turned sharply left onto Manitou Avenue, driving slowly but still aimlessly.

"Silas, you're always so forgiving of others," Victoria said, "but you stubbornly refuse to forgive yourself, even for what you didn't do."

Silas looked at her for a second, then thoughtfully turned back toward the road.

Ahead, at Ruxton Avenue, a trolley car was turning around on the loop, preparing to head back down Manitou Avenue toward Colorado Springs. When Silas reached the loop, on an impulse, he turned right, driving the carriage uphill on Ruxton. He and Victoria sat quietly for a while, their shoulders leaning together, watching their surroundings pass slowly by as the horse continued trudging up the hill.

Eventually, as they saw the little depot for the Pikes Peak Cog Railway ahead on their left, Silas pulled the carriage up next to the building.

"What are you doing?" Victoria asked.

"Have you been up to the top?" Silas asked, and he climbed down from the carriage.

"No, I haven't," she replied as Silas helped her down.

"John took me up there a couple of years ago. Everyone should see it."

After that, Silas was quiet as they went inside where he purchased their tickets, and made livery arrangements for the horse and carriage. They didn't have to wait long as the train was preparing to make the climb.

They approached the track and passed the odd-looking little locomotive, raised up in the back and slanted forward to keep its boilers level on the inclined track. Ahead of it was the passenger car, and Silas helped Victoria up onto it. They walked down the aisle, looking at the people who were anxiously awaiting the trip. The car was almost full, but they found two seats together and sat down.

Within just a few minutes, the little locomotive began chugging, belching black smoke into the air. The cog wheel on the engine engaged with the toothed rail in the middle of the track, slowly propelling the locomotive forward. Silas and Victoria felt the car jerk a little as the locomotive, in turn, began pushing the car of passengers ahead of it.

The climb up the side of the mountain was punctuated by "oohs" and "aahs" from the passengers. The journey took them through beautiful forests of spruce and pine. Victoria took Silas' hand as they passed a waterfall, and they could feel each other relaxing, letting go of the tension they had felt just an hour before with Stewart.

Chipmunks could be seen, by those with quick eyes, scampering in all directions away from the tracks. As the train traveled farther up the mountain, Silas and Victoria were able to spot larger wildlife. A number of mule deer, some with fawns, were drinking from a stream in the dappled shade of the forest. They were alert, their large ears erect, as the train continued climbing up the track.

About halfway up the mountain, the little train came to a stop at a large log structure called the Halfway House, a hotel and restaurant. At this point, a few people got off the train, but many of them stayed on, Silas and Victoria included, while others boarded here.

As they continued the climb, the scenery gradually changed, the dense forest giving way to more rocky terrain, dotted here and there with ancient gnarled bristlecone pine trees. The passengers uttered a collective "aah" as a large herd of bighorn sheep came into view. The sheep watched the strange vehicle continuing its climb, cautious but curious.

Watching the animals, Victoria leaned closer to Silas who put his arm around her shoulders. They traveled the rest of the way to the summit like that.

§

The Pikes Peak Cog Railway was established by Zalmon Simmons, a mattress maker from Wisconsin who, in 1888, had endured a difficult two-day climb to the summit by mule. Construction began in 1889, and limited service to the Halfway House was undertaken in 1890. The train completed a trip to the summit the following year.

There had been a structure on the peak of the great mountain, though, as far back as 1873, when the United States Army's Signal Service branch built a telegraph station there to monitor the weather. Within only a few years, the structure was abandoned by the Army, but it was later reoccupied when the Department of the Interior allowed the railway to operate a train terminal and guest house on the site.

At the turn of the century, the Summit House was upgraded and enlarged to accommodate more guests and facilities. The upgrades included an elevated tower, which allowed adventurous visitors who wanted to climb even higher to see the complete panoramic view.

So after a couple of hours, this stone building is what Silas and Victoria saw as the little train came to a jerky stop at the summit of Pikes Peak. They stood up and stretched, feeling a little unsteady after the lurching and vibration of the ride up the mountain, and it felt good to get out and stand on the ground again.

It was considerably cooler up here, but after the summer heat down below, it felt good to them. The summit was bare, a rock-strewn dome, high above the timberline.

But the view was magnificent.

They strolled around aimlessly for a few minutes, as many others of the passengers did. Then, taking Victoria's hand, Silas led her toward the observation tower. The tower was nothing more than a bare metal framework with a few flights of stairs leading to a platform at the top.

"Two bits, please," said the man at the base of the stairs. "Per person."

Silas fished fifty cents from his pocket, though Victoria objected that it was a totally unnecessary extravagance, which Silas ignored.

They began climbing and, at over fourteen thousand feet, they were feeling fatigue from the altitude, and they were panting for breath before they reached the top.

But . . .

"Oh, Silas!" Victoria exclaimed. "It's beautiful!"

Silas smiled as he watched her face.

The tower raised them up just enough to be able to see over most of the curve of the dome-topped mountain, giving them an unobstructed view all around them. At the moment, they had the platform to themselves.

Toward the east, the land lay spread out before them in a patchwork of farmland and wilderness. For the most part, it was flat, but Silas and Victoria were so high up that they could see the curve of the earth. The horizon was so far away as to become invisible to them, ultimately blending with the sky in a misty blue.

To the west, the Rocky Mountains stretched out in receding rows of peaks and valleys, finally disappearing in the blue haze of the distance.

Victoria looked at Silas, wisps of henna-colored hair blowing across her face in the wind.

"We're so small, so tiny and insignificant," she said in awe, her voice barely louder than a whisper. She looked again at the views around her. She sighed. "There's so much more to the world than what we see in our limited little environment down in Manitou."

Silas followed her gaze, appreciating the vistas with a new perspective.

"The things we worry about," Victoria continued, "the problems that fill our everyday lives, they really mean so little, don't they?

"We let those worries become so large in our minds that we sometimes fail to see the good things. Like holding a baby in your arms and hearing her laugh when you make a face at her." She smiled for a moment as she thought about Emily, but then she looked around her again. "Or the little animals we saw on the way up here. Even this impossibly blue sky!" She turned her face up toward the sun, closing her eyes and holding her arms out at her side.

Silas was no longer looking at the scenery. He was, as usual, captivated by Victoria, by her face, her voice, the depth of her mind and intellect.

"There are people who have traveled the world," she said. "They've discovered new lands, new animals, new peoples. They've seen wonders that we can scarcely imagine. They describe them in phrases that sound almost magical to our ears. And then we sit in our houses and feel indignant about people

next door who aren't doing things the way we think they should."

"The issues **are** important," Silas said.

"They are," Victoria agreed with a knowing smile. "But Silas, sometimes, people focus so much attention on solving an important problem that they fail to see how other things connect to it. They think the ends justify the means, and they don't bother to see how the means cause even more problems that they didn't, or couldn't, foresee."

Silas, already feeling guilty about the part he played in the Independence bombing, smarted at this indictment. Victoria saw the fleeting pained expression on his face, and she put her hand gently on his chest.

"I'm certainly not trying to diminish the importance of those problems, or the things that you and my father have been working for. But there's so much more. Sometimes we just get so absorbed in the problems that affect us, significant as they are, that we end up missing the beauty of the whole world."

"You're right," Silas said. "Earlier today, and this past week, I was feeling low, lower than I've felt since my mother died. But now, I feel like I'm on top of the world." He looked out at the crags and canyons, stretching out farther than his eye could see. "And I really am."

Then he turned and focused on Victoria, taking her hand from his chest and holding it in his hands. "I know I haven't fully appreciated the possibilities that were open to me until now. I don't want to miss out on them. And I want to realize them with someone I love."

Victoria stood close to Silas, her head turned up toward him, her eyes expectant.

"I don't know if I'll ever be able to travel the world," Silas continued, "but wherever I am able to go, I want you to be there with me."

"What are you saying?"

"I'm saying that I want you to change your name." He smiled at her confused expression. "I love you, and I want you to become Victoria Baskin. Will you marry me?"

Victoria, already short-winded from the altitude, now gasped a little. But she smiled and, with her free hand, brushed the hair out of her eyes.

"Silas Baskin," she said in a hushed tone, "I love you, too. I would be honored to be your wife."

Silas was exuberant. Wrapping his arms around her, he picked her up, spinning her around. Victoria grinned, then laughed as she buried her face in Silas' neck. When he put her down, she looked up at him and he kissed her, holding her face gently in his hands.

They parted reluctantly, only because they were short of breath, and Silas moved his hands down her arms. They felt rough, and he noticed the goose flesh of her cold skin.

"I'm so sorry," he said as he quickly took his coat off and put it around her shoulders.

"Thank you," Victoria said as she pulled it closed around her. "It is rather chilly up here."

"Why don't we go down below and see what they have to eat in the Summit House?"

"That's a good idea," she said as he guided her toward the stairs.

§

Tom Gardner was 'in a state.' Having just buried his only son, Frank, the day before, he was feeling bitter about how unfair life was.

His wife had died several years before. Frank was the only family he had left.

The boy had so much to live for. At sixteen years of age, he had just taken a job at the Liberty Bell mine in Independence, filling in for striking miners.

Gardner was so proud of him, and had personally taken him to Independence a week ago, on Sunday. Frank's first shift started early the next morning.

But he didn't make it.

Frank had been among those standing on the train platform, waiting to board the train, when the depot exploded.

The explosion shook the town, waking Gardner from sleep in his hotel room. He had planned on going back home to Cripple Creek that morning, but he ended up staying throughout the day, clearing rubble, looking for survivors.

Frank wasn't one of them.

The sight of his broken and bloody body would haunt Gardner for the rest of his life. But something else had begun haunting him, too. The memory of the guilty expression on Silas Baskin's face when he saw him at the site of the explosion.

Amid his grief at the loss of his son, Gardner had managed to ask around in Independence about Baskin. Nobody seemed to know anything about him. Nobody knew of any business he would have had there.

He remembered Baskin from when he worked at Hodges' Mill in Colorado City. He had been a very polite and quiet young man, and a conscientious worker.

He was also polite and quiet when he came to Gardner a few months ago, stumping for the Western Federation of Miners. But behind his polite and quiet words, Gardner detected a determined forcefulness. Almost a threatening stance. Gardner wanted the WFM to keep their noses out of his business, and had said as much to Silas Baskin. Baskin had politely acknowledged his wishes and left.

Gardner's mine was blown up that night.

There had been no physical evidence to determine who had been responsible. He had thought at the time about the timing of the explosion, immediately after Baskin's failed negotiations with him. But the thought of Baskin being involved was fleeting, quickly dismissed from his mind based on his knowledge of the young man.

But now, seeing him near the depot at the time of the bombing seemed like too much of a coincidence. Especially when he apparently had no business in town.

The memory of him riding away so quickly from the depot, instead of going toward it to help, was enough for Gardner to reach a verdict.

Baskin was guilty.

Today, after asking around Manitou about him, somebody told Gardner that they saw Baskin and the Stewart girl driving up Ruxton Avenue. Further questioning led Gardner to the Pikes Peak Cog Railway.

He knew that they wouldn't be back for a few more hours. Gardner decided that he was hungry and went back down into town for lunch.

He could wait.

The train took Silas and Victoria back down the mountain, but Silas still felt as if he was on top of the world. As their train gradually descended, the temperature rose, and Victoria took off Silas' coat and gave it back to him.

But still, he kept his arm around her shoulders for the entire ride.

"Up at the summit," Victoria said as they neared the station, "you mentioned your mother."

Silas nodded, remembering the moment.

"What was she like?"

"She was a good mother." Silas was not trying to be evasive, but thought it prudent to not say too much about her.

"Well, I would have to agree," Victoria said, leaning her head on his shoulder. "You turned out very well. But what kind of person was she? And your father?"

"I don't know my father."

"I'm sorry," Victoria said softly. She lifted her head and looked up at him. "He's dead too?"

"No. I mean, I don't know. I don't know who he is." Silas could see that he was getting in too deep, but then he decided that, as his future wife, Victoria deserved to know. "My mother was a prostitute."

"Oh."

Silas wasn't sure what that simple expression indicated. The couple sitting in front of them, though, turned briefly, then shifted nervously in their seats.

Silas looked at Victoria's face. She smiled and put her head back on his shoulder, so he continued, more quietly. "She worked at a saloon called Goldie's, in Colorado City. When I was younger, I divided my time between Goldie's and the boarding house where I lived with my mother."

The little train was approaching the station and chugged to a stop, and the conversation was interrupted as they filed off with the other passengers. But after Silas got the horse and carriage and helped Victoria up onto it, she continued.

"I'd like to see it."

"See what?" Silas had lost track of the conversation and was concentrating on driving the carriage downhill on Ruxton.

"Where you lived. Where you spent your childhood."

"They're not really places for a lady," Silas said with a little embarrassment.

"Silas, this is the twentieth century," Victoria said in a mildly scolding tone. "Ladies are not the weak, demure little creatures they used to be. Not all of us, anyway. I'd like to think I'm progressive enough to be able to accept somebody's less than perfect family history. Especially somebody I love, and especially when they had nothing to say about that history."

"It will take a little while to get there."

Victoria smiled. "You said up there on the summit that wherever you go, you want me to be there, too. Well, I feel the same way. If I'm with you, Silas Baskin, I don't care how long it takes. Besides, we still have a little bit of the evening left to spend together."

Silas looked at Victoria for a moment. He felt himself being drawn into her eyes, as if they had a gravity all their own. Helplessly giving in to the pull, he leaned toward her and kissed her, not caring if anyone was watching. As they approached Manitou Avenue, he flicked the reins and turned right, heading east through town.

In time, after they had traveled through Manitou and into Colorado City, he pointed out the boarding house, where he had spent his childhood with his mother, until Mr. Wilcox kicked him out after she died. It was a nondescript place, a little more ragged and broken down now than when he had lived there.

Victoria had her arm through his, and he felt her pull it closer to her. Her other hand was caressing his arm, unconsciously, as she looked at the rough dwelling.

They continued through town, past the turn toward Hodges' Mill, and reached the eastern edge of town. Silas pulled the carriage up in front of Goldie's, and he felt a brief pang in his heart. He hadn't been back here since his mother was killed.

He turned toward the right and leaned on the back of the seat to get a better look at the establishment. The shadows were becoming more intense as the sun was down behind the mountains now, but there was light shining out a little high window on the main floor, and in one of the windows upstairs.

"Silas Baskin!"

Silas looked around but couldn't see who had called him. He could see the deepening shadows of twilight, but no details. Then he saw a large form in a deep shadow by the door, and recognized it as Odin, the big bartender, apparently taking a break out front. But Silas knew that that's not where the voice had come from. He could just barely make out Odin turning toward the voice, too.

He glanced around again but, not seeing anybody else, he was just about to call a greeting to Odin, when he heard the voice again.

"You killed my son, you bastard!"

Silas turned toward the voice. He still couldn't see anyone, though he did notice movement in the shadow by the door, where he had recognized Odin.

Victoria was looking around too, apprehensive in this rough and, to her, unfamiliar territory. Silas decided not to take any further chances. Still holding the reins in his left hand, he snapped them against the horse's neck to drive away.

As the horse started forward, the carriage jerked, just as Silas heard a shot behind them. In the same moment, he felt a burning pain in his right arm.

The Odin shadow moved again, coming a little into the light, looking toward the direction of the gunshot. Having pulled his own gun, the big Colt 45 from his belt, there was a flash as he fired and Tom Gardner fell dead, his revolver clattering on the sidewalk in front of him.

"It's alright, Silas," Odin called out, his wild hair flying, as the carriage slowed down.

Silas, his right arm in pain, had slacked up on the reins, and the horse seemed confused as to what to do. Silas pulled back with his left hand and brought the carriage to a stop.

Odin rushed to the carriage and grabbed onto the bridle and harness as the horse reared up, startled. Silas barely noticed him, though.

All he saw was Victoria slumped forward. A widening stain of blood, black in the dim twilight, was spreading on her dress. The bullet, having passed through Silas' arm, had entered her side, a few inches below her left shoulder.

She was dead.

Silas collapsed sobbing next to her in an agony much greater than the pain in his arm.

§

In the hills southeast of Manitou, a sad congregation was gathered around a new grave in Crystal Valley Cemetery.

William Stewart seemed a little smaller than his usual towering self. His shoulders slumped, his head bowed, he was flanked by George and Elizabeth, who were also mourning the loss of their sister.

Others who knew Victoria were there, as the minister paid sad tribute to her caring nature, her sweet disposition, and even her progressive inclination, though not everyone at the turn of the twentieth century considered that a virtue.

But the saddest one in attendance had his right arm in a sling. Silas Baskin was not crying now. He felt as if he were dried up. But his eyes showed very clearly the tremendous sense of loss *that he felt. His sadness was deeper than tears could express, though he had shed plenty of them.*

John and Abbie Hodges stood beside Silas at the grave, with Emily cooing in Abbie's arms.

Silas barely noticed them, though. Lost in a deep, cold sadness stronger than any he had felt since the death of his mother, he was oblivious to others.

Silas had lost the woman who meant the most to him in the whole world.

Again.

ell, thank you, Dorie. That was delicious." Aside from a few shallow pleasantries, dinner had been a quiet affair. Clark Baskin sat back in his chair on the deck, and as he came out from under the umbrella a little, he felt the almost summer sun on the back of his head.

"Thank you," Dora said quietly. She felt herself withdrawing a little with the continued presence of her father, and she tried to fight it, remembering the outcome of her morbidly depressed mother. Having found her several years ago, dead in the bathtub, her wrists slashed, Dora was especially sensitive to her own tendency toward depression. She tried hard to resist things that threatened her own peace of mind.

"What do you do for a living, Mr. Baskin?" Shawn asked.

"I'm retired now, but I used to be a lawyer."

"Oh, really?" Shawn asked. "What kind of law?"

"I started out as a corporate lawyer, but later on, I got more into estate planning."

"Estate planning? What a coincidence," Shawn said. "My brother and I own an estate liquidation company. It's a small business, but it pays the bills. In fact, that's how Dora and I met."

"Yes, I saw on the news about that coin collection," Clark said, seemingly a bit more attentive now. "That was really something!"

"Yeah. Unfortunately, though, we didn't handle that. I'm the one who lined up Sotheby's, but they were a little better equipped to take care of the actual auction on something of that magnitude."

"Hmm." Clark took a drink of his beer, then looked at Dora. "And then you just gave away all of that money? What the hell were you thinking, Dorie?"

Dora thought his tone changed slightly, developing almost an angry edge to it. And it was as if something clicked into place in her mind.

"So that's why you just happened to show up now," she said. "You're wanting a piece of it." Shawn looked up at her with a nervous expression.

"What are you talking about?" Clark asked indignantly. "Why would I think I could get any of the money when I already knew you gave it away?"

Dora looked at him for a moment, trying to puzzle it out. She realized that she hadn't thought it all the way through before speaking.

"But you likely knew about Gramma's stock portfolio. And of course this house."

"I don't want this house, Dorie," he said, shaking his head.

After a pause, Dora said, "I notice you didn't mention the stocks and bonds."

Clark scoffed at that, shaking his head again. "I didn't know about a stock portfolio either."

"You know what?" Dora said with an exasperated voice. "Take it. I don't need it."

"Dorie, come on," Clark said quietly, in a placating tone. "Don't be like that."

"I mean it," she said, throwing up her hands. "Just take the whole damn thing. I don't care."

"Honey, that's not why I came here," he said. "I mean, sure, it would be nice to finish out my days with a little spending cash. But I came here to see you."

"I'm sorry. But I just can't seem to get past the fact that, in all these years, you never had the urge to come and see me until I had some money."

Shawn sat there, trying to keep from squirming in his seat, not knowing whether to say anything or not. Listening to their argument, he decided that Mr. Baskin seemed, to his inexperienced eye, to be a nice but down-on-his-luck guy. But he had to admit, having heard Dora express it, that the timing was indeed suspicious.

"Like I told you earlier, Dorie," Clark said, "I'm sorry about the past. I really am. But there's nothing I can do now to change it, regardless of how much regret I'm carrying around."

Dora stared at him for a few moments, her eyes filled with a dark mood, but she said nothing.

Clark finally broke the silence. "You didn't say anything about it, but a little while ago I noticed that ring on your finger. I didn't see it earlier."

Dora looked at the engagement ring, and then glanced at Shawn. She saw the uncomfortable expression on his face and immediately felt bad about putting him in the middle of this.

"Yes," she said. "Shawn asked me to marry him."

"You're wearing the ring," Clark replied with an easy smile. "I assume you said yes."

"Yes, I did," she said and, despite the smoldering animosity she still felt toward her father, she couldn't resist the urge to smile. Shawn, happy now to be on a more pleasant and comfortable subject, reached over and placed his hand on hers.

"Well, congratulations, you two," Clark said. "When is the wedding going to happen?"

"We haven't gotten that far, yet," Shawn said.

Dora opened her hand and allowed her fingers to interlock with Shawn's. She immediately felt some of her anger wash away.

In a fleeting thought, she wondered if she might be able to keep him with her until her father left.

§

Clark Baskin quietly excused himself shortly after the sun dipped below the mountains. Saying something about

105

giving Shawn and Dora time to themselves, he was glad to be alone again.

Leaving them on the deck, he went in the house and slowly climbed the stairs. He went back into his room, closing and locking the door. Then he leaned against it and sighed.

"Fucking idiot," he thought to himself. He needed to be more careful. He had almost ruined everything. That one stupid remark he made about Dora giving away the money was enough to make her suspicious about his reason for being here.

Clark walked over to the chair that was situated by the window and sat down. The window faced south, with a view of the side yard and stream. There were numerous flower beds, with chairs and benches scattered in little aesthetic groupings.

A hedge of lilacs lined the back edge of the property. While the flowers had passed their peak in the spring, there were roses and cosmos still in bloom, providing a riot of color.

Directly down below the window where Clark sat was the south side of the wraparound deck, and the table where they had just eaten dinner. Shawn and Dora were still there, but with the umbrella opened, they could not be seen, even if he had looked.

But he didn't see any of it. Or he didn't focus on it.

Clark decided that he didn't feel like sitting up. He was so tired, and he discerned that it was probably the altitude.

He wasn't accustomed to it any longer. He stood up and went to the bed, easing himself down.

Then he realized that it wasn't just the altitude. He was an old man now. Fatigue just seemed to be much more common these days.

Dora had said he could have the stocks and bonds, and that could work in his favor. True, she was angry at the time, and he had implied that he didn't want it, to smooth things over with her.

If his trip here was successful, though, maybe he wouldn't need the stock portfolio anyway. The other things that had lured him here had not even been mentioned. Which led him to the conclusion that Dora didn't know anything about them.

But at least now, the thought had been introduced into her mind to give him the money. As long as the thought was there, it could resurface.

But he had to make her want to. It was not like cash, something he could just pick up, stick in his pocket and leave with. She had to voluntarily sign it over to him. Granted, it would be just as effective if she did it angrily. Her hatred would not diminish the value.

But he had to admit, he did still care about Dora. There would always be that. And he even cared about what she thought of him. He didn't want her to see him as just a selfish, opportunistic asshole.

What he had told Dora was true. He really did regret how he had treated her.

God, he regretted so many things!

§

Bridget Lindstrom sat under the awning of her back porch. The phone call had been completely unexpected. She hadn't thought about him in years and had pretty much given up on ever hearing about him again.

She had been only twenty-one years old at the time. She could easily have blamed her youth, her inexperience. Her relative unfamiliarity with the new country.

But no, there had been something about him. She thought he seemed sweet and compassionate, really caring, but with an element of danger. Excitement. Something she couldn't quite put her finger on.

Whatever it was, the appeal was there, so when he approached her table at The Ancient Mariner restaurant and offered to buy her a drink, she accepted. They ended up talking and drinking all evening.

She had spoken extensively about her reason for coming to America in the first place. He seemed genuinely interested in her family tree project, and said that he admired her bravery. Traveling alone to a new country must have been scary.

He also said he loved her accent.

The mid-80s had been a little looser. At least as far as "safe sex" was concerned. AIDS had barely even been heard of yet, and at the time was primarily associated with gay men and intravenous drug users.

So when he asked if she wanted to leave with him, she accepted. Maybe it was the alcohol. Maybe it was the aforementioned personal appeal.

But when he offered to get a room for them at a motel, she said it wouldn't be necessary. She was staying at the Silver Saddle Motel just down the road.

She still couldn't believe that she had done that. She would never dream of doing that now. Apparently she had learned her lesson at some point since that night in 1986.

But she still remembered the fluttering feeling in her stomach as she unlocked and opened the door. A simple motel room. A bed with a gaudy bedspread. A table and two uncomfortable chairs in front of the window. A dresser unit with a TV on it.

Nothing really out of the ordinary.

But she was bringing a strange man into it with her. She had a quick, transitory thought that perhaps she was not doing the right thing. But then she felt his fingers on her back as he came in behind her. And the caution turned into a tingling excitement.

They made a little small talk as Bridget nervously tried to work up the courage to follow through. But he seemed to recognize her nervousness and came to her rescue.

When he kissed her, the tingle turned into an electrical sizzle. She opened her mouth and accepted his tongue, and she tasted a trace of the bourbon he had been drinking.

She felt his hands all over her body, and truth be told, she was exploring his too. She felt his hand under her blouse, and the sudden release as her bra was unfastened. Then she felt one of his hands on her buttocks, pressing her groin hard against his, and she could feel the size and hardness of his erection already pressing against her. His other hand was at the back of her neck, supporting her head.

All she could do was hold on.

By the time they were both naked, Bridget felt a little dizzy, no doubt a combination of alcohol and stimulation. Her need to lie down only accommodated his desire.

And hers, too, she had to admit.

Flames crawled relentlessly up the dry wood, crackling and popping, finally erupting into a respectable fire. Silas stepped back away from the heat. He watched as the column of smoke rose into the sky, then about forty feet high, it was whipped away by a cold current of wind.

"Run fast, my friend," Silas said softly as the smoke curved away from him and a tear slipped down his cheek, disappearing into his beard.

The smoke blended with the lead grey clouds overhead, the mixture steadily making its way eastward across the late autumn sky. Silas sat down on the ground, leaning back against a tree.

"Don't worry, Bella," he said toward the fire. "I'll be here till it's all over."

The world had changed. The industrial revolution of the nineteenth century had shrunk the world. New technologies of the early twentieth century made it even smaller and faster.

In a matter of just a few years, strange terms had crept into the American vocabulary and become household words. Words like relativity, cubism, radioactivity. Proper names like Titanic, Chevrolet, Chaplin, Versailles.

Silas Baskin, in late November of 1919, was all but oblivious to this new world.

After Victoria's death in 1904, John Hodges had cautioned him against isolating himself. And Silas had tried. He really had. He stayed on at their inn while his arm healed. But he found that the guests constantly coming and going offered no appeal to him. He just wanted to be alone, so he spent much of his time in his room.

He tried after his arm was healed, too. But there was just too much that reminded him. All of the places that he and Victoria had gone to in Manitou. And Colorado City, which now inflicted the double pain of being where both his mother and Victoria had been killed.

Even the sitting room next to his room at the inn was a painful reminder.

The worst of what would later become known as the Colorado Labor Wars was over, but many conflicts continued. Hearing about that brought back the guilt of his involvement in the bombings, which were also, ultimately, responsible for Victoria's death.

There was just too much.

So in December of 1904, Silas found and purchased some remote property near Eastonville, Colorado, on the edge of an area known as the Black Forest. There wasn't much to it — a small cabin, with a small stable and barn, on several acres of land. The land was partly covered with dense pine forest and partly with farmland for growing potatoes.

But it was secluded.

A few miles northeast of Colorado Springs, it was unfamiliar, and relatively far away from anybody Silas knew.

He thought that farming might be just the thing for him. The fact was that he was ready for anything, as long as it wasn't in the mining industry.

Not wanting to try to explain or justify the move to John and Abbie, and likely have them try to talk him out of it, he had quietly packed up his things very early one morning, even before they were up, and disappeared sadly in the dark.

The isolation of his new life suited his state of mind. He had contact with a few people in Eastonville early on when he was getting himself set up on the property, buying certain things he needed. But he was far enough outside of the tiny town that gradually his association with people reduced to the point that he rarely saw anybody.

In his seclusion, he had started talking to Bella, his horse, or to himself when she wasn't around. He had little contact with other people, and after a while, he found that he didn't really miss them, aside from feeling a yearning for the adopted family he had left behind in Manitou. Growing or killing whatever food he needed, Silas settled into a peaceful life. A lonely but comfortable reclusive existence.

One day followed another, each year turned into the next.

That's not to say that he never noticed any changes. From a distance, for example, he had begun seeing strange-looking carriages going past the perimeter of his property, driven without horses. He saw them a little more closely on those very rare occasions when he went into town for clothing or other items he

114

couldn't provide himself. He was mildly curious, but that was the extent of it.

At least until Bella died.

The mare had been with Silas since John Hodges had first given her to him eighteen years earlier. Now, deprived of her companionship, Silas mourned her loss. And without Bella around, he also began feeling more acutely the absence of human companionship.

As the fire gradually died down to embers and the smoke from Bella's funeral pyre dissipated, Silas, now thirty-three years old, stood up.

Lacking a mode of transportation which Bella had always afforded him before, Silas realized that he had to take action. He sighed as he cast one last look at the charred remains of the fire.

"Don't get mad at me, old girl," he said, "but it looks like I need to get another horse."

His acreage wasn't that large, but he wanted to be able to get around faster than he could on foot. And for the first time in years, he began considering the possibility of visiting friends in Manitou.

When he had moved here, Silas brought all the money he had saved. It wasn't a fortune, but he had used only a small portion of it in getting settled, and in those few shopping trips. The rest had remained untouched.

So a couple of days after Bella's death, on a sunny late autumn morning, Silas gathered his money and started walking toward town.

§

While he was walking toward Eastonville to buy a horse, Silas had passed the Bruner farm where a hand-lettered "For Sale" sign mounted on the fence at the front of the property caught his eye. Silas stopped and pondered for a moment, then he went back and looked at the sign again. He went inside the gate and found Mr. Bruner to inquire.

"It's a few years old," Mr. Bruner said. Leaning against a fence post, the old farmer lowered his head a little, lifting his hat and scratching his head. "It belonged to my son. He was killed in the war."

"I'm sorry," Silas said, wondering what war Bruner was referring to.

"I got no need for it," the man continued.

Silas looked now at the Ford Model T. The shiny black metal had been polished recently, with only the slightest film of dust on it, practically unavoidable on a farm, he realized. The glass sparkled, the wood spokes gleamed, and the brass trim glowed almost blindingly in the late autumn sunlight.

"It's a beautiful machine," Silas said with a note of awe in his voice. However, he had an expression of doubt on his face, feeling far out of his element. "But I don't really know anything about them. How do you work it?"

"Oh, it's the easiest thing in the world," Bruner said. He waved his hand in a gesture that indicated that there was nothing to it. "Here, let me show you."

He demonstrated turning the crank to start the engine, and invited Silas to get in the automobile with him. Silas was excited as he climbed in, and he watched Bruner carefully. Taking it for a few turns around his property, Bruner showed Silas how to use the pedals to shift gears, how to control the throttle with the lever on the steering column, how to turn with the steering wheel, how to stop with the brake pedal.

When Bruner allowed Silas to take the automobile for a spin himself to try it out, Silas was captivated!

He paid Bruner for the car and drove it away.

Driving his new motorcar through Eastonville, surprisingly, did not turn as many heads as Silas had expected. There were other automobiles in the area, as he already knew, having seen them drive past his property. But even though it may have been old news to the rest of the world, it was new and wonderful to Silas. He loved it.

It wasn't long before his new mode of transportation, in addition to his more intensely-felt lack of companionship, motivated Silas to point his Model T to the southwest and head back toward Manitou.

But navigating the new route was confusing at first. He had to follow roads, some of which had not been there when he had travelled here fifteen years earlier. And some roads were paved while others were not. To add to the confusion, Colorado Springs had become more heavily populated in the intervening years.

Eventually, though, he made his way through Colorado City, then Manitou. Choked with other automobiles, travel was sometimes slow, and often he found that the appeal of driving his newfangled contraption was waning.

When he finally drove the gravel-covered road up the mountain west of Manitou and parked in front of the inn, he exhaled audibly, turning the motor off and relishing the sudden quiet. The area in front of the log house had been cleared for a parking area, and there were several other motorcars parked here as well. Silas decided that the Hodges' inn must be doing very well.

As he looked at the structure, though, he saw a window, the one in the den on the right, broken and boarded up. Apparently some kind of accident had occurred and had not yet been repaired. He figured it must have been recent and they just had not had a chance to rectify it yet, as something like that might detract from their business.

He waited in the car for a few moments, relaxing after the jarring ride, wondering what kind of reception he would receive. Remembering how he had left, Silas steeled himself for well-deserved anger, and stepped down out of his car. He climbed the steps to the porch and took a deep breath.

He reached for the doorknob, but before he could get a grip on it, the front door was whisked open. Abbie, fifteen years older but still beautiful, and apparently pregnant, stood there looking at him.

"Hi, Abbie," Silas said quietly.

Without a word, she stepped forward and threw her arms around his neck.

§

"All this time, and you've only been about thirty miles away," Hodges said. Silas simply nodded.

He was sitting in the parlor – or what they now called the living room – with John and Abbie. He felt right at home, almost as if he had never left.

And yet so much had changed.

Sixteen-year-old Emily was there. She had been a baby the last time he saw her, but now was a young, grown-up beauty with dark skin and hair the color of honey. With her were her younger sisters, thirteen-year-old Jane and eleven-year-old Olivia, both possessing similar beauty.

"So you just moved away from us and made new friends, did you?" Abbie asked. Her tone was scolding, but it was softened by a bit of a smile.

"No," Silas replied. "I mean you're only half right. I had virtually no contact with any other people. It was a lonely existence, but that's exactly what I wanted after I lost Victoria. As time passed, my solitary life just became a routine. I became accustomed to it. Then, before I knew it, fifteen years had gone by and I was officially a hermit."

"Well, we're very glad to have you back," Abbie said, as she laboriously stood up from her chair. "Just promise us that you won't ever do that again!" She leaned over and kissed Silas on the cheek.

"I promise."

"Come on, girls, help me with dinner." As the girls got up, Abbie smiled again at Silas and they filed out of the room, leaving him and John alone.

"Would you like a drink?" Hodges asked as he stood and walked across the room to his liquor cabinet.

"I don't know," Silas said with a smile. "I don't know if I can handle it anymore. I haven't had alcohol in fifteen years."

"There's talk about outlawing alcohol. I can't believe that it will actually happen, but we might want to use up what I have, just in case."

"Alright, I guess I'll have one. So, what happened to the window in the den?"

"Oh, we just had a visit from our old friends, Fian Rúnda," Hodges said in a dismissing tone as he poured two glasses of whiskey.

"Who?"

"Long story. I'll tell you later."

Before Hodges went back toward Silas, he saw an envelope that was stuck in the back of the cabinet, behind the bottles. He pulled it out and looked at it for a second, then he put it under his arm. He picked up the drinks and walked back toward Silas, handing him a glass.

Silas sipped the whiskey, feeling the old familiar warmth as it slipped down his throat.

Hodges sat down and took a sip, holding the envelope in his other hand.

"Having been away for so long," he said, "you probably haven't heard the news. William Stewart died about five years ago. He was a sad old man. He aged quickly. Like you, he never really got over Victoria's death.

"I don't know how far his sorrow went, but he did finally feel bad about the way he left things with you. So when he died, he left something to you in his will."

Hodges handed him the envelope. Silas accepted it gingerly and looked at Hodges.

"I'll leave you alone with that," Hodges said. "Take however much time you need to look it over." Then he stood and left the room.

Silas placed his drink down on the table beside his chair and looked at the envelope. On the front was typed:

Silas Baskin
In care of:
John Edward Hodges
24 Elk Run
City

Silas slipped his finger under the flap and tore the envelope open, pulling the contents from it. The first thing he saw was a letter, written in longhand.

Dear Silas,

I hope you will take the time to read this letter, and not just throw it away when you see who it is from. I am a man full of regrets. I don't expect for you to feel sympathetic, knowing how badly I treated you on our last meeting. But let me state that, had I to do it over again, that meeting would go much differently.

Victoria loved you. I know that. To my shame, I knew it then. But I allowed my attention to be too fixed on my own affairs, and I gave too little care to those of others. For that, Silas, I offer you my sincerest apology, and I hope that you can find it in your heart to forgive me.

I hear that you have gone away, and nobody knows your whereabouts. I know that this is largely due to your intense sorrow over losing Victoria, but in hindsight, I also know that I didn't make it easy for you. And for that, again, I apologize.

I will leave this gift in the hands of your good friend John Hodges, in the hopes that, should you reappear, you may benefit from my own sorrow. You may feel that I'm just trying to salve my own conscience, and indeed that may be partly the case. But I do genuinely hope that this gift will lighten your burden, and that you will find some measure of happiness.

Your humble and penitent friend,
William Joseph Stewart

Silas stared at the letter for a few moments, reluctantly revisiting that last morning. Then he sighed and refolded the letter, putting it on his lap. The next item that had been in the envelope was a map, showing a detailed area north of Cripple Creek, with a small rectangular plot outlined in red ink.

Unsure of the point of the map, he put it aside as well. He unfolded the last item and saw the words "Mining Deed" at the top. Signed over to Silas Baskin from William J. Stewart was the deed to the Victoria gold mine. Following that were coordinates to its location north of Cripple Creek. A smaller folded piece of paper was inside it, and Silas opened it up. It was a handwritten note from Stewart.

> The Victoria mine had started producing good color. A rich vein was discovered just before the main tunnel collapsed. Two men died in the cave-in, and I closed the mine temporarily. But then, after my little girl died, I never revisited the mine. I hope you can profit from it.
> William

Silas looked at the items again, unsure how he felt about them. But a tear formed in his eye over yet another late reminder of Victoria's death.

§

"I hope you decide to stay," Hodges said, placing his hand on Silas' shoulder. "I could really use your help."

"I don't know, John. I got out of the mining business years ago, and I didn't want to go back." Silas stood before the living room window, watching a car pulling up in front. Guests were returning for the evening as snow started to fall.

"I understand. But the business has changed. It's not so volatile anymore. Some of the mines have played out and several mills have shut down. But we're still doing very well, and my people are happy."

"Well, that's great. But why do you need me?"

"I need a capable manager. You're good with people, and you know the processes and the business."

A young couple came in the front door, laughing and brushing snowflakes from their shoulders. They wiped their feet on the rug inside the door and they nodded and smiled a greeting when they saw Hodges. Then they went upstairs.

"That was a long time ago, John."

"I know, but the milling procedures really haven't changed much at all since then." John paused and looked down for a moment. He took a deep breath before looking back up at Silas. He continued, but he spoke a little quieter. "The truth is Abbie's having a harder time with this pregnancy. She's forty-five years old, and it took us by surprise."

"She's alright, isn't she?" Silas asked.

"She's fine, but she just gets tired quickly. The girls help her out around here, but they're too young to be completely responsible for the inn. I want to be able to spend a little more time here and carry some of the load. So I need a manager I can trust at the mill."

Silas felt a flutter of anxiety at the thought of reentering the mining business. But unless he was going to remain in exile in his cabin, he did need to be able to support himself. And Hodges was right; Silas did know the mill inside and out.

"Alright," he said as he turned and extended his right hand. Hodges took it enthusiastically.

"Oh Silas, that's swell! I'll pay you a sawbuck a day, with free room and board."

"What? Are you crazy? You really do need a manager. You'll go broke in no time if you pay me ten dollars a day."

"I'm happy to do it, Silas," Hodges smiled. "It will be worth it to me to know that someone I can depend on is taking care of the mill for me."

Silas turned back to the window as he heard another car drive up. He hoped he was doing the right thing.

S hawn turned out the bathroom light and came into the bedroom. The year before, Dora had completely renovated the unfinished basement and turned it into a nice master suite, leaving all of the upstairs rooms for guests.

She was sitting up in bed, now, her elbows on her knees, looking pensively at the engagement ring.

"You're not having second thoughts, are you?" Shawn asked. Dora looked up at him, then smiled and shook her head.

"No. I just . . . I don't know. I hope we can do it better than my parents did."

Shawn pulled the covers down and got into bed under the sheet. Leaning on his elbow, he looked at Dora.

"No two marriages are alike, babe."

"I know," she replied. "And I know we're getting off to a better start than they did. Mom's depression showed up pretty early, but I guess Dad thought he could handle it, that he could take care of her."

"And you're afraid that it will show up in you."

"Actually, it already has. I *know* I have the tendency. Kind of a double-whammy, because I think my Dad was depressed, too. Of course, he never saw anybody about it or had it diagnosed. Men were supposed to be strong and 'get over it.' But about the time that Grampa died, even though I was only six and a half years old, I remember seeing a change in him."

"What kind of change?"

Dora furrowed her brow, thinking about it. "It varied. Sometimes sad, sometimes angry.

"Angry at you, or just in general?"

"Sometimes at me, although it could have been in general and I just happened to be there at the time."

She sat back against her pillows as she reflected.

"I do remember the very first time I noticed it, though. We were living in kind of a dumpy place in south Denver, but at least it was still a house. That was before we had to move into an apartment.

"My dad went on occasional business trips. Come to think of it, I'm not really sure why. I never thought to question it when I was a kid. He may have been doing estate planning by then, and maybe he had to travel to see some of his clients.

"Anyway, he had just come back from one of his trips a couple of weeks before, and suddenly we had to move. We'd moved once or twice before that, but this is the first time I remember being really aware of it. At the time, it just seemed like an adventure to me.

"I was actually looking forward to it, to living in a new home, having a new room, a new neighborhood. To a little kid, it was exciting.

"My mom wasn't happy about it, though. She and Dad were fighting a lot more, and I remember the dejected look on her face when she instructed me to pack up anything I wouldn't be using in the next week. I was six years old and it was summertime, so that meant a few indoor toys and my winter clothes. I got it done quickly.

"But I was a sensitive kid, and I could see that the move wasn't having as good an effect on my parents, so I wanted to help them out. I decided that I would pack up some of their things, too."

"Trying to be a relief worker even back then," Shawn said. Dora nodded, somewhat lost in thought.

"Dad had a workshop in the garage where he would putter around sometimes. He'd do minor appliance repairs, or even occasionally build small, simple pieces of furniture." Dora smiled wistfully. "I remember I had a little rocking chair in my room that he had built for me. He let me paint it myself.

"But I had heard him lament a few times that he just didn't have the time to spend in his workshop like he used to. So I thought I would be safe packing up some of those things. I knew he wouldn't be needing them in the next week.

"So I found an empty box and dragged it to a cabinet by his work bench. I knew he kept paints, glues and finishes in there. I remember feeling really good about helping my parents, easing their strain, and I had just opened that cabinet when Dad came into the garage.

"He started yelling at me, to stay out of that cabinet. I tried to explain to him that I was only trying to help, but he slapped me. I ran back into the house crying."

Shawn instinctively caressed her arm sympathetically.

"That night, he came into my room. He said, 'I'm sorry I slapped you, Dorie.' He hadn't hit me that hard, but I was still smarting emotionally, and I didn't say anything. He said, 'I was afraid for you because there are a lot of things in that cabinet that can hurt you.'

"Well, I was indignant. I said, 'I know I'm not supposed to drink that stuff, Daddy. I'm not a baby.'

"He said, 'I know you're not. I was just afraid for you. But I was wrong to slap you.'

"I accepted his apology, but I was pretty wary after that."

"And you said that was around the time your grandfather died?" Shawn asked.

"Mm-hmm," Dora nodded. "I didn't know what it was back then when I was a kid, but looking back in later years, I recognized the signs of depression in him. The melancholy, the sudden bursts of anger.

"In time, it got better, but never really went away."

"He seems like a sad old man now," Shawn said.

Dora nodded again, then looked at Shawn and kissed him.

"We *are* going to do it better," she said.

"Absolutely!" Shawn agreed. "The tendency you mentioned doesn't mean it will ever turn into full-blown clinical depression. And I don't have any tendency toward depression myself. In fact, nobody in my family ever has. I'll be a good influence," he smiled.

Dora peered into Shawn's eyes, and seemed to draw strength from them.

"We're going to have a good life," she concluded.

"Yes, we are." Shawn reached over to the bedside lamp and turned it off, and they both slid down under the sheet. Shawn molded himself into Dora's back, and with his arms around her, she fell asleep feeling content, but with an undercurrent of sadness for her parents.

§

Down in Colorado Springs, Bridget Lindstrom turned her toothbrush off and placed it back on its charger. She blotted her mouth on the towel and, after one last look in the mirror, turned out the light.

The bed felt particularly good when she lay down on it. Her memories had been plaguing her since she received the phone call. They didn't appear to be letting up yet, and she felt fatigued. Really dead tired.

The morning after her one night stand back in 1986 had been tough. Besides the hangover, she had an empty bed next to her. He had left the motel sometime before she woke up.

She kicked herself for being so stupid. She had just met the guy. After a couple of hours of drinking with him, she takes him to her motel room and has sex with him. And having gotten what he wanted, he was gone.

Bridget wondered how differently her life would have turned out if she had never met him. She had to admit that it really hadn't been such a bad life. But there were some things she had issues with.

She still did, even now.

§

Clark Baskin lay on his bed, somewhere between sleep and wakefulness. Racked with anxiety about his future, his mind kept tumbling into the past.

When he was young, he had heard the stories of his father's life so many times that, through the years, he had come to be able to visualize them. The mental movies were showing more and more, the higher his stress levels rose.

But he shouldn't let his stress get so high. Anxiety clouded his thinking.

He needed to think clearly.

He needed to stay alive.

Silas Baskin closed his eyes and kneaded the side of his head with his knuckles. He took a deep breath and sighed, wishing for a break in the routine. The headache was worse today.

Since he had started working at the mill again, he hadn't been sleeping very well. The job itself, the responsibility he bore, the interaction with so many people, it was all such a great and sudden change from the previous fifteen years that he figured it was just going to require a period of adjustment.

He allowed some time for the adjustment, and his sleep did eventually improve, but then, in the late spring of 1920, it had become a little more fitful again. Most days, he was tired and had a headache.

At John and Abbie's suggestion, he had visited a doctor who, upon learning of his connection to the Hodges, an influential family in the area, conducted a rather extensive interview with Silas. The doctor was something of an admirer of practitioners of the emerging psychiatric and psychological sciences. His interview introduced the thought that Silas' return to his old surroundings was making him feel the approaching anniversary of Victoria's death more acutely.

Silas didn't know much about these new sciences, but the doctor's theory made sense to him. The laudanum that he had given Silas helped him to sleep better, and he got past Victoria's anniversary unscathed.

But the headaches and sleepiness continued. It turned out that Hodges had begun having them too.

A revelation came one day in late June.

Hodges had been spending less time at the mill and more time home at the inn. Silas was a good manager, though, so Hodges' time at the mill was often spent just walking around, watching what was going on. One day, he was called to his office for a telephone call.

He wasn't in there very long.

"Silas," Hodges said as he rushed out of his office, "Emily just called. Abbie's gone into labor. She's having the baby! I have to go."

"Of course," Silas said with a smile. "Good luck! I look forward to meeting your son when I get home."

Hodges smiled and slapped him on the shoulder, rushing out the door. After Hodges drove away, Silas turned when he heard a commotion behind him on the mill floor.

"What's going on?" he asked as he ran toward a cluster of workers.

"It's Clyde!" said Billy Benson, one of the ore crusher operators. "He's having some kind of fit!"

Silas shouldered his way through the crowd and found Clyde Rankin having seizures on the floor. Silas knelt down beside him. Clyde's skin was very pink.

"Billy, you and Otis get him over to Doc Howard's!" The doctor's office was only a block away.

He watched as the two men struggled to pick up their companion, an arm over each of their shoulders, and they rushed out the door with him.

Silas stood back up and felt dizzy, and his head throbbed.

The doctor immediately admitted Clyde to the hospital with cyanide poisoning, but by that time, he was in a coma. Clyde would eventually end up dying later that afternoon.

A cursory investigation revealed a mislabeled cyanide drum. Cyanide was used in the gold extraction process, and great care was taken in the use and storage of the chemical. But this particular drum had not been cared for properly. Either due to an error at the supplier or here at the mill, it was labeled incorrectly. It had been slowly leaking for an indeterminate time, possibly months. The unfiltered fumes had been gradually infiltrating the mill.

Upon questioning, a number of the mill workers admitted to experiencing headaches, weakness, shortness of breath and occasional dizziness. Had the leak occurred during the colder months, when the building was closed up tighter, the result could have been even more disastrous than it was.

All of the workers were sent home, or to the doctor for examination, and Hodges' Mill was closed down that afternoon to await decontamination.

§

Silas drove his Model T home from the mill. He was feeling better now, being out in the fresh air. As he thought back about it now, he realized that he usually felt a little better when he left the mill. He had always thought that it was just relief at the work day being over.

As he drove through Manitou and up the mountain, he thought about how best to break the news to Hodges about the mill, and about Clyde. He would probably be somewhat distracted anyway, with the baby's arrival. Silas decided that the direct approach would probably be best. Get his attention, then just come out and tell him.

Silas forgot all about the problems at the mill, though, when he arrived at the inn and saw Doctor Young driving away in his car. He didn't seem happy.

The girls were all sitting on the divan in the living room when Silas walked in. Emily was in the middle, holding the other two, and all three were crying. Silas was about to ask them what was wrong when he heard a door close upstairs. Hodges started slowly down the staircase, leaning heavily on the polished yellow pine handrail.

Silas had never seen him looking so sad.

As Hodges neared the bottom of the stairs, he noticed Silas standing in the entryway.

"John, what's wrong?" Silas asked.

"It's Abbie," John said quietly. He was struggling to hold back the tears.

He looked toward the living room, at the girls, and he lowered his voice. "She's dead, Silas. Abbie's dead."

Silas took a step back and suddenly felt as if someone had punched him in the stomach. He stood there in shock for a moment, unable to take a breath, feeling the tears coming to his own eyes.

Even though Abbie was only thirteen years older than Silas, she was the closest thing he had to a mother since his own mother was killed. She had loved and cared for him as a son, and though he had never actually told her, he loved her deeply.

"What happened?" he whispered.

"She hemorrhaged." Hodges seemed exhausted. His eyes were dry, but they were red and swollen, and Silas knew that he had been crying. He gave a brief shudder before he continued. "I admit this pregnancy came as a surprise to both of us. We knew there was a greater possibility of complications at her age. Her blood pressure was pretty high when she was in labor, and when she started bleeding, the doctor just couldn't stop it."

"Oh, John, I'm so sorry." Silas walked toward him and wrapped his arms around him, and the contact caused them both to start sobbing.

The girls saw them from the living room and, still weeping, joined them in a sad huddle. Hodges finally broke the silence.

"But, as bad as this news is," he said to Silas and the girls, "it's not all bad. The baby is fine." Caught up in their shared grief, Silas hadn't even given a thought to the newborn.

"He's alright?" Silas asked, wiping his eyes.

"She. We had another girl." Hodges managed a bit of a smile for his three daughters gathered around him. "She's asleep now. Her name is Isadora."

§

In July of 1922, when she was almost twenty years old, Emily Hodges married a young jeweler from Colorado Springs with the serendipitous name of Russell Silverman. The happy day was marred only by Abbie's absence. John Hodges escorted Emily down the aisle with a smile on his face.

Friends remarked that it was the happiest they had seen him in a couple of years.

Hodges had been experiencing some breathing complaints. In January of 1923, he developed a cough which proved to be debilitating to him. He spent some time in the hospital, fighting pneumonia, while Silas managed the mill.

Gwenn, the young lady they had hired to help with the inn back in 1901 had gotten married ten years later, so they had hired Mary, a widow, to take her place. Still with them, she now took on more responsibility, along with Jane and Olivia, to manage the inn.

Jane was eighteen years old in 1924 when she married a cattle rancher from Cheyenne, Wyoming. John Hodges was present, but his lung issues continued.

His doctor speculated that the cyanide leak at the mill had caused damage that might afflict him for the rest of his life. He had spent a week in the hospital, battling another respiratory infection, and had been discharged only a few days before.

Jane had postponed the wedding for a week to allow her father to be present. Too weak to escort her down the aisle, though, the happy job was delegated to Silas, now a deeply loved and trusted member of the family.

Silas himself experienced occasional respiratory problems as a result of his continuous exposure to the cyanide, but not to the extent that Hodges did. Winter was the hardest time, when the air was cold. Outside, his inhalations felt like a knife in his chest, and he sometimes had to stop in his tracks when a coughing fit seized him.

During a cold spell in late November, John Hodges began coughing up blood, and was admitted to the hospital. Silas arranged for the girls to be able to visit him, even after visiting hours. Silas himself spent hours with him in his hospital room. He was holding Hodges' hand when he died. Hodges was fifty years old.

In his will, he bequeathed generous cash sums to both Emily and Jane, and trust funds for sixteen-year-old Olivia and four-year-old Isadora. Silas was also left cash, as well as the smaller log home south of the inn.

And he was given ownership of the mill and the inn, with the request that, should he ever wish to divest himself of the responsibility, they be left to Hodges' daughters.

Silas was also named the legal guardian of Olivia and Isadora. Considering that, by now, he loved them as if they were his own flesh and blood, he did not find that to be too onerous a task.

At thirty-eight years old, Silas was now the wealthy heir of a family dynasty.

ora woke up early Thursday morning ready to work. Before falling asleep the night before, she decided that she didn't like the direction her thoughts had been going yesterday. Her father's surprise appearance had thrown her for a loop. She decided that she was going to focus her attention on her guests and her other responsibilities in the bed and breakfast, and try to give as little thought to his presence as possible. The weekend was approaching, and weekends were always a busier time anyway.

The problem was, with the Black Forest fire still raging, there were fewer guests showing up. Two more had cancelled their reservation yesterday afternoon, the phone call that had come in just after Shawn had proposed to her, which meant that she still had only one couple staying in the B&B.

And her father.

Her duties would be pretty light again today, so there would be little to distract her from the disquietude she had been feeling with him here.

But she was also scheduled to do a volunteer shift at the orphanage today. That should help.

She went upstairs to the kitchen and turned on the light. The first order of business was coffee. The first coffee maker was brewing and the second just starting when Robin arrived to help with breakfast.

"Morning," she said, her eyes half closed.

"Hi," Dora replied with a smile. Robin usually arrived in that condition, but perked up as she drank coffee and got to work on the food.

"Four for breakfast?" Robin asked.

"Actually, two cancelled yesterday afternoon."

"Oh," Robin said, and she managed to say it with a little sympathy despite her flagging motivation. She went to the first coffee maker as it beeped and poured herself a cup of coffee. "So just two again."

"No, it's three." Robin looked up at Dora through her early morning fog, confused. "My father showed up just after you left yesterday."

Robin's eyes opened wider, without the help of her coffee, which she put down on the counter.

"Oh my God! I thought he was dead!"

"I never knew for sure. It just seemed that, for all intents and purposes, he was *probably* dead. Turns out I was wrong."

Robin looked at Dora's face for a moment, studying her expression, before responding.

"You don't seem happy about it. Was it rough?"

Dora hesitated, with a furrowed brow, taking a moment to get eggs out of the refrigerator.

"Just internally," she sighed. "You know how I am. He seemed very sad and contrite about what he did. And I almost feel sorry for him about that. But I'm having a hard time knowing what to do about it. I mean, how do you just forgive someone who supposedly loved you, and then left without a trace? Leaving you to deal with the most difficult time of your life all alone?"

Robin shook her head and took a sip of coffee.

"I love him as my father," Dora concluded, "but I hate him for what he did to my mother and me."

Robin nodded her understanding and took another sip, but she stopped when a flash of light caught her eye.

"Uh, Dora?" she said, pointing at Dora's hand on the counter. "What's that?"

Dora looked at where Robin was pointing and saw the engagement ring. In spite of the dark thoughts she had just been expressing, she smiled.

§

Gash Seever directed his black BMW Z4 convertible northward on the Garden State Parkway. He maneuvered back and forth across the lanes, deftly cutting through traffic with the precision and self-confidence of a veteran brain surgeon.

Trees rushed past on both sides of the road as Gash left the other cars behind him. He hated being stuck in traffic, but he loved driving when he could really move. In fact, there was only one thing that he did by himself that he liked more than driving, and that was flying.

Having acquired his pilot's license several years ago, and then buying his Cessna 172 single engine plane a year after that, his business had 'taken off,' as he liked to say. Being able to get to targets across the country without having to depend on the big airlines saved him a lot of time and money.

Not to mention simplifying the transporting of the tools of his trade.

The only thing he knew of that would improve his situation would be if he could afford a jet. Seeing the private Learjets at the airport was enough to get him salivating.

Maybe someday.

It had been so freeing when he went freelance. Gash could take on jobs for anybody who could pay his price, and he didn't have to pretend he liked his employers, or their politics. But he had demonstrated over the years that once contracted, his loyalty was unquestioned. The job would be done, clean and quick.

Gash didn't like the term 'hit man.' He felt that it belittled his talents. It was such a crude word, so beneath the amount of attention and finesse that he devoted to the job. Besides, he wasn't always hired to kill. Sometimes he was hired simply as a go-between. Occasionally people would forget where their loyalties lie and just needed to be convinced to do the right thing. Many of his previous marks had been thus persuaded, and were still alive.

Gash preferred the term 'enforcer.' It seemed to convey the nuances of what his job really entailed. He had liked that term ever since he saw the Clint Eastwood movie of the same name years ago. Gash didn't care about the incongruity, the fact that Dirty Harry was a cop and not a mob enforcer.

The trees thinned out as the road rose up a little, turning into a bridge across the bay. In time, the trees returned, giving the illusion that he was driving on a country road. But it wasn't long before he took the cloverleaf to switch over to the Atlantic City Expressway, a busier and more crowded highway.

With the early morning sun at his back now, the heavier traffic irritated him, but he only had to drive a couple more miles before he came to his exit, taking him to the Atlantic City International Airport.

He had been in the New Jersey area for quite a while now. It would do him good to get away.

Colorado sounded nice this time of year.

§

Bridget Lindstrom was up after a fitful night. Normally she would be sleeping in on a Thursday in June, but this year she had opted to teach summer school classes.

She wished now that she hadn't.

She couldn't get her past mistakes out of her mind. Those memories were what had interrupted her sleep.

Bridget vividly remembered the disappointment she had felt when she discovered that he had left before she woke up that morning in 1986. As she lay there in bed, she could still smell him on the pillow next to her. She could still feel his hands on her body.

And she could feel the tidal wave of regret washing over her.

But time heals all wounds, as the saying goes. During the weeks that followed, the regret gradually eased a little as she distanced herself from the event. She got a job in Colorado Springs and moved into an apartment, ready to take on her new life with gusto.

But as much as her life had changed, it was nothing compared to the mutation that was brought on by a little bit of blue water.

The instructions for the First Response home pregnancy test said to wait twenty minutes for the result. She remembered the anxiety she felt as she paced around her apartment, trying to focus her attention on other things instead of just watching the little glass test tube.

But the blue water was unmistakable. She was pregnant.

That weekend, she went up to the Garden of the Gods. She needed to be in a place where she could think clearly about what to do. She found the forest and the ancient red rock formations to be a good place to do that, away from the city, and totally immersed in primeval nature.

After spending a few hours there, though, she was still undecided. From Garden of the Gods, she drove west a little ways into nearby Manitou Springs. Revisiting the 'scene of the crime' was the phrase that came to mind.

And she saw him again.

She had wanted him to know about the baby, but she didn't know how to find him. She didn't know his last name. So as she ate dinner in the Ancient Mariner, she felt a disorienting blend of relief and anger when she saw him walk in.

If he was surprised to see her, he didn't show it. When he saw her, he just walked over to her table as if she had been waiting for him. He smiled easily as he sat down, as if it was expected.

"How are you doing?" he asked.

"Pregnant," Bridget responded, going for the shock factor. Now the surprise showed, but only for a moment. He got past it quickly.

"Is it mine?" he asked quietly. Bridget just nodded. "What are you going to do?"

"That's what I've been trying to decide. The idea of getting an abortion doesn't appeal to me, but as a young single girl in a foreign country, I have far from ideal circumstances for raising a child."

"I'm sorry, Bridget," he said quietly. "But I'm not in a position to marry you."

"Who the hell asked you to?" she exclaimed. Belatedly, she self-consciously looked around the tavern as a few people looked up at her. She took a breath and lowered her voice. "I don't want to get married yet either. We had fun a few weeks ago, but I'm not looking to settle down in the American Dream just yet."

"It *was* fun, wasn't it?" he asked, a bit of a smile adorning his lips. "God, you were an outstanding lover!"

"Not really the point of the conversation," she replied, but feeling his eyes on her, hearing his smooth voice telling her what a great lover she was, she didn't say it with as much conviction as she had planned.

Instead, she was looking at his face. My God, he's so good looking! Sitting there at her table, she could feel his hands on her again, caressing her skin. She tasted his lips on hers, felt his tongue probing her mouth. She could feel their naked bodies pressed together.

And as the evening progressed, she hated the fact that her resolve was crumbling once again.

She heard the clock in the living room chime, yanking her back to the present. With a gasp, she gulped down the coffee in her cup. Then she grabbed her keys and her purse and rushed out the door.

Silas stuffed the last box into a gap at the back of his flatbed truck. He slipped the rear gate down in its slots onto the back of the truck and secured it. The day was blazing hot and it was not even noon yet. He pulled a handkerchief from his back pocket and wiped the sweat from his face.

He looked around and saw the river a few feet in front of him, on the other side of the road. He was tempted to slip into it and cool off, but then he remembered that he wasn't alone. He reached up and got his shirt off the stake side rail of the flatbed where he had hung it earlier. It was a bit of a chore to pull it back on over his sweaty arms and shoulders.

It was July, 1928. Only a few months before, Charles Lindbergh had been presented a Medal of Honor for his flight across the Atlantic Ocean. A couple of months later, Amelia Earhart became the first woman to fly across the Atlantic, but as a passenger. Just this month, the very first machine-sliced and wrapped loaf of bread was sold in Chillicothe, Missouri, thus establishing a benchmark against which the greatness of virtually every technological advancement henceforth would be measured. Prohibition, which John Hodges didn't think would ever actually happen, was now in its eighth year. Women's hair had gotten shorter, and so had their skirts.

Olivia was twenty years old and was getting married in three days. Chester Faraday was a young man who lived in Manitou. He had worked at a competing gold mill in Colorado City for a couple of years. But then the mill closed up shop and Chet came to Hodges' Mill looking for work. Silas knew Chet to be a good, honest man, and a hard worker, and there just happened to be an opening at the mill. He hired Chet on the spot.

Silas was something of an anomaly in the area, an owner and manager who was also a union supporter. Having spent time in the work force himself, and fighting for the union, he held onto the memory of what it was like to be poor, the realization of which struck him after his mother was killed.

Silas was extremely conscientious in taking care of his employees, even more than Hodges had been. Because of that, he had people who had been with the company for many years. Knowing his character, his employees were loyal, not just to the mill, but to Silas himself.

Chet was one of those loyal employees. Having been on his own for only a short time, he had only recently paid off a rather large debt that his father owed when he died. The young man had little to offer Olivia, other than his love, but she returned it wholeheartedly. He lived in a boarding house in Manitou while he saved up to buy his own home, and he had proven, to Silas' satisfaction, his ability to manage his money.

Silas was only too happy to give his blessing to their marriage, though he was certainly going to miss having Olivia around. In the time since John and Abbie had died, Silas had come to love 'his girls' as if they were his own.

He didn't want Olivia living in a boarding house, though. So as a wedding present, he was giving them the smaller log house, just up the road from the inn, the one where Silas first lived after the Hodges took him in. It had been sitting empty for a few years, being used for nothing more than storage space.

Silas had spent several days sorting things in the house, throwing away some items, taking some to the inn to store them down in the cellar. Other things that he was sure would not be needed, he was taking to his old cabin near Eastonville. Since it had been sitting vacant since he moved back to Manitou, it seemed the perfect place to store seldom-needed items.

He walked back up to the house, looking around one last time to be sure he had gotten everything he needed. Olivia and a friend would be coming this afternoon, to clean the place and to make a list of things that were needed.

Finding nothing else that had to be moved, Silas went out the back door. Isadora was playing there where he had left her. He stood there and watched her for a moment. She was sitting on the ground, and at first, Silas couldn't tell what she was doing. Then he saw a couple of ladybugs crawling on her arm. She watched as they crawled up her arm, then she gently transferred them to a hand, talking to them the whole time.

As pretty as her sisters were, at eight years old, Silas thought that Isadora was the most beautiful one of the lot. And with the sweetest disposition. As if John and Abbie had poured their very best qualities into their final offspring.

"Come on, Little Bit," he said. "Time to go."

The little girl looked up at him and smiled, pushing her golden hair out of her dark brown eyes. Gently brushing the ladybugs off her arm and into the grass, she stood up and came inside, and Silas closed the door.

§

"Oh, Silas, he's beautiful!" Isadora gushed. "Thank you!"

"You're welcome, sweetheart," he smiled.

They looked back into the corral behind the inn where her new palomino colt gamboled about. Silas had just bought him from a rancher south of Colorado Springs. It was June of 1935, the year that Manitou officially changed its name to Manitou Springs. It was also a time when many people across the country were hurting.

An extended period of drought, followed by massive wind storms, had blown away the topsoil of many farms in the central part of the country, including many in eastern Colorado. Farmers already suffering from the economic hardships of the last few years of depression were moving away, hoping to find better conditions elsewhere.

Among those critically affected was Eastonville, the town near Silas' old cabin. First, a blight had afflicted the potato crop, which in itself was devastating to the little potato-growing community. Then when the railroad that went through Eastonville was abandoned, the town could not survive.

Silas was doing well enough, though. Many of the small gold mines had been bought by larger mining corporations, and while some of those companies did their own extraction, many still used outside mills. Since Hodges' Mill had contracts with several of those large corporations, as well as many of the independent mines still in operation, they were kept busy.

Isadora had always had a great love of living things. Silas had gotten her a cat a couple of years before, but that had ended disastrously when it was killed by a mountain lion. Isadora was an emotional wreck for a while after that. Silas decided that if he got her another cat, it would remain inside.

Then he saw an ad in the newspaper about a sale. A rancher south of Colorado Springs was pulling up stakes and leaving. Everything must go.

Silas remembered Bella, the horse he had the whole time he lived near Eastonville, and he remembered with some amusement the last time he went to buy a horse. He came back with a Model T. While he did enjoy driving his automobiles, he realized when he saw that ad how much he missed riding a horse. He missed the interaction between horse and rider, and being able to go places where the car could not.

The stable and corral behind the inn were essentially unused and had begun to fall into disrepair. When he saw the bay mare for sale, he knew it was time to repair them. And when he saw the palomino colt for sale by the same rancher, Silas knew that Isadora's fifteenth birthday was the perfect time to introduce her to the joys of riding.

Now, as the colt trotted around the enclosure, Silas looked at Isadora's face again. From her continued beaming smile, he decided that he had made the right decision.

§

Isadora Hodges, at eighteen years old, was the most popular girl in El Paso County. This was quite a feat for someone who was not in the larger metropolitan areas, but rather lived outside one of the smaller towns in the county. Her beauty was widely known, though, as was her sweet personality.

Still a caring, soft-hearted person, she spent whatever time she had available riding her horse, Cochise. Knowing her own mixed Indian background, and knowing that the Apache name Cochise meant "the color of oak," she thought it was an appropriate name for her spirited palomino.

Although Olivia still came from her home a few houses down to work at the inn, in 1938 Isadora was the last Hodges girl still living there. Besides the time she spent working at the inn and riding Cochise, she also volunteered frequently at soup kitchens and other charities in Manitou Springs, and sometimes Colorado Springs.

Deeply disturbed by the suffering being endured by so many, the young beauty established herself as a warm and kind individual. So Silas was not surprised when the boys came calling, but one in particular ended up making quite a deep impression on Isadora.

Phillip Brandt was the son of a Colorado Springs banker. His father's bank was one that had survived the great crash in 1929, as well as the continuing depression that followed. Despite the financial issues so many suffered, the bank was thriving.

Silas' first knowledge of him was when he showed up at the inn to call on Isadora, and to talk to Silas. A few years before, Silas had turned Isadora O'Riordan's old bedroom on the ground floor at the back of the inn into a sun room. The three of them were seated there now.

"How did you and Isadora meet, Phil?" Silas asked.

The handsome young man smiled.

"Not much to tell, really," Brandt replied. "There's a soup kitchen a couple of doors down from the main entrance to our bank. One day, it seemed they were doing a booming business." He smiled at his little joke. "The line to their door was stretching in front of ours. My father was concerned that our bank customers might be aggravated about having to push through this line of dirty, unkempt people, and he was getting irritated himself."

Isadora looked down, seemingly embarrassed by Brandt's father's description of the unfortunate people.

"Well, I told him to calm down and I would take care of it," Brandt continued. "So I went down to the entrance to the soup kitchen. And when I squeezed past the people and into the door, I saw this lovely creature dishing up soup. I was instantly taken with her."

He glanced at Isadora and took her hand. Isadora looked back up at him and smiled. Silas glowered at Brandt.

"But my reason for calling today, sir," Brandt said, "is to ask for your blessing on our marriage."

"Your marriage?" Silas asked, thoroughly surprised. Isadora glanced down again, but then she looked up at Silas. "When was it that you met?" he asked.

"It was a little over a month ago," Isadora replied.

"You've known each other for a month and you're getting married? What do you know of each other?"

"We know we love each other, sir," Brandt was quick to say. He looked at Isadora, then back up at Silas. "I know that Isadora is the kind of person who can make me a better person."

"It was my hope that Isadora would find and marry someone who was already a better person," Silas returned, trying somewhat unsuccessfully to keep the tone of censure from overpowering the statement.

"Phillip is a good person, Silas," Isadora said, and Silas could hear the irritation in her voice. "I'm sorry I didn't tell you about him before, but honestly, it all happened very quickly. And besides, you aren't around here that much either. You're always so busy at the mill. You and I don't really see that much of each other anymore."

Silas stood up, uneasy with the direction the conversation had taken.

"Yes, I am busy at the mill. I feel a certain sense of responsibility to your father, and to his offspring, to keep his company strong and successful. And to make a living, to support myself. And you."

"You have a very skilled and trustworthy crew of employees, some of whom could manage the company without requiring your constant supervision."

"It's a man's duty to work and earn a living!" Silas said, raising his voice. Isadora stood up, followed by Brandt who looked nervously back and forth from Silas to Isadora. Silas noticed the fire building in Isadora's eyes.

"That's just an excuse men make for spending so much time away from home," Isadora said as her irritation grew.

"What is this? You're sounding like a wife, now. Besides, the amount of time I work is not at issue here. I think you could have found a minute to let me know that one of these twits was getting serious with you."

"Phillip is not a twit!" Isadora spat back.

Beneath his own anger, Silas subconsciously noted surprise at Isadora's building rage. It was so rare. But caught up in the heat of the argument as he was, the thought was quickly lost as he made his next response.

"He's a twit if he thinks that marrying you after only knowing you for a month is a good idea!"

"Look, Pops," Brandt said, his voice shaking in anger, "I think you better watch who you're calling a twit. You're a big guy, but I still think I can kick the shit out of you!"

"Pops?" Silas mocked, bristling at the epithet. He turned toward Brandt, standing up a little taller. "You think you can kick the shit out of me, do you? Why don't we go outside, you little bastard! I'd like to see you try."

"Stop it!" Isadora cried. "You're both acting like twits now. I expected better than this from both of you!"

"Do you really love him, Isadora?" Silas asked angrily. He turned from Brandt to face her.

With a growl of exasperation issuing from her throat, she turned and headed for the back door.

"Isadora, wait," Brandt called out.

"No!" she said. She turned toward Brandt and looked as if she was about to say something, but she stopped. She closed her eyes and took a deep breath. Letting it out, she opened her eyes and, struggling to stay calm, she looked at Brandt. "Why don't you go home, Phillip? I just want to be alone right now."

The door slammed behind her, leaving the two men facing each other. The object of their argument having fled out the door, they looked at each other angrily, but they both felt their hostility gradually cooling.

Finally, Brandt turned without a word and went out the front door. He got into his car and drove away.

§

"Cochise, stand still!" Isadora said impatiently.

Knowing that it would help to calm her down, Isadora was attempting to saddle Cochise for a ride. The connection between Isadora and the horse was deep, almost spiritual. Cochise always seemed to understand when Isadora was upset, and this time was no exception.

He was a high-spirited horse, and Isadora loved giving him the reins and letting him run. But his spirit was sometimes elevated when Isadora herself was agitated. In the stable, Cochise kept shuffling back and forth. Isadora, still feeling impatient from the heated exchange with the two men, was getting terse with the horse as well.

Cochise had just reared up a little and the blanket slid off his back. Isadora uttered a low growl, similar to the impatient sound she had just made in the house, and she went behind the horse to pick up the blanket.

§

Silas, feeling bad about the argument, had gone looking for Isadora. He didn't know how their discussion had gotten so out of hand. There was just something about Brandt that he didn't like. Still, he hadn't meant to upset Isadora, and he wanted to patch things up with her.

Knowing Isadora, he figured she went to the stable. He pulled the door open to look in and Cochise was startled by the noise and kicked.

Isadora, despite knowing better, was leaning over behind the horse to pick up the blanket. She took the full force of the horse's kick on the right side of her face. Thrown against the stall, she crumpled to the ground.

Silas saw immediately what had happened and rushed into the stable, his heart pounding. In the time it took him to cross the stable and come into the stall where Isadora lay, Cochise had apparently sensed what he had done. He was nickering softly and gently nudging the girl with his nose.

Silas pushed the horse away and knelt down beside Isadora. She was in a little heap, unconscious, facing the lower slat of the stall. Silas gently turned her and, to his horror, he saw that her face was caved in on the right side, the bones shattered.

Silas led Cochise to a different stall and enclosed him there. Then, struggling to stay calm, he ran to his car and drove it up to the stable.

Chafing at his slowness, he forced himself to move Isadora slowly and deliberately. He gathered up the injured girl and placed her in the back seat of his car.

§

Silas paced the dingy tiles of the hospital waiting room, his stomach churning from the nervousness and guilt coursing through him. Emily and Olivia, with their respective husbands, sat in the hard chairs lining the walls.

Dr. Young had told Silas that Isadora's injuries were just too great for him to treat in his office. He had immobilized her head and administered an anesthetic to keep her unconscious. Then he had her transferred by ambulance to a hospital in Colorado Springs.

Emily and her husband, Russell, had arrived only a few minutes after Silas called them. Olivia and Chet got there about a half hour later. Isadora had been in surgery for almost four hours now and Silas was becoming even more impatient.

At almost seven o'clock in the evening, Silas heard footsteps shuffle into the room and looked up.

"Are you Silas Baskin?" the doctor asked. Silas quickly responded in the affirmative, while the others stood up to hear the news.

"I'm Dr. Charles. I'm the chief surgeon here. Isadora is out of surgery now, and she's going to be alright. But I'll be honest with you. There was an awful lot of damage done. Several bones – around her right eye, her cheek, her jaw – were crushed. We did our best to piece them back together, but I'm afraid it will never be like it was.

"There will also be some permanent scarring. The bones will fuse back together, but there will likely always be a certain – " he

paused as if searching for the right word, "deformity to the right side of her face.

"Obviously, we did everything we could to keep that to a minimum, but with injuries this severe, I'm afraid there's just no way to avoid it. That abnormality is something that will always be there."

Silas, his eyes swimming in tears, had been holding his breath as Dr. Charles spoke. Focused on the doctor, he didn't see Olivia and Emily dabbing their eyes behind him.

"She's not going to die?" Silas asked.

"No," Dr. Charles said with a sympathetic smile. "That I can tell you. She's not going to die. We've given her antibiotics to fight infection, and she is going to be in quite a bit of pain for a while, so we will also be administering pain medication as needed. But she will for a certainty survive this."

The tears rolled down Silas' face now, and he finally let out his breath as he shook the doctor's hand and thanked him.

"Can we see her?" Emily asked.

"I think it's best if you all go home for now. Isadora's going to be sleeping through the night. Once the surgical anesthesia wears off, she'll still be very sleepy from the pain medication. So go home and get some rest yourselves, and we'll see how she's doing in the morning."

The doctor turned and walked away, and the five relieved relatives engaged in a group hug.

§

The next morning, Silas felt Isadora squeeze his fingers. He had been at her bedside, gently holding her hand, for an hour

161

already. It pained him to look at her. Only the left side of her face was visible, and even it looked bruised and swollen. Silas hated to think about what the right side of Isadora's beautiful face must look like under the bandages.

But he was attentive when he felt the pressure on his hand. He saw that her left eye, though swollen and discolored, was open and looking at him.

"Hey, Little Bit," he said. "How are you feeling?"

She mumbled something, but Silas couldn't understand her, partly because of the drugs and partly because her jaw had been immobilized.

"Are you in pain?" Silas asked. She moved her head slightly from side to side. Silas followed up with additional 'yes' or 'no' questions, concerning whether she was thirsty, warm enough, and so on.

Finally Isadora squeezed his hand again and gave him a piercing look with her one visible eye. Then she turned it down toward herself in the bed. Without a word, she made Silas understand that she wanted to know about her condition.

"Cochise kicked you in the face," he explained softly. Isadora gave a slight shake of her head again, and Silas continued, in a consoling tone. "I know, honey, he didn't mean to. If anything, it was my fault."

Isadora saw the tears in his eyes and squeezed his hand, shaking her head again. Bearing the load of his guilt, Silas ignored her response and went on.

"The doctor said you're going to be alright, though." He squeezed her hand gently as the tears tumbled down his cheeks.

"Baby, I'm so sorry. I didn't mean to upset you. I don't know what got into me."

Isadora moved her lips slightly, attempting to speak again, but no discernible sound came out. A tear rolled out of her eye and slipped down her cheek, finally disappearing in the gauze wrapped around her neck under her jaw.

There was a soft knock on the door and Phillip Brandt stuck his head in. Isadora looked from him back to Silas, and Silas nodded.

"I called him." Silas stood up and let go of her hand. "I'll be here," he said, and he walked toward the door.

Brandt came into the room, looking apprehensively at Silas, but Silas spoke softly to him on his way out.

"Don't ask her too many questions," he said. "She can't speak, so just talk to her."

Brandt nodded his understanding. Silas looked back one more time at Isadora, then he went out into the hallway.

W hat's on the agenda for today?" Dora asked cheerfully as she picked up the final dishes from the table. The only guests were the Jurgenssens, a nice young couple visiting from Minnesota.

"We were hoping to check out the Cave of the Winds," Steve Jurgenssen said. "We've heard it's pretty fascinating." They slid their chairs back from the table and stood up, gathering their cell phones and other belongings.

"Oh, it's beautiful," Dora nodded.

"That's not near the fire, is it?" his wife, Jamie asked with a concerned expression on her face.

"No, it's not," Dora replied. "The fire is miles away. You should have a beautiful day for it."

"Great!" Steve said with relief. "We've been looking forward to it."

"Breakfast was delicious, Dora," Jamie said. "Thank you so much."

"You're welcome. Have a nice time."

Dora carried the dishes into the kitchen where Robin was putting away the griddle that had been used to make the raspberry French toast. Shawn had left for work a couple of hours ago, so they were alone.

"This is the last of it," Dora said as she put the dishes down on the counter.

"You know, I can see the disadvantages of having only two guests," Robin said. "It may not pay you very well, but it sure lightens *my* workload." Robin smiled and Dora gave her a good-natured sneer as she pulled off the white smock she wore when serving breakfast. Robin took it from her and hung it on a hook along with her own in the little cubbyhole office.

"Well, it's time for me to go now," Dora said. "I put a serving of the French toast in the fridge for whenever my dad comes down." Robin nodded as Dora paused, in thought about her father. Dora's hesitation continued, though, as she stood there silently, apparently lost in thought. Robin looked up expectantly at her. Dora sighed and looked at Robin. "He's really not that bad," she finally continued. "It's just that . . ."

"I know, honey," Robin said. "Your feelings about him are colored by your own personal experience with him. Your relationship has history, baggage."

"Right. But still, I'm sorry to leave him to you."

"It's fine. He'll be just another guest. You don't feel bad about leaving me in charge while you go to the orphanage *other* times. Don't feel bad about it now."

Dora smiled and kissed her lightly on the cheek.

§

Clark got up out of bed and washed his face. The sun was shining brightly, and he knew even before he looked at the clock that he had slept late. At 10:00, he was aware that he had missed breakfast, but he didn't mind. He hadn't wanted to have to socialize with other guests anyway.

He hadn't brought much in the way of luggage, only a hastily-packed overnight case. So he put on the same pants he had worn yesterday, with a fresh shirt.

He left his room and started down the stairs, pausing to look nostalgically at the paintings that filled the wall. He remembered them from growing up in this house, and he knew all the stories. He looked at the portrait of Mahaley Franklin, the beautiful Cherokee who had been a good friend and adopted mother of Isadora O'Riordan. And there was Isadora herself, with her first husband Atsila, a Cherokee, and their daughter Clara.

Clark came to the bottom of the stairs and turned to walk back toward the dining room. As he had anticipated, there was nobody there. Continuing into the kitchen, he saw a mousy young lady with short black hair reading the newspaper on the countertop. As Clark came in, she looked up at him.

"Hi, Mr. Baskin. I'm Robin. I'm Dora's assistant."

"Oh, hi Robin," Clark said, taken off-guard for a moment.

"Dora had to leave. She volunteers on Thursdays at an orphanage in Colorado Springs. But she *did* put a breakfast in the refrigerator for you." She pointed to the coffee maker. "There's coffee right there. Go ahead and pour yourself a cup and make yourself comfortable. I'll heat up your breakfast."

Robin turned on the toaster oven and got something wrapped in aluminum foil out of the refrigerator. Clark poured a cup of coffee and sipped it as he wandered back into the dining room. He looked at the familiar décor, feeling another wave of nostalgia wash over him.

The enormous century-old table made of yellow pine nearly filled the room, its varnished surface showing the patina of the years. He didn't think his mother had ever had more than eight chairs around the table, though it was big enough for more. Dora had added an eclectic collection of chairs that were different from the original eight, yet they all went together well, and now comfortably seated twelve people.

On the walls, Clark saw several framed pieces. Some he recognized, others were unfamiliar. Going to one wall which contained a grouping of old photographs, he focused on one of them, a hand-tinted photograph of a very pretty girl, about sixteen years old, on the back of a palomino horse. The girl was smiling, and Clark, without realizing it, was smiling too. In the background, behind the girl and the horse, was the inn, Dora's B&B almost eighty years ago.

He heard a sound behind him, and he turned to see Robin setting a plate down on the table.

"Raspberry French toast," she said.

"It smells delicious," Clark replied as he sat down. "Do you know when Dora will be back?"

"When she works at the orphanage, she usually gets back here around six o'clock."

"Six o'clock," he repeated distantly, somewhat surprised. "Thanks."

"Can I get you anything else, Mr. Baskin?"

"No, thank you." Clark quietly began eating. As he didn't seem to want to visit, Robin excused herself and went back into the kitchen.

§

Gash Seever was looking forward to lunch in Chicago. He was still about an hour away and would be landing his Cessna there to refuel. Gibsons Bar and Steakhouse, located at O'Hare International Airport, served up a fine steak. Gash could almost taste it.

Looking below him, he saw what he had been seeing for a while now, a seemingly endless patchwork of farmland, with occasional small towns. Northern Ohio, northern Indiana, southern Michigan – without border markers, they were all blending together.

But soon, he would start to see larger settlements, he would pass over the southern tip of Lake Michigan, and be scooting up to a table at Gibsons by 12:30.

Interesting that it was a steak dinner that had marked his entrance into this business in the first place.

Twelve years ago, Gary Seever had been a young, soft-spoken Rutgers law student in Newark, New Jersey. But he was struggling with his studies. Reviewing case histories, as he had been doing, revealed to him just how many criminals got off on technicalities. Or by being able to afford the best attorneys money could buy.

Gary was feeling inadequate. He had never been a very persuasive speaker and he doubted his ability to ever really make a difference.

When Gary met, gingerly fell in love with and then married Antonia Martinelli, he was very well aware of her family connections. The Martinellis were a prominent crime family in New Jersey. Antonia, though, had never wanted anything do with it. So when she agreed to marry Gary Seever, she made her wishes known to them, particularly to Vittorio, her uncle and the head of the organization.

Vittorio loved Antonia. He respected her wishes and kept his distance. Hence, Gary was surprised when, after his classes one day, he saw a big black limousine waiting. The back window came down, revealing Vittorio in the back seat, and Gary realized that the limo was there for him.

His brows furrowed, he cautiously but curiously approached the stretch Cadillac. The back door opened and Vittorio slid over, making room for Gary, motioning for him to enter. When Gary hesitated, Vittorio was more forceful and said, "Get in!"

Vittorio was silent during the entire trip, despite Gary's attempts to find out the reason for this ride. It took less than ten minutes to reach their destination, stopping in front of Vittorio's restaurant. Vittorio had bucked a fairly common Italian crime boss stereotype. Instead of running an Italian restaurant, he opened a steak house.

The table was already set when they went inside, and within two minutes after taking their seats, their meals were served. Completely mystified by the strange and silent ordeal, but hungry after a tough, nerve-racking day in his classes, Gary dug into his medium-rare filet.

Near the end of the meal, Vittorio put his silverware down and looked at Gary.

"I thought this should be done on a full stomach," he said. He dabbed his mouth with his napkin and placed it back in his lap. "I'm afraid I've got some bad news for you, Gary."

Gary followed suit and put his silverware down. He looked at Vittorio, his stomach now comfortably filled, but fluttering with nervousness.

"As you know, I've respected Antonia's wishes and have not involved the two of you in any of my business. Unfortunately, my enemies have not made such an agreement. Someone has been trying to force my hand on something for a while now. I won't bore you with the details. But today, this person took the unwise step of touching someone I care about."

Gary's nervousness was increasing, but Vittorio didn't make him wait any longer.

"I'm afraid Antonia's dead. She was gunned down a couple of hours ago."

Gary's eyes glazed over with tears, but looking around the restaurant, he attempted to keep his emotions in check, to not make a scene.

"As you may imagine," Vittorio continued, his voice hardening, "this does not sit well with me. This person will be dealt with. I just wanted you to know that."

Gary was flooded with thoughts and emotions at that moment. He felt intense grief and sadness, of course, for Antonia. But also, amid those acute emotions, he had memories of all the criminals he had studied about, who had gotten away with their crimes. People who had destroyed other people's lives, and went on with their own because they could afford the best attorneys.

Better attorneys than Gary would ever be.

He didn't want vengeance. He wanted justice. Antonia had been a beautiful innocent, her life taken from her as nothing more than a worthless pawn in the eyes of her killer. Gary wanted to see that he paid.

"I want to help," Gary said.

"Excuse me?" Vittorio replied, a confused, even surprised expression on his face.

"Antonia was my life. Someone took her away from me." Gary was struggling to keep from breaking down in tears. "I want to help make them pay."

"Hold on, Gary. Don't fuck up your life. You're not thinking straight. You got your whole future ahead of you. You're going to be a lawyer."

"No, Vittorio, I already know I'd be a shitty lawyer. I know only too well how the court system works."

"I can assure you," Vittorio interrupted, "this person will not be going to court."

"I want to *see* him pay for what he did to Antonia!"

The conversation went on a little while longer, but eventually Gary convinced Vittorio to let him accompany him and his men. Vittorio himself was going because he loved Antonia.

So was Gary.

When the time came, gathered in the home of the man who had Antonia killed, Gary still didn't know what beef the man had with Vittorio. He also wasn't sure what steps Vittorio's men had taken to get them into the fortress of a house. He didn't care. He just wanted to be there to see justice carried out.

Vittorio himself pulled the trigger, and when the man fell in a heap on the floor, Gary felt the anger ease a bit. They went to Vittorio's place after that where they drank to Antonia.

That night, after he was dropped off at his apartment, Gary was able to mourn Antonia without uncertainty about the fate of her killer, without the nagging feeling that there was unfinished business.

He never went back to Rutgers.

He worked for Vittorio initially, but within a couple of years, the family dynamic got to be too much for him. Without the blood relation, Gary didn't feel the connection to the Martinellis that he thought he needed to be a part of the family business. He decided to go freelance.

And business had been good.

He found that he could be persuasive after all.

A few months after Isadora's accident, on the first cold day of autumn, 1938, Silas stepped outside the inn to go to work at the mill. His first breaths of the cold air felt like knives in his lungs, and in just a few seconds, he was doubled over coughing. Since he was unable to stop, Olivia insisted that he stay home.

Silas had almost forgotten about the cyanide poisoning from eighteen years before. At fifty-two years old, he was otherwise in very good health, and he looked younger than most men ten years his junior. But when the weather turned cold, the effects of that old cyanide poisoning reappeared.

On this morning, though, Olivia was busy with the guests, and with caring for her two children whom she brought to the inn with her, so Isadora took care of Silas. She had been staying in her room most of the time, her face still in bandages. The swelling and discoloration on the exposed left side of her face was gone now, and it looked just as beautiful as before. She was able to talk now, though her jaw movement was still quite restricted.

Silas, exhausted from his coughing attack, was in his bed, feeling somewhat better in the warm air of home. His throat raw, he was able to speak only when absolutely necessary. Isadora was tireless in caring for his needs, giving him bourbon with honey to sip, to ease his throat, bringing him food, or whatever else he might need.

Isadora mercilessly forced Silas to stay inside during the cold weather, while Bill Benson oversaw the mill. Under her loving care, his ailment subsided in just a few days.

The day after the weather warmed up, Isadora had an appointment to have her bandages removed. Silas, feeling better now, offered to drive her to the hospital.

Isadora's excitement was almost palpable as she sat on the examination table. The doctor and a nurse carefully cut away and removed the bandages, placing them on a tray, as Silas watched. Isadora was scrutinizing their faces, and Silas knew that she was watching for any clues concerning the results of her surgeries.

Finally, the last piece of gauze removed, Silas could see her whole face again for the first time in months. The right side of her face was pasty white and slightly wrinkled from being bandaged for so long. There were visible scars, still reddened in some places. And there was a drooping quality to her expression. As if the skin was sagging.

He smiled encouragingly, but she didn't seem to buy it.

"What is it, Silas?" she asked. "Is it bad?"

"No, Little Bit, it's not bad," Silas replied, mustering as much sincerity as he could.

"We knew there would be some permanent damage," the doctor reminded her. "But actually, I'm pretty happy with the way it's turned out."

"Really?" Isadora asked hopefully. "May I see?"

The doctor nodded to the nurse who handed Isadora a mirror. Looking at her reflection, Isadora sat immobile, holding her breath, and her eyes filled with tears. Silas rushed to her and put his arm around her.

"Oh, Silas, I look hideous!"

"No, you don't, honey," he said. "You don't look hideous at all. You're still my beautiful girl."

"Look at me!" she cried. "My right eye and my eyebrow look like they're melting. My cheek still looks like it's caved in. My face looks – unfinished."

"It will probably get better, right doctor?" Silas asked.

"The paleness will go away and the skin will firm up, now that it's exposed to the air again. That in itself may improve your features a bit." He gently prodded the bones around her eyebrow and her cheekbone. "But the bones have healed. The pieces have knitted together as well as we had hoped. Their shape won't change. As we said, there is unavoidable permanent damage with an injury like this."

Silas' heart fell, not because of how Isadora looked, but because of the way she felt. She was inconsolable, her face buried in his neck, as she cried.

Silas didn't notice when the doctor and nurse left the room.

§

On a sunny late fall afternoon in early November, Phillip Brandt was waiting in the living room, as bright, warming sunlight streamed in through the window. During Isadora's convalescence, he had visited her on numerous occasions, and

Silas had made it a point to stay out of the way. There was still something about Brandt that Silas didn't like, but Isadora loved him, so he didn't try to keep the boy away from her.

Isadora had dressed in what she considered her most attractive outfit, a slim-fitting dress with shoulder pads, in a warm brown color that highlighted her golden hair very well. Her hair came to just below her shoulders, and she had been accustomed to wearing it up and swept back, in a fashion similar to that of many movie stars of the time.

Now, though, she wore it down, parted on the left and partly covering the right side of her face. She hadn't noticed, but she had also started carrying her head tilted down slightly, causing the hair to hang forward.

That was the way she came down the stairs this afternoon. Sitting on the divan in the living room, Brandt heard the footsteps and he turned to see her through the doorway as she reached the bottom of the stairs.

With a smile, he stood up and walked toward her.

"Wow, honey," he said enthusiastically. "What a looker!"

"Really?" Isadora asked hopefully. As the doctor had predicted, the skin had firmed up, and some of the redness of the scars had faded. But she still didn't like the shape of the features on the right side of her face. It still looked sunken and misshapen, as if it was sagging. Hearing Brandt's affirmation, though, was encouraging. "You really think I look good?"

She lifted her head up a little, unconsciously flipping her hair back, and Brandt stopped. He stood still and caught his breath for a moment as he looked at the misshapen structure that was the right side of her face, visible now from behind her hair.

"Phillip?" she said, seeing his hesitation, and the tears started to come.

"Uh, no, it's great to see you again," he said, attempting to recover from his temporary lapse.

"Yeah?" she replied, a little incredulous.

"Yeah." He paused for just a moment. "You're still healing, though, right?"

"A little," she said in a bit of a monotone, seeing the new trajectory of the conversation. "But this is pretty much the way it's going to be."

Brandt stood still, trying to think of what to say.

"I – I thought you told me it was all healed up."

"It is, Phillip. The shattered bones have knitted back together. The stitches have healed. The inflammation is gone. This is me from now on."

The disappointment on his face was unmistakable.

Isadora's tears left glistening tracks down her cheeks as she started to turn, but Brandt grabbed her hand. As she turned back toward him, he got a close up look at her face, and he took a deep breath. He put his arms around her and held her, keeping his face on her left side.

He held her like that for a few moments, then he pulled away, kissing her quickly on her left cheek.

"I'm sorry," he whispered, as he walked out the front door, pulling it closed behind him.

§

"If you will excuse my language, the man is an asshole!" Silas said with a cold edge to his voice.

Isadora was lying across her bed, sobbing. The late afternoon sun shining through her windows cast long, stark shadows across the bed. Silas, his heart breaking for her, was almost in tears himself.

"No, he's not," Isadora said through the sobs. "It was a perfectly normal reaction to the way I look."

"If he can't see your beauty, then I feel sorry for him."

"Beauty?" Isadora said almost angrily as she sat up. "Beauty? This isn't beautiful! This is disgusting!"

"Isadora," Silas said firmly, looking deep into her eyes, "you could never be disgusting. Honey, you are the most beautiful person I've ever known."

"But – "

"But nothing. You're beautiful on the inside where it counts the most."

"That's what they always say about ugly girls."

"You are one of the most selfless people in the world," Silas continued, ignoring her remark. "You give your time and energy to help other people, and anybody who doesn't see that beauty is pitiable.

"You have a beautiful, caring heart. If you see someone in need, your heart goes out to help them before you even take the time to think about yourself.

"I can see it when you work here at the inn. You're always the favorite of every guest, because they can sense that you really care. I see it every time you go down to help out in the soup kitchen. I saw it when I was sick and you were always there to help me, taking such good care of me. That's true beauty.

"But you're also beautiful on the outside, too," he continued softly.

"No, I'm not, Silas," she said, the tears welling up in her eyes again. "My face is horrible. I'm ugly. No man would ever want me now."

Silas pushed her hair away from her face, and Isadora self-consciously pulled back, wiping her eyes and nose with a tissue. Silas leaned forward and purposefully kissed her right eyebrow. Isadora pulled back again, but this time to look at him.

"Silas," she said, but beyond that, she was at a loss for words.

Silas caressed her face, while Isadora studied his. He leaned forward again, and this time he kissed her right cheek. He felt her body start to shake with sobs and he pulled her close, holding her tightly as she cried.

§

Isadora Hodges slipped noiselessly through the dark hallway. She tapped quietly on Silas' door, listening for his response. No response came for a few seconds, and she was considering whether to tap again when the door opened.

Silas looked at her through the doorway, as a thin finger of moonlight traced the contours of Isadora's face.

"Is everything alright?" he asked.

Isadora didn't respond but gazed at Silas, his form simply a black silhouette in front of the window in his room, the backlit edges of his head and body showing as a blue outline against the shadows. In the dim light, Silas could see her conflicting emotions reflected on her face. He opened the door wider to allow her to come inside.

"Isadora?" He closed the door and turned toward her. She was near the window now, still facing away from him, still silent. Hesitantly, he came up behind her and put his hands on her shoulders. At the feel of his hands, she leaned back, her head next to his chin, her back against his chest.

Silas put his arms around her, pressing his face against her hair. He could feel her breasts rising and falling, her heart pounding with emotion. And he felt a tear fall on his forearm.

He turned her around to face him.

"What is it?" he asked softly.

She looked up at him, her asymmetrical features illuminated by the moonlight, her tears twinkling like stars in the darkness.

"This can't be right," she said.

"Why?"

"You're like my father. I'm your Little Bit."

"You'll always be my Little Bit," he said with a gentle smile. "But I'm not your father, honey. We're not related in any way."

"Won't people talk?"

"Probably. But do you love me?"

"Oh, Silas, I've always loved you."

"I don't mean like that."

She leaned against him and held him tightly, her face pressed against his chest. He kissed the top of her head and he felt her relax a little. Then she pulled away and looked up at him, opening her robe and letting it drop at her feet.

Silas let out a little gasp as he looked at her, the moonlight pouring through his window caressing the smooth curves of her body. The sharp, rectangular panes were rounded as the light traced over her breasts and down her belly, disappearing into the shadows below. She was the image of perfection except for her marred right cheek and brow. And even that – it was Isadora, so Silas loved it.

He stepped toward her and held her body in his arms, stroking the soft skin of her back and shoulders. She turned her head up toward his face and they looked into each other's eyes for just a moment. Then Silas leaned down, pressing his lips hungrily against hers.

Isadora uttered a soft whimpering sound and Silas cradled the back of her head in his hand. After a couple of minutes, feeling their energy drain away, as if their legs were about to topple over, they collapsed onto Silas' bed. They paused to look at each other again, and Isadora smiled at the unconcealed love she saw in his eyes.

And somehow they found the energy.

§

In a simple ceremony, Silas Baskin and Isadora Hodges were married in December of 1938, with a small gathering of their family and closest friends. Silas was fifty-two, Isadora was 18. People did indeed talk, some disapprovingly. But Silas and Isadora were oblivious to it in their love for each other, immune to the criticisms of others. There were more who were happy for them, and these were congratulatory, wishing them much happiness.

At Isadora's insistence, Silas arranged for Bill Benson to oversee the mill full time, but particularly in the colder months. As Olivia was now pregnant with her third child and decided that it was time to stay home and raise them, this came at a perfect time.

Silas was around to help Isadora with the inn.

It also came at a time when, during the past nine years of depression, the number of vacationers had gradually dropped off and the inn was not as busy as before.

But the mill was successful enough that it helped make up for the lack at the inn. Silas, though, was surprised to find that he didn't mind.

In 1939, Amelia Earhart was officially declared dead after her mysterious disappearance over the Pacific Ocean. Hitler continued his rampage through much of Europe, while Franco seized control of Spain. The Wizard of Oz premiered in Grauman's Chinese Theatre in Hollywood.

1939 also began what Silas called his domestic phase. With Isadora by his side, he had all he needed. In fact, he was almost happy about the sluggish business at the inn. It allowed him more time with Isadora.

When the weather warmed up, Silas busied himself with an outdoor project. He enlarged the front porch, creating a large platform that wrapped almost all the way around the inn. In time, he and Isadora would grow to love spending time together outside on the veranda in good weather. In bad weather, they found things to do indoors.

As a result of those inclement weather activities, in June, Isadora discovered that she was pregnant.

T he El Paso County Sheriff's office this morning has named the Black Forest fire the most destructive fire in Colorado history," the radio announcer said. "In just over two days since its beginning, it has already surpassed last year's Waldo Canyon fire.

"Sheriff Terry Maketa reported that containment of the fire stands now at about five percent, and that so far, 379 homes have burned. Besides the massive amount of damage, the fire has also now claimed two human lives. The victims appear to have died while attempting to evacuate their home.

"Over 38,000 residents have been evacuated so far, and with these recent fatalities, and the fire's relentless destruction, authorities are hoping to step up evacuation proceedings, to avoid any additional loss of life.

"It's been reported that over 450 firefighters are currently working the fireline, including local urban fire departments, personnel from the Colorado Air National Guard, Fort Carson and the Air Force Academy, as well as firefighters from around the state."

Robin clicked the radio off and turned to see Clark standing behind her. He had placed his dishes on the counter and had been listening to the broadcast. His face was lined with worry.

"Mr. Baskin, is everything okay?" Robin asked.

"Yes, fine," Clark replied. Robin wasn't convinced. Seemingly deep in thought, he turned. Walking out of the kitchen, Clark turned slightly, as an afterthought, and muttered, "I'll be back later."

He went out the front door and got in his old Datsun, driving away in a cloud of blue smoke.

§

Bridget Lindstrom, finished now with her summer school classes, drove up toward Manitou Springs. It had been on her mind all day, distracting her from her work, and yet she still wasn't sure what she was going to say. She hoped that something would come to her by the time she got there.

No longer having to concentrate on her work, she allowed the memories to flood back. As her pregnancy had progressed, she hadn't seen him anymore. She gave birth to a baby girl early in 1987, and she gave her up for adoption.

It wasn't until the summer that she saw him again, and again, it was at The Ancient Mariner.

He was already there when she walked in this time. She was slim once again after working off her pregnancy weight gain. As usual, he looked as if he was happy to see her, but there also seemed to be an undercurrent of – what? Sadness? Worry?

His father had died since he had seen her last, so that would account for the sadness, and he apologized for not having been around. But now, he had other concerns, too. He gave her a sob story. At least that's the way she thought of it now.

She couldn't even remember the details about it. Something about the devaluation of his real estate. She hadn't really understood what it was all about. But back then, in one final demonstration of epic stupidity, she gave him money. He insisted that it was a loan, but it had to be in cash.

She never saw him again.

Now, with her mind back in the present, she drove through Manitou Springs and parked her car near The Ancient Mariner. He wasn't there.

She ordered a drink and waited.

§

Gash Seever got out and stretched his legs as his plane was refueled at Wichita Mid-Continent Airport. It was too early for dinner, so he just stayed near the plane. But his belly was still relatively full from the filet he had eaten in Chicago. The lunch hour had taken a little longer than he had hoped, but it was worth it.

He looked around him at the flat terrain. Aside from the patchwork design of the farmland, it had been pretty featureless from the air, too.

He decided that he could never be a flatlander. He liked a landscape that gave him something to look at. Hills, forest, ocean, mountains.

He was looking forward to seeing Colorado. It had been a long time. He had been hearing about the forest fires in Colorado, and that made him sad. It was such beautiful country.

He hoped the fires wouldn't interfere with his job. He wanted to get back home to Jersey.

Then again, maybe a little R&R in the Rockies would be in order.

In February of 1940, Isadora went into labor. Being a cold month, it was a difficult time for Silas. Childbirth methods had changed. Women seldom gave birth at home anymore, or used midwives. That meant that Silas needed to go outside in the cold, to take Isadora to the hospital.

But even while Isadora was in labor, between the pains and contractions, she was directing Silas on how to dress. A warm coat, a knit hat pulled down over his ears, a scarf arranged over his mouth and nose, all with a view to keeping the cold air from afflicting his lungs again.

On the drive to the hospital, Isadora worried.

"Oh, Silas, what if the baby looks like me?"

"Then the baby will be very lucky, indeed." He smiled at her, but Isadora couldn't see it, as his mouth was still covered with the scarf.

"I mean my face," Isadora said insistently.

"I know what you meant, Little Bit," he said calmly, "and we've talked about that. Physical injuries are not genetic and are not passed on to offspring. The baby can't inherit an external injury that you suffered."

"But what if the injury altered my DNA in some way? I've been reading about the discovery of DNA a few years ago, and I'm afraid that such a traumatic injury might have changed it. Scientists have talked about different things being able to cause mutations in the DNA."

"I don't think it works that way, honey," Silas said patiently.

Before Isadora could argue, another contraction began, demanding her full attention.

They arrived at the hospital where Silas took care of getting Isadora admitted. After a short, and thankfully relatively easy labor, Isadora gave birth to a perfect, beautiful baby boy.

They named him Clark.

§

War had been raging in Europe for a while now. But it was only after a US Navy base in Hawaii was bombed by the Japanese in 1941 that America entered the fray.

In War Production Board Order L-208, the United States government ordered gold mines to be closed to free up resources for the war effort. Gold production dropped and Hodges Mill all but closed.

The mines were opened again after the war ended in 1945. Production was not as great as in the early years, but due largely to Silas' good and fair treatment of his employees and his clients, his mill did better than most.

Mining corporations continued buying up mines and mills. When Silas was approached in 1950 with a generous offer, he seriously considered it for a short time – long enough to consult with Isadora and her sisters.

Silas had arranged a meeting when all of the sisters were able to attend. They had gathered in the living room at the inn, while the older children played together back in the sunroom.

"Your father stipulated in his will," Silas said, "that should I ever wish to divest myself of the business of the mill, that I should consult the four of you first.

"As you know," he continued, "I've been unable to continue working there and have left the duties of management to trusted employees, while retaining ownership of the operation.

"Now, though, in the post-war boom, I've been offered a sizable sum for the mill by a gold mining corporation. While it's tempting to accept the offer, I'm concerned about my employees, and how they might fare in the deal. I'm also concerned with how you ladies feel about the business."

Firstborn Emily spoke first, without hesitation.

"Silas, you have tirelessly and conscientiously run the business and managed the employees for all these years, much better than I ever could have."

"I agree," Olivia said. "Your name is connected to the mill almost as closely as Father's."

Jane nodded in agreement.

"As far as I'm concerned," Emily said, "your fair and equitable management of the mill and the employees puts you in a much better position to determine what is to be done with it."

"The mill is yours, Silas," Jane said. "You've earned it."

Isadora looked at Silas, smiling proudly at him.

So Silas made his own decision and turned down the generous offer. Instead, he helped his employees form their own corporation, after which he sold the mill to them for much less than the mining corporation had offered him.

Still, it was more than Silas needed. He had the added satisfaction of knowing that his employees were well taken care of.

When he retired from the mining industry in 1950, he was 64 years old. He had become a homebody again, but now, instead of his home being a lonely place, it provided him greater happiness than he had ever enjoyed.

In their idyllic life and marriage, even those who had initially spoken ill of their relationship came around. They could see the love and regard that Silas and Isadora felt for each other and, in time, were able to feel happy for them.

Isadora was indeed the love of Silas' life, and she felt happy and content in that role. She had gradually come to accept the facial deformity that looked back at her every morning and every evening from her mirror. There was little that she could do about it anyway. Silas' undying love certainly helped.

Late in 1950, though, Silas gave her an unusual present. The horrors of war had necessitated certain advancements in reconstructive surgery. Now, in peacetime, those advancements were making inroads into conventional medicine, being improved upon, and were being made available to civilian patients with gross deformities or injuries.

After enduring the unavoidable pain and post-surgery recovery time, Isadora eventually emerged from her bandages like a butterfly from its chrysalis. Modern 'plastic surgery' was still *only a little past its infancy, so the result was not a total transformation, although it was a drastic improvement.*

Some of the earlier scarring remained, but the bones had been reshaped, bringing her face more into balance, giving it a symmetry that it had lacked for the previous twelve years. Isadora immediately decided that the pain had been worth it.

Silas could once again see the complete, beautiful face he had fallen in love with.

And he could better see the resemblance of Clark's handsome features.

§

In the post-war prosperity, Americans were getting out and vacationing more. Manitou Springs once again became a popular tourist destination, and Silas and Isadora decided to take advantage of it.

Silas constructed an actual sign for the inn, and they changed the name to The Log Cabin Inn. Considering the size of the structure, it was an inaccurate label, but the quaint name appealed to American travelers at the time.

Business was once again booming. In some ways, it was an exciting time for Clark. He was able to meet people from all over the country.

But Isadora had less time for him.

Isadora adored Clark. Next to Silas, her son was the most important person in the world to her. She had always hoped to be able to give him a little brother or sister, but it had never happened. So Clark enjoyed her devotion without having to share it with anybody else.

When Isadora was busy with guests, though, she seemed to Clark to be more distracted. He had to share her attention with these strangers. They almost always remarked on what a handsome boy he was. Clark liked that, but still, he missed his mother's attention.

In the spring of 1951, her attention was again required elsewhere. That's when the weather changed quickly.

On a fairly warm early spring day, Silas had gone down into town for necessary supplies for the inn. He was reveling in his freedom, happy to be outside again after the cold winter months. But he was taken by surprise as a fast moving cold front rapidly swept in from the north, plunging the area back into a deep freeze before he had finished up in town.

He drove back home, coughing all the way. By the time he got back to the inn, it was all he could do to pull himself upstairs to his bed.

"Clark, be a dear and unload the supplies," Isadora instructed tensely. "If there's anything too big for you, just leave it, and I'll help you with it later."

Clark had never seen his mother looking so worried. He slipped his coat on and zipped it up, pulling up the hood. He went out the front door to carry in the supplies as Isadora helped Silas to bed.

Isadora turned up the wall furnace in their room as Silas continued his painful hacking, and she got out the electric vaporizer from a cabinet. They hadn't needed it for several years. After she got the vaporizer filled with water and plugged in, she rushed downstairs to get Silas' favorite treatment for cough, bourbon with honey.

"Is Dad going to be okay?" Clark asked Isadora after Silas had relaxed and fallen asleep.

"He'll be fine, honey," Isadora replied. "This is why he has to stay in during the cold weather."

"What's wrong with him?"

"It's because of something that happened a long time ago. Thirty-one years ago, in fact, the day I was born. There was an accident down at the gold mill where he worked and he breathed some poison. It damaged his lungs, and that damage never really went away. Now, he just has to be really careful."

"That's the same thing that killed Granddad, isn't it?" Clark asked. He had never known his grandfather, but had heard much about him.

"Yes, it is, honey. But don't worry, your Dad's very strong, and he takes good care of himself. I have a feeling he's going to be with us for a long time."

§

During his father's convalescence, since his mother was not able to do everything, eleven-year-old Clark took on more responsibility at the inn. His mother had already taught him how to clean the rooms, but she had always supervised him before. Now, she decided it was time to try him out unsupervised. So while she took care of breakfast and cleaning up the kitchen, Clark worked in the rooms.

One morning, he was in the room of some guests who were staying over, so their things were still in the room. Clark always thought it was interesting to see what other people brought with them when they travelled. But as his mother taught him, he focused on his cleaning work and not on the guests' personal property.

Until Clark saw a rather large wad of money partially exposed on a table.

Clark had never wanted for anything in his life. But he had never seen that much cash before, and he had certainly never had cash like that himself.

At first, he ignored it, going about his business. But he kept coming back to it. It was a struggle, one he had never had to deal with before. He knew it was wrong – his parents had taught him that – but he took some of the money for himself.

He didn't take it all. He was intuitive enough to know that if he did, the guests would likely notice it missing and Clark would get in trouble. But if he only took part of it, they might not miss it. They might think they had just miscounted.

Clark stuffed the bills into his pocket and finished with the room, locking the door behind him.

He was nervous at first, afraid that God would be unhappy with him and punish him. He had heard his father tell about the apple he stole after his mother died, and how he felt so terribly guilty about it. Clark was feeling similar pangs of a guilty conscience.

But he also felt a bit of a thrill.

etting through Colorado Springs wasn't a problem at all. It seemed like business as usual. People were driving, going about their affairs as if it was just another day. Clark was relieved to see that.

Based on what he had seen on the news, he was expecting practically a state-wide war zone. It almost wouldn't have surprised him to see tanks and armed soldiers blocking the streets, with curfews and martial law in effect. Surely near the fire, it *was* something of a war zone, but the news seemed to blow it out of proportion. Traffic was flowing through town nicely.

As he drove farther east, though, he could see the massive cloud of smoke on his left. Occasionally he saw planes or helicopters heading toward the burn area, likely to drop a load of water or fire retardant on the burn.

There were other helicopters, too, TV or radio news choppers, hovering here and there, outside the perimeter of the burn area, relaying the information back to their respective stations.

To be further blown out of proportion.

The radio was telling him about road closures. He was starting to see barricades and signs about closures, too. But he was trying to remain hopeful. He had to.

It had been years since he had been in this area, so he had Googled it and printed out the map before he came. He pulled the map out of his wallet and unfolded it. His air conditioner didn't work and he had the windows rolled down, so he pulled the passenger side seatbelt, which also didn't work, across the map to hold it down and keep it from blowing away.

Heading east on Woodmen Road, he came to Meridian and was going to turn left. But he saw that they had it blocked off. He got onto U.S. 24 heading northeast, hoping to turn onto Elbert Road, but he found it closed as well.

With a sigh, he continued on. Eventually, a few miles farther, he came to Bradshaw Road. It was open so he turned there, going north. But each road he came to which headed west was either closed at Bradshaw, or closed after he had been on it for only a short time.

He spent the better part of the afternoon driving around the fire, but finding no way in.

His hope was quickly dissipating.

By the beginning of the evening, he was tired after having accomplished nothing. He decided to go into town to get something to eat. Then back to the B&B, to bed.

§

Dora climbed into her Prius and started it up. She kept her door open for a minute until the air conditioner started blowing cool air. Then she closed the door and put on her seat belt.

She felt better now. Having spent some time with the orphans – reading to them, playing with them – as always, it recharged her. She thought it helped her as much as it did them. Maybe more.

Dora almost felt as if she could handle being around her father for a little longer now. But the next thought that occurred to her was, "I wonder how much longer he's staying."

The thought of her father reminded her of her grandmother, and of a question that had occurred to Dora, about the inheritance. She realized that, with her father actually alive, he would have been the rightful heir. She didn't know how the law would work in this case, and as she drove through western Colorado Springs, she decided to stop at the lawyer's office.

She pulled up in front of the small office building and went inside. It had been almost a year since she had been here, just after Gramma Izzy was killed. She went down a hallway, past other businesses, to a door with a sign that said, "Taylor, Benson and Schulmann, Attorneys at Law." It was a small firm. Dora had never seen more than three people at a time in there, including the receptionist.

Eric Benson himself was walking through the office when Dora went in. He paused for a moment when he saw her, as if he was trying to place her. It had been almost a year for him, too. Then he recognized her.

"Ms. Baskin?"

"Hi, Mr. Benson," she said. They shook hands and exchanged pleasantries.

"What can I do for you?" he asked.

"I won't take much of your time," Dora said. "I know I don't have an appointment, but I just wondered if I could ask you a question about my grandmother's estate."

"Well, it's *your* estate now, but yes, of course. Come on into my office."

"Thanks."

Benson closed the door behind Dora and motioned her into a seat in front of his desk. As she sat down, he opened a file cabinet drawer. He flipped through the files, pulled out a file folder, and opened it on his desk.

"So, what's your question?" he asked.

Dora paused for a moment, trying to arrange her thoughts.

"My father showed up yesterday," she said.

"Well, great! That's good news!" Benson replied in a happy tone.

"I guess," Dora replied. Knowing nothing about their shaky relationship, Benson looked at her with a puzzled expression, but Dora ignored it. "Long story. My question is: What happens to my grandmother's estate now? And to the Cherokee trust fund I opened with the money from the coin collection? Does it all go to him, or what?"

"Well, let me see," Benson said as he flipped through papers in the folder. Coming to the will itself, he read the wording. "No, the will doesn't name your father as a beneficiary at all."

"But he's next of kin. Even if she thought he might have been dead when she drew up the will, wouldn't he still be entitled to it now that he has turned up alive?"

"No. Even if your grandmother thought that there was a chance he might be alive, she didn't provide any condition or qualification in the event that he showed up. She specifically named you, not 'next of kin,' as the beneficiary."

"Hmm." She sat there processing his answer for a moment. "On the chance that I decided to turn over the stock portfolio to him, is that a difficult process?"

"No, not at all. You would want to be absolutely certain that you wanted to do that. But if so, I could help you with that, or your financial advisor could. It can be done fairly easily."

"Okay, good. Well thank you, Mr. Benson. That's all I needed to know. I appreciate your help." She started to stand up.

"Not a problem." He continued looking through the folder. "I see here that my partner, Jack Taylor, called you several months ago."

Dora puckered her brows, trying to recall.

"I vaguely remember that," she said. "I don't remember what it was about, though."

"It seems there was something else that showed up from your grandmother that was not directly connected to her

Last Will and Testament. A different piece of business that she did with Mr. Taylor, for some reason." There was a PostIt note stuck to a sealed envelope. He followed the handwriting with his finger as he told Dora what it said. "It was to be handed over to you personally, and you said that you would come in to pick it up."

"Wow, I forgot all about that. I was pretty busy back then, starting up my bed & breakfast, and I guess it slipped my mind."

"Well, it's fortunate you came in today," Benson smiled. He made a note of the date on the PostIt, then pulled it off the envelope and placed it back in the file. He handed the envelope to Dora and closed the file folder.

"Thank you," she said as she looked at it, unsure of what to make of this latest development.

Back in her car, she decided to wait until she got back home to open it. Maybe when Shawn was with her.

§

Gash Seever took the rental car agreement and the key and walked out to the parking space specified in the paperwork, where a silver Lincoln MKZ sedan was parked. He had finally made it to Colorado Springs, but it had been a long trip, nearly a twelve hour flight, and he was tired.

He had seen the fire on his way in, and all the choppers and airplanes involved in fighting it, or covering the news about it. He had been routed around the fire activity and had to circle a few times. With the added air traffic he encountered up there, landing took a little longer.

He was just glad to be back on the ground now.

He drove to the Marriott, about a mile away from the airport, and checked in. He decided that, after a shower and a light dinner in his room, he would go online to check for any updates to his information.

But that would be the extent of his work tonight.

§

"Come on, you bloody wanker!" Bridget Lindstrom said under her breath. So far, he hadn't shown up.

She wondered if she would even recognize him now. It had been over twenty-five years since she had seen him last. A person can change a lot in that time.

But after scrutinizing every face she saw that evening, she was getting pretty tired of it. The longer she sat there, the more doubts she developed. Even if he did show up, what were the chances that anything would come of it? She wasn't sure what she hoped to accomplish by being here.

Her butt was sore from sitting in the chair, and she was tired of being hit on by guys looking for a hookup.

Been there, done that.

She just wanted to go home.

She got the check from her waiter. It wasn't much. She had been nursing two glasses of wine all evening. With a sigh, she paid it, picked up her purse and left.

It's just as well, she thought as she opened the door to her car and got in. It's getting late, and I have to get up for school in the morning.

Just as she was thinking that and fastening her seat belt, she saw someone who looked a little familiar. He had gotten out of a junky, rusty old car, parked a couple of spaces ahead of her.

Good God! Could that old man be him? she thought.

He was a little stooped over. He had white hair and a scruffy white beard, but the way he walked – it did look like him.

She did the math in her head. This guy looks like he's around seventy. Subtract about twenty-five years, and he would have been around forty-five, which she realized would have been about right. He was an older man. That's partly what had appealed to her.

Bridget was still tired, and she still had to get up for school. But she had to know. After the day she'd had, and then the long, tiring evening, she knew she wasn't up to confronting him now. She didn't think she had the patience to attempt a coherent conversation with him. But she decided to wait, to see where he goes. It was only seven o'clock. Not that late. But he's an old man now. He probably has to go to bed within the next hour or so. She realized she was being snarky, but she didn't care.

Forty-five minutes later, she saw him come back out, and she smiled a self-satisfied smile.

He got into his car and started it up, and a cloud of smoke erupted around it.

That should be easy to follow!

He pulled out of his space, heading west on Manitou Avenue. Bridget pulled out after him, and she kept her distance, not just to avoid being detected, but to keep from breathing his smoke. It was still light, so there was little danger of losing him. They went past the roundabout at Manitou and Ruxton, and up out of town.

He drives like an old man, Bridget thought, as he slowly followed Manitou Avenue to where it finally merged with Highway 24. After a few minutes, Bridget felt a sense of *déjà vu* as he took an exit that seemed familiar. Then he turned onto a road marked Elk Run, past a few old houses, and pulled into a parking area in front of an enormous log house. *The* log house, Bridget realized, the one she had visited back in 1986. There was now a sign in front that said, "Isadora's Bed and Breakfast."

Oh, my God, she thought, *the old lady started a bed and breakfast. She must be in her 90s by now! And what are the chances that he'd be staying here?*

Based on the junk heap of a car he was driving, this B&B seemed like it would be too expensive for him. Maybe one of the little motels on the east side of town, like the Silver Saddle, where she herself had stayed back in 1986. But not this classy looking place.

Bridget wasn't sure what to make of it. But at least she knew where he was staying. She hoped he wouldn't be leaving in the morning, but she was tired. She needed to get back to Colorado Springs and into bed if she was going to be any good at work tomorrow.

But she would definitely call Jack when she got home, to update him on what she had found out, and to see if he had anything to add.

§

"Sorry, babe," Shawn said on the phone. "I meant to call you sooner. It's just been pretty crazy."

"It's okay," Dora replied. She was relaxing on her bed but hadn't actually gotten in it yet. "What's going on?"

"We've had some issues with an estate we're working on. The auction is on Saturday and we have to get these problems all ironed out before then."

"So, you're going to stay at your place tonight?"

"Yeah, I'm afraid so. Colin and I are trying to get this done, but it's going to be pretty late. I know you have to get up early to make breakfast, so I don't want to disturb your sleep."

"No problem," Dora said. "Come over tomorrow if you have a chance."

"I will, sweetie. I love you."

"I love you, too," Dora said, and with a sigh, she disconnected and put her cell phone down.

She looked at the envelope she had gotten from her lawyer this afternoon. It was on her bedside table, unopened.

Oh well, she thought. It can wait till tomorrow.

She was too tired now. She got up and went in the bathroom to get ready for bed.

Jenny Putnam sniffed as Clark related the story about Cochise, her brows puckered with concern. She was a pretty fifteen-year-old brunette, her hair styled in a soft pixie cut, similar to Audrey Hepburn's hairstyle in Roman Holiday, *one of Jenny's favorite movies.*

Clark's story was heart-rending, told with tears in his eyes, and Clark knew that Jenny had a soft spot for horses. And for good-looking boys. Clark Baskin was one of the best-looking boys she had ever seen. Clark knew that, too, and he knew very well how to use it.

"Cochise was only twenty-one years old," Clark said. "That's young for a horse, but Dad thinks he ate some bad feed. He was dead when I woke up this morning."

"You were pretty close to the horse?"

"All my life. My Mom taught me to ride on him."

To outward appearances, they had been wandering aimlessly down Canon Avenue. But as sixteen-year-old Clark began telling his story, he subtly aimed toward Lovers Lane which ran somewhat parallel to Manitou Avenue. It was a narrow, secluded, heavily forested road.

They were now walking behind the Stagecoach Inn, a restaurant that delivered its food with a nostalgic flair, its waitresses dressed in Old West costumes. What Clark especially liked about this area was the fact that the trees became a little thicker, the seclusion a little more complete. A little more romantic, as Fountain Creek angled toward the road, adding its gentle sound to the ambiance.

It was June, 1956. Cochise had actually died a few months before, and even though Clark had not really cared that much about riding, he still managed to work up some tears in his eyes as he told the story, updating it to make it sound as if it was a recent, traumatic occurrence. He kept his head down most of the time, his hands at his sides.

Jenny was looking at Clark's face as he spoke, and when Clark hazarded a glance at her, he could see tears forming in her eyes as well.

"Oh, Clark, I'm so sorry," she responded. She took his hand in hers and squeezed.

Clark shook his head and squeezed his eyes closed just enough to make the tears roll down his cheek.

"I just keep seeing him lying there on the floor of the stable," he sniffed. "He was kicking and gasping. The poor thing." That was a new addition to the story, and he realized too late that he had told her that Cochise was already dead when Clark woke up. He needed to be careful with his embellishments! But Jenny didn't seem to notice the change in his story.

Jenny moved closer to Clark and put her arm around him. In response, he put his arm around her waist.

"It must have been horrible!" Jenny said, and she leaned against him. Clark could feel her breast against his side, her hip pressed into his. He was already becoming aroused.

He stopped walking and he turned his head toward Jenny's face, now only inches from his own. He looked into her eyes and she looked into his, and he could see that she was just oozing with sympathy. He waited for only a moment, then he slowly leaned toward her. Their lips met and Clark pulled her closer. He opened his mouth, probing gently with his tongue, coaxing her to open hers.

Jenny pulled away just a little to look at him, and he was careful to display just the right mix of sadness and longing. A well timed tear just happened to slip down his cheek at that moment. Jenny sighed and put her head against his chest, and Clark held her, stroking her back.

He could now feel her breasts pressed against his chest. In his caressing motions, he casually ran one hand across the fastener of her bra, feeling where it was located, taking note of how many hooks. His other hand was just grazing the small of her back, and lower, where her back started to flare out into her buttocks. With that hand, he increased the pressure just slightly, pressing her against his groin.

They stayed like that for a few moments, and Clark wasn't sure if she was being sympathetic or affectionate, or if she was hesitating. He didn't want to risk having her curtail their intimate adventure, so he let her stay there for a bit longer. Just before he was about to make a move, Jenny looked up at him, and as he leaned in closer, her lips parted.

Clark kissed her deeply, and she responded, leaning into him. She put one hand on the back of his neck and held him tightly, pulling his head down to her.

As he continued caressing her lower back, he gently pulled her blouse out of her skirt, touching the bare skin of her back with just his thumb to start with. When Jenny didn't hesitate, he slipped his hand under her blouse, caressing her skin. He ran his hand up along her back, slowly and casually unfastening her bra. He could feel the release of her breasts against his chest as the undergarment loosened. Then he slipped his hand down inside the back of her skirt and under her panties. He gently but firmly pulled her against him. By then, he was so hard, he was sure she must be able to notice his arousal. And thinking about that certainty aroused him even more.

With the soft, smooth contour of one of her buttocks in his hand now, Jenny's breathing was fast and hard, but she kept kissing him.

And Clark knew he had her.

§

"You have to talk to him, Silas," Isadora said after she hung up the receiver of the new wall mounted telephone. They were in the kitchen.

"Honey, I have talked to him," Silas said.

"Well, it obviously hasn't done any good." Isadora nodded toward the phone. "That was Joan Adamson. Her daughter, Christina, said that – " Isadora looked around and lowered her voice, "that he had relations with her behind the Congregational Church."

Silas fought a smile and tried to hide it by covering his mouth and coughing. But he wasn't fast enough.

"Silas, it's not funny,"

"I know, Little Bit. But you're forgetting that you and I had relations before we were married."

"No, Silas, I'm not forgetting that at all," Isadora replied indignantly. "And I'm not saying it was right. But we didn't do it outside, where somebody who happened to be walking by might see. And we certainly did not do it in the shadow of a church!

"Besides, we were in love, and we got married. Clark is not in love with any of these girls, and doesn't seem to have any interest in getting married."

"You're right. I know."

"He's lying to them and then just using them to satisfy his own lustful appetite. Silas, he's my son and I love him, but Clark can be just plain nasty."

Silas nodded. He knew she was right.

Clark was a lothario, and he was only sixteen years old. Silas just wasn't sure he had what it took to be a father in these new and changing times, especially at his age. He was seventy years old, too old, he felt, to be trying to keep a twentieth century teenager in line.

Isadora was only thirty-six, a much more normal age for keeping up with a teenager. Silas sometimes wondered if he had done the right thing in marrying Isadora. The difference in their ages was more apparent at times. They loved each other dearly, but she clearly had more energy and stamina in some things than he had, such as in raising a child.

But she was right. This was his job.

"You've worked so hard to establish a good reputation in the community," Isadora continued, her tone becoming warmer and more beseeching, "and to set a moral example for Clark. You started out as the poor, orphaned son of a prostitute and made something of yourself. You took the mill that my father started and made it even better. And now, people look up to you as a pillar of the community.

"But in a very short time, the reputation that you and Father built over the years, Clark has managed to demolish it. Some of those people who used to look up to us now avoid us.

"I hate to say it, Silas, but I am often ashamed that Clark is my son."

"I know, Honey," Silas acknowledged. "I feel the same way." He just didn't know how to get through to Clark.

He also didn't know that Clark was quietly listening out in the hallway.

§

Clark Baskin, now a first-year law student at Yale, was lounging in bed on a Friday morning. The room was bright. He looked at the clock on the bedside table. It was after one o'clock. He turned back and closed his eyes. He wasn't really that sleepy anymore, but he just felt lazy. He may have dozed a little more after that, but he couldn't be sure.

It didn't matter.

He had nowhere to go. He did have one class that day, but he had decided to skip it. He had been up late the night before and needed to sleep in, but it would be fine. As with high school and his undergraduate studies, Clark practically absorbed the information with little effort on his part.

New Haven, Connecticut was a far cry from Manitou Springs, Colorado, so that's where Clark decided he wanted to go. He had argued that Yale was a much better university than all the little podunk cow-town colleges in Colorado. Yes, the tuition was considerably higher, but they could afford it.

But the fact was that he wanted distance. His parents had been riding him so much about his social life. And not just them. The whole town was so backwards and old-fashioned. Sure, he liked the ladies. But the ladies liked him, too.

The problem with the small town was that the occasional girl who wanted him to settle down with her and get married went crying to her mother when that didn't happen. Word spreads quickly in a small town.

Here in the city, things were different. And New Haven wasn't even that big of a city. Like New York City. He hadn't gotten to New York yet, but he was planning on it. But even here in New Haven, some of the chicks practically begged him to take them to bed. Like this one. He looked at the blonde sleeping with her head on his shoulder.

What the hell was her name? Peggy Sue? Barbara Ann? It was one of those names from a song.

Clark had let a friend talk him into going with him to some Beat joint last night. It had turned out to be really boring. Just a bunch of sad cats sitting around griping and complaining about rich people, saying that everybody needed to shed their materialism. Some even talked about a revolution of some kind.

Some of them were sincere. But considering that several of them were Yale students too, that meant that they had money. Clark was turned off by the hypocrisy. Besides, he liked having money. He liked what he could do with money.

He liked the girls, too.

Like Betty Jean, here. She had been sitting alone in that Beat joint, chin resting on her hand, nursing a Manhattan, while some weird jazz music droned on in the background. She seemed just about as interested in the whole scene as Clark was. She perked up when he approached her, though.

"I'm Clark," he said.

"Ann-Marie," she replied, or something like that.

"Are you here alone?"

She nodded and took another sip. Clark glanced over at the group he had left, then back at her.

"You want to split?"

"Sure," she said. "You want to go make out? We can go to my place. It's just a block away."

Clark smiled and nodded. Yes, he definitely liked the modern city mentality.

Turned out she wanted to do more than just make out. Clark didn't take much convincing. They were in bed within just a few minutes.

She stirred next to him now and opened her eyes.

"Morning, stud," she said as she snuggled up closer. Clark turned his head, making a show of looking at the clock again. It was one-thirty.

"Nope," he said. "I'm an afternoon stud now."

"Why don't you turn on the radio, smartass?" she smiled.

With his free hand, he reached over and turned the knob on the radio. Can't Get Used to Losing You *by Andy Williams* was playing.

"Bitchin' station," Clark said with a sarcastic edge to his voice.

"Shut up." She squirmed for a moment and stretched. The first thing Clark noticed were her gorgeous breasts. Then, as she stretched, her left hand came out from under the covers and into view, and Clark saw the gold ring.

"I didn't notice this last night," he said as he took her hand. "You're married?"

"Yeah," she said. She looked at the ring for a moment, then pulled her hand away. "He's an asshole. We'll probably be splitting soon."

Clark had never had a married woman before. He realized that she didn't feel any different than a single one. But his main concern was the husband.

"Where is he?"

"He's away on business. Again." She looked at Clark's face. Then she squinted her eyes as if concentrating. "Damn it. What was your name?"

"Clark," he replied with a smile. "I'm glad you asked, because I can't remember yours either."

"Mary Lou."

"Well, hello Mary Lou. I knew it was in a song."

The pizzicato violins of the Andy Williams song faded out. After that, Johnny Angel *by Shelley Fabares began. Clark* turned and looked at Mary Lou and raised his eyebrows questioningly.

"Find another station," she said, rolling her eyes, and she got up and walked toward the bathroom. Clark smiled as her naked body glided easily and uninhibited across the room.

"Nice to see you go," he said. She casually raised her middle finger at him over her shoulder without bothering to turn and look at him.

Clark rolled over and sat up on the edge of the bed, turning the tuning knob on the radio. He stopped when he heard Dion's The Wanderer.

He got up and stretched, walking naked around the room. He was looking at a little display of ceramic figurines on top of Mary Lou's dresser when she emerged from the bathroom.

"Hmm," she said when she saw Clark standing there undressed. Her eyes lingered on his crotch, and Clark thought she almost licked her lips. He looked Mary Lou's body up and down, too.

"I'd have to agree," he said. "And as much as I'd like to stay and pick up where we left off earlier this morning, I'm afraid I have to go."

"Yeah, me too." She picked up her bra from the chair and put it on, while Clark found his underwear on the floor. As they were putting their clothing back on, Ring of Fire by Johnny Cash was playing on the radio. Suddenly, before the song was over, it stopped.

"We interrupt this musical program," the announcer said, "with a special bulletin out of Dallas, Texas. Three shots were *fired at President Kennedy's motorcade just a little while ago. At the beginning of a two-day speaking tour in Dallas, gunshots rang out, and first reports say that President Kennedy has been seriously wounded.*

"We will continue to keep you updated as more details are received."

I Can't Stop Loving You *by Ray Charles started playing as Clark and Mary Lou looked at each other. They each had a shocked expression on their faces.*

Clark had never had much of an interest in politics, but he liked Kennedy. The man was rich, and he was rumored to have had a lot of women. The latter detail was not something that others admired very much, but Clark had to admit that Kennedy was a man after his own heart.

His first thought was, I wonder if it was a jealous husband who shot him.

§

"We gotta get out of here," Jerry Barnham told Clark. "This place is such a drag now."

Clark had met his friend shortly after he left Mary Lou's apartment. They were now in one of their favorite bars, their second one of the afternoon. It was usually a swinging place, but this afternoon, it seemed that wherever they went, the mood was morose.

"I'm sure it'll be like this everywhere," Clark said. "He was a popular president. People are sad."

"It won't be like this everywhere."

"What do you have in mind?"

"I heard about this place downtown," Jerry started.

"Not another one," Clark interrupted. "That place you took me to last night was bad news."

"Well, you seemed to do alright, Romeo. No, this place has card games."

"What kind of card games?" Clark asked, his interest now aroused.

"Poker, Blackjack, you name it. With higher stakes than the ones you beat us at all the time."

"That's against the law, isn't it? What happens if we get caught?"

"We say we're from out of town," Jerry replied. "We didn't know."

"Yeah, I'm sure that will make a difference. I'm a law student. I'm supposed to know the law."

"You're only first-year," Jerry said, waving it off. "Nobody expects you to know anything yet."

Clark shook his head and smiled at Jerry's easy excuses, but he was still interested.

"Look," Jerry continued, "obviously, the best thing to do would be to not get caught. Besides, I heard this place was really secure. It's in a back room behind a legitimate and expensive restaurant, with some serious security. It'll be fine. Come on, what do you say?"

Clark drained his bourbon.

"Let's go have a look."

§

The restaurant was on the ground floor of a hotel. Jerry had mentioned his interest in the games to the maitre d', reinforcing it with a folded twenty dollar bill and the name of the person who told him about them.

But even though Jerry had taken the lead in getting them in there, once they were inside, Clark clearly had the upper hand when it came to the games themselves.

Jerry had dabbled in a few games that evening, winning and losing, emerging in pretty much the same condition in which he had started. Clark, though, had joined a table of Five Card Draw and had stayed with it. In the early morning hours, he was still at it, while Jerry and a few others gathered around to watch. Including a pretty redhead named Tierney that Clark had been keeping his eye on.

Clark had done quite well, as attested to by the stacks of chips in front of him. He had lost a few hands, like the one very early in the evening. Joe, the man sitting across from him with the black hair slicked straight back, had played a straight flush, easily beating Clark's full house. Clark had bet, and lost, quite a bit on that one.

But Clark's luck, while fluctuating a bit, had generally been good. He looked again at his hand. He had three aces, a face card and the four of hearts. He had already bet a thousand dollars. If he didn't get what he needed, he would still have three of a kind. It would be a respectable hand, but it could also be beaten by any number of other hands.

Clark was feeling tired and was struggling to keep his wits about him. He had stopped drinking an hour before, but was still *feeling the effects of the alcohol he had already imbibed. He had to concentrate.*

He pulled the two worthless cards from his hand and discarded them. Joe dealt him two more.

He slid them toward his hand and lifted the corners. The "A" he saw in the corner of the front card made him breathe easier. Four aces was definitely a potential winning hand, though it could still be beaten by a straight flush. Clark looked around at the other players.

Mike, the nervous-looking man to his right, looked at his hand, sighed and shook his head. He tossed his cards face down and scooted his chair back a little.

"I'm out," he said.

That left Gus, the tall man with the droopy eyes to Clark's left, and Joe. Clark studied their faces. Gus seemed undecided, which told Clark that he didn't have a clear winner, certainly nothing better than Clark's four aces. Joe, on the other hand, was characteristically cool.

Joe studied Clark's face as well, and apparently reached a decision.

Clark didn't like the smile on Joe's face as he pushed all of his chips to the center of the table.

Gus blew out his breath as if he had been holding it, and put his cards down.

"I'm out, too," he said.

Clark sighed and pushed all of his chips in.

Joe seemed very pleased with his four kings, until Clark turned up his four aces.

Joe, his eyes moving between Clark's face and the pile of chips on the table, shook his head slightly. But then he smiled and stood up, extending his hand to Clark.

"Well played," he said.

"Thank you," Clark said with a giddy smile as he shook Joe's hand.

He noticed Tierney smiling too.

Jerry helped Clark gather up his chips and take them to the cashier, who then counted out thirty-five thousand dollars. Jerry was astonished watching the stack of several five hundred dollar bills followed by several more one hundred dollar bills growing in front of Clark.

"God, I'm so tired," Jerry said, rubbing his face. "I think I'm hearing things. I could have sworn she said thirty-five thousand dollars."

Clark picked up the money, snapped a hundred dollar bill off the top and slipped it into Jerry's shirt pocket, giving it a pat.

"Thirty-four nine," Clark said. "Go home, Jerry. Get some sleep." Jerry's expression was a little confused, intensified by the alcoholic fog.

The rest of the bills Clark stuffed in his own pocket. Then he turned around. There was Tierney watching from a distance. He smiled and walked toward her.

§

During the remaining years of Clark's schooling, he found several illicit gaming parlors in and around New Haven. Visiting them on weekends, he sharpened his skills, becoming well-known among his peers. He also made a few weekend or holiday trips to Las Vegas where he was able to experience gambling on a much larger scale.

Although the gambling was enticing, and often lucrative, Clark managed to keep it confined to the weekends. He was able to keep the two primary parts of his life compartmentalized, so his studies did not suffer too dramatically.

Eventually, Clark found Jerry to be boring and stifling, and discarded him. He was dealt new friends occasionally, but he usually outgrew them quickly.

The women came and went as well, seldom lasting longer than a single night.

Clark graduated in 1966 with his Juris Doctor degree from Yale. He received multiple job offers and, feeling a surge of homesickness, he accepted a position in a Denver law firm. In July, he passed the bar exam within the top five percentile.

Bridget Lindstrom had made it a point to wake up early on Friday morning. The information she found waiting in her e-mail was interesting. After she had followed Clark to the B&B last night, she had called Jack and told him about what details she had found out.

He had already followed up this morning.

His e-mail said:

> Hello Bridget. I went online just after you called me last night. I found another charge at The Ancient Mariner, from last night, but none at the B&B you mentioned.
>
> After doing further research, I found that the B&B was owned by Isadora Baskin, Clark's daughter. Clark is also the son of the Isadora you met there years ago. So he's probably staying there free of charge.
>
> Don't know what kind of relationship the daughter has with him, but seeing as how

he's her father, she's very possibly sympathetic.

Let me know if you need anything further.

Good luck.

Jack.

Interesting. Bridget had never made that connection. She hadn't realized until this moment that Clark was connected in any way to the old woman she had spoken to back then.

So their first meeting probably hadn't been an accident. Bridget remembered meeting his mother Isadora, and hearing that her husband was sick inside.

She didn't see Clark at that time, but he must have seen her. Did he follow her to The Ancient Mariner? Had he specifically targeted her for some reason?

Whatever the case, she had to get her mind off of it long enough to take care of her summer school class. She would think about this later.

§

Gash Seever was up early and went online. His search last night hadn't revealed much. There had been another charge at The Ancient Mariner restaurant, but nothing else. No hotel or motel charges. And this morning, no change.

The limited information he had *did* tell Gash one thing, though. Multiple charges at The Ancient Mariner meant that it was a favorite spot.

And that meant that it was a good place to start his search. It would probably be more fruitful than just making the rounds of the local motels showing around a photograph.

He saw on their website that The Ancient Mariner didn't open till 11:00, though. So he had plenty of time for a nice leisurely breakfast.

And maybe a walk around town.

§

Dora and Robin had the kitchen cleaned up before 10:00. Breakfast for three really was pretty easy.

The Jurgenssens had checked out and had begun their drive back home to Minnesota. Dora's father had been down for breakfast, but he avoided the Jurgenssens, preferring to eat by himself. He had been very quiet, and left immediately after finishing his breakfast.

Dora wasn't sure what to make of his behavior, but at least he was out of her hair for a while.

Robin turned on the radio in time for the end of the local news.

"The fire is only about five percent contained. Sheriff Terry Maketa has announced that nineteen more homes have burned, now totaling 379. The National Weather Service is predicting a third day of hot, dry, windy weather for the area, especially in the late afternoon. So for now, there appears to be little relief in sight."

§

Clark, like yesterday, was heading east again. He knew he had to remain calm, but with each passing day, the dread he had been feeling grew a little stronger.

Also like yesterday, he kept passing roadblock after roadblock. He could see the smoke on his left, at times even the flames, but he wasn't seeing any way to get in there. Not that he *wanted* to get closer to the fire, but he had to.

So far, he was following his same route as yesterday, and by the time he was heading north on Bradshaw, the feeling of dread was starting to turn to panic.

Then he saw it. The barbed wire fence on his left had a gap. He hit the brakes and skidded to a stop. It wasn't actually a complete gap. Only the upper strand of wire was broken. The lower one was still intact, but it gave him an idea.

He looked ahead and behind, and saw the empty road stretching into the distance both directions. It was deserted.

He got out of his car and went to the fence. Inside it was a large expanse of vacant field as far as he could see. He examined the barbed wire and saw that, while the lower strand was not broken, the fasteners that held it to the posts were old and rusted, and somewhat loose. The barbed wire itself was also old and slack. When he stepped on the wire next to one of the posts, the fastener snapped off easily. Same with the other one.

The loose wire was now dangling barely an inch above the ground.

Before he lost his nerve, Clark got back in his car and turned toward the gap in the fence, hoping the ground was not too bumpy. He didn't know if his old Datsun could handle too much shaking.

He drove off the road, between the posts, and headed west, toward the smoke and fire. Yesterday, he had made notes on his printed map showing where the roadblocks were located. So he hoped that once he actually got inside the evacuation zone, he would be able to drive on the deserted roads.

The ride was bumpy. It was acres of undeveloped land, pasture ground, and he knew it was hard on his old car. But he took it slow and steady, avoiding rocks and other obstacles, and eventually came to what appeared to be a dry river bed. He slowed even more, picking his way through the smoothest area he could find.

His progress was painfully slow. Looking at his map, it appeared that it was almost three miles from Bradshaw Road to Elbert Road, where he hoped he could get out of the fields. Clark took a deep breath and exhaled it, willing himself to be patient, as he continued on.

His route through the field was meandering as he had to keep turning constantly to negotiate the smoothest route and avoid obstacles. But about forty-five minutes into his traversing of the field, he reached an impassible obstacle. A miniature canyon, carved through the field by a now extinct river, or possibly severe erosion, stretched out across his path. There was no way his car could navigate that.

Looking both directions, Clark shook his head and sighed, and he turned to the right, following the canyon. He was happy to see that this route, while going mostly north, was also still going west a bit. So at least it wasn't entirely out of the way.

But then it started turning back, forcing Clark to head east once again, and the frustration brought tears to his eyes. Finally, though, an hour and a half after he entered the large enclosed area, he came to the western boundary, and Elbert Road.

Here, the fence was in better condition, and he spent fifteen minutes breaking the barbed wire loose from several posts, to get it low enough to drive over. He wished he had had the foresight to bring wire cutters with him.

Once he was on the road, tears came to his eyes again, this time from relief. He hadn't reached his destination yet, but just being able to drive on a road and to move faster felt as if an immense burden had been lifted. His old Datsun was rattling now, and smoking a little. He hoped he would be able to get back into town.

Going north on Elbert, he turned left onto Murphy Road, and in a matter of minutes, the smoke and fire was looming in front of him. Pasturage gave way to large forested lots with expensive homes, and always the trees growing thicker around him.

Clark could see how dangerous it was to be in this area.

Eventually, he turned off of Murphy Road, onto a gravel road, making turns that he barely remembered. But finally, he arrived.

There in front of him stood the old cabin. His father's secluded home from a century ago.

The old wood was weathered and grey, with small gaps showing through in places. But it was still standing.

Of greater concern to Clark was the proximity of the fire. The forest came to just behind the cabin, and he could see the billowing smoke above the trees. He couldn't tell how far away it was. He couldn't see the fire for the trees, and despite his concern, he smiled grimly at the paraphrasing of the old saying.

He got out of his car and walked toward the door, the smell of smoke almost overpowering.

He didn't have a key, but he hoped that the door would be old and weak enough that he could force it open. Indeed, by ramming his shoulder against it, on the third attempt, the door crashed open.

He went inside and looked around, as the memories washed over him.

"This is impressive," Clark said. He was sitting behind his desk reviewing a bundle of documents supplied to him by one of his clients Joshua Garrett, a Denver entrepreneur and founder of 24 Garrett Gold Investments, Inc. "Are these numbers accurate?" he asked, looking up at Garrett.

"Absolutely," Garrett said. "Since Tricky Dick broke us loose from Bretton Woods, the price of gold has been climbing."

The Bretton Woods Agreements was a system established after World War II whereby many countries fixed their exchange rates relative to the US dollar. Dollars could be exchanged for gold at the official exchange rate of $35 per ounce.

In August of 1971, due to a number of factors including federal expenditures for the Vietnam War and persistent budget deficits, President Nixon put an end to the direct international convertibility of dollars to gold. This was meant to stabilize the value of the dollar, but within just a few years, the dollar ended up being devalued a number of times in relation to gold.

In October of 1976, the US government officially changed the definition of the dollar. Gold no longer had anything to do with it. From this point on, the American monetary system was purely fiat money, or money that had value simply because the government said so, instead of by gold backing.

"So gold is a good investment," Clark said. "And instead of just buying gold, why not make your own?"

"Exactly." Garrett smiled.

Garrett's plan was to buy up companies involved in gold mining and production, with the hope of acquiring gold at a cost well below market value, then selling it as the value topped out.

"I've had my best financial people look it all over," Garrett continued. "I just need it looked at from a legal standpoint." He lowered his voice conspiratorially. "And I know how you like a good investment tip."

"I appreciate that, Josh. I always like an interesting gamble."

"No gamble here, Clark. This is a sure thing!"

"That's what they all say." Clark smiled and extended his hand as he and Garrett stood up. "I'll have a look at it."

He walked Garrett to the door where they said their goodbyes. Settling back behind his desk, Clark glanced briefly at the documents, then he pivoted his leather chair so he could look out his window.

It was November, 1976. The year the first commercial Concord flight was made. Patty Hearst had been found guilty of armed robbery, and a young geek named Steve Jobs started up a little unassuming computer company in his parents' garage along with a friend. North and South Vietnam had finally united to form the Socialist Republic of Vietnam, and the Viking 2 spacecraft had landed, taking the first close-up color photographs of the surface of Mars.

Clark's window looked southward from downtown Denver, with a view of the Greek Amphitheater in Civic Center Park. Despite the southern exposure, it was cold and grey.

Dad will be staying in today, Clark thought to himself. Silas was ninety years old, and while still pretty spry for someone his age, the respiratory attacks took a much greater toll on him. He was always very conscientious about taking the needed precautions where his health was concerned.

Clark hadn't been down to Manitou Springs to see them in several months. His work as a corporate lawyer kept him quite busy. But he did make it for the family reunion they had in June. That had been mildly interesting.

They had closed the inn a while before. Silas was too old to help with it, and Isadora devoted herself to taking care of Silas. So they closed off several rooms, except when they had relatives or friends visiting.

Clark's father didn't have any family, so all the relatives at the reunion were from his mother's side. He had met cousins, aunts and uncles from various parts of the country, including a few Indians – Arapahoe who were related to his grandmother, and Cherokee from farther back in the family tree. But ultimately, he had little in common with any of them.

He was finding that he had little in common with his parents, either.

Silas, while proud of Clark's achievements, was disappointed in the direction Clark had taken his career, and was often quite critical of him. Silas, still a major union advocate, had hoped that Clark might practice in support of labor. Or perhaps Indian

235

rights, environmental issues, homeless and underprivileged people – there were so many segments of the country, and even of the local and regional communities, that could benefit from a highly skilled lawyer.

Instead, he served corporations, the modern equivalent of what Silas had spent his younger years fighting against.

Clark's mother was a little more forgiving. Isadora was fifty-six years old and still a beauty. With age had come a few lines, but those lines, interestingly, helped to hide what few scars she retained from the horse kick all those years ago, and the subsequent plastic surgery. Her face displayed a lovely and delicate serenity, perfectly matching her sweet disposition.

Clark dearly loved his mother. But being around her meant being around his father as well.

It was just easier to stay busy and stay away.

§

In August of 1977, Clark sat at a table at the Wazee Supper Club, a restaurant in Lower Downtown Denver. Until just a few years ago, the area was something of a slum, but had recently begun revitalization efforts. Clark had arrived early to get a table and was waiting for Joshua Garrett.

As he sat there, he noticed a pretty young woman at the end of the bar. She had a pencil in her right hand and was drawing. As she did, she would slowly tilt her head back and forth, as if she was looking at her drawing from different angles. This repeatedly caused her long hair, the color of dark chocolate, to slip down over her shoulder, and she kept unconsciously flipping it back with her left hand.

236

Clark watched her for a few moments with a slight smile. He glanced at his watch. It was still nearly ten minutes before his appointment. He stood up, watching her as he walked toward her.

She rested her chin on her left hand for a moment as she thoughtfully studied what she had drawn, absently fingering the flowered choker around her throat.

"I haven't seen anybody wear clothing like that in almost ten years," Clark said. The woman was wearing a long tunic over floor-length culottes. The effect reminded Clark of hippie girls in the late sixties.

She looked up at him with deep brown eyes, then she looked down at what she was wearing.

"I like to be comfortable," she said. "I don't like the clothing they're wearing nowadays. Polyester just makes me sweat and rubs me raw in the crotch."

Clark was a little taken aback by her forthrightness, but he smiled, intrigued. She really was beautiful, with fine features and a dark complexion.

"We wouldn't want that, would we?" he said. "I'm Clark Baskin."

"Vanessa Beleza," she replied. Her voice was soft and smooth, but with a somewhat throaty quality. The sound was extremely sensuous.

"Beleza?"

"It's Portuguese. My father is from Brazil."

Clark motioned to the stool next to her. Vanessa nodded and he sat down, looking at her picture. It was a line drawing of a pair of herons standing in a pond, with cattails arranged around them.

"That's beautiful," Clark said.

"Thanks."

"Is it finished?"

"The drawing is, I think," she replied, squinting a little as she looked at the picture critically. She tilted her head again, pursing her lips, and Clark almost couldn't drag his eyes away from those lips. "Pretty close, anyway. But it's actually just a design sketch for a stained glass window. That's what I do."

"Really? I'm impressed."

"Are you? Why?"

She seemed almost as if she was toying with Clark, and that intrigued him even more.

"I've just never really known anybody who was artistic."

"Hmm. And what do you do, Clark Baskin?"

"I'm a lawyer. I'm actually waiting for a client." He looked down at his watch. "I have a meeting, but it shouldn't take too long. Are you going to be here for a while?"

Vanessa looked intently at Clark's face, dwelling for a moment on his eyes, then his mouth. Clark felt almost as if she were touching him with her eyes, and the effect was somewhat disconcerting. He realized to his surprise, though, that he actually felt physically aroused by it.

"I'll be here," she nodded.

§

"Well, I've got the mines, now," Garrett said, "and they're producing well. But I need more processors. I've got too much gold ore."

"I guess that's a good problem to have."

"You could say that. But I only have one mill and it's not keeping up."

"I don't understand what I can do," Clark said, taking a sip of his bourbon. "I'm just your lawyer." He glanced up toward the bar where Vanessa was still tinkering with her sketch. As if she felt his eyes on her, she looked up at him and smiled a sultry smile.

"I've heard that you have connections to a mill near Colorado Springs," Garrett said.

"Well, I wouldn't say I have connections. My father used to own and manage the mill. But he sold it to the employees something like twenty-five years ago. I never had anything at all to do with it."

"Still, you might be better able to convince them to sell it than a complete outsider like myself."

"Are you suffering an attack of humility, Josh?" Clark asked in a needling tone.

"More like recognizing my limitations." Garrett selected an onion ring and pushed it into his mouth, washing it down with a swallow of beer. "I've had my people look into the mill. They moved and expanded about twenty-five years ago, but since then, it's gone to hell.

"Gold processing hasn't changed much in the last century, but for God's sake, the equipment should be updated once in a while. The fucking mill's falling apart and it's poorly managed. Frankly, I think it could definitely benefit from having some money and some know-how pumped into it."

"Makes sense," Clark said, taking a sip of his drink. "So what's the problem?"

"The 'employees slash owners' are stubborn and don't want to sell. They think it's fine as it is."

"Well, again, what can I do?"

"Talk to them. Or talk to your father. Whatever you think might help to convince them that selling to a wealthy benefactor would be good for them."

"And you're willing to pay top dollar?"

"I don't know about 'top dollar.' Honestly, the mill's not worth a whole lot anymore, but it would be cheaper for me than to try to start up my own."

Clark thought for a moment, taking another drink of bourbon, while keeping his eyes on Garrett. He put his glass down and nodded.

"I'll see what I can do."

"Great! I knew I could count on you." Garrett put his hand out and Clark shook it. Garrett shifted in his seat and looked around for their waitress.

"Don't worry about it," Clark said, waving him off. "I've got this."

"Thanks," Garrett said. Then he smiled. "I'm sure it's probably an expense. It'll likely just show up on my bill anyway."

"See you, Josh," Clark said dismissively. Garrett smiled and finished his beer.

"Thanks, Clark. Let me know what you find out."

Clark nodded as Garrett walked away. He sat there for a few moments, thinking about the mill, and about his father. He wasn't sure how he would pull that off.

But right now, he had other business to attend to.

He picked up his glass and moved to the bar. Vanessa watched him approach and smiled.

§

"You know, you're almost harder work than the deal with the mill," Clark said. He and Vanessa were lying naked on his bed, the sheets rumpled and damp, even though it was cold outside. It had snowed the night before, but the sky had cleared and the sun was reflecting brightly off the snow. A bright swash of sunlight curved warmly over their bodies from the skylight.

"What are you talking about?" she asked in her husky voice. But she smiled slyly as if she already knew the answer. "I've given you everything you wanted."

"But I want more. I can't get enough of you." His voice carried a tone of amazement. "I'm completely unaccustomed to that."

Lying on his side, he gently brushed damp strands of hair from her face and shoulders. He let his eyes travel slowly down her body, appreciating the sensuous curves, perfect in proportion and exotic in their light umber coloring.

Vanessa had been in Haight-Ashbury in 1967 for the Summer of Love, handing out flowers to passersby, promoted free love in

Greenwich Village in 1968, and made it to Woodstock in 1969. But by the early '70s, she began feeling discouraged about how little influence the various factions of the so-called hippie movement were having on things that really mattered. Nobody seemed to take them seriously.

She began moving within more traditional circles, though she still retained much of her earlier philosophy. She donated cash and time to charities. She still occasionally protested things she felt very strongly about, such as the Vietnam War, until it finally came to a definite yet unsatisfying end.

And she was totally uninhibited about sex. There didn't seem to be anything that she wasn't willing to try. Her energy level amazed Clark, and it seemed that the more he got, the more he wanted. They had been together for four months, longer than any relationship he had ever had with a woman.

He was addicted.

Vanessa turned on her side to face him.

"So, what's your problem with the mill?" she asked.

"Well, it's not a problem. Not really. I mean, the deal went through."

Clark had started working on it the day after Garrett had proposed it to him, the same night he met Vanessa. Four months later, the deal was done. Much faster than many corporate takeovers, but it was also more emotional.

His father had opposed it from the start, but he also saw the need for changes at the mill. Garrett was right. The mill had gone to hell. There was no longer any real management. The equipment was dated, some of it dangerously neglected.

242

After hearing the proposal from Clark, Silas had gone to the mill to talk to them about it. He let them know that he opposed it, and he tried to motivate them to take steps to improve the operation on their own. But he was discouraged by the level of apathy among the employee-owners.

They were intrigued by the proposal, and agreed with Clark's assessment that the infusion of outside money into the mill is what was needed to improve the business. In the end, they accepted the offer. The transfer of ownership was facilitated quickly and without a hitch.

Then, Garrett fired everybody and brought in his own people.

That had been a surprise, and had resulted in some pretty negative press.

"Yeah, the deal went through," Vanessa said, "but a lot of people lost their jobs."

"I know," Clark said in a mollifying tone. "That wasn't my intention. Josh made that decision on his own, after the deal was all done."

"And you took a lot of shit for it, too."

"I'm a lawyer. Nobody likes lawyers."

The disgruntled former employees were shown on the TV news angrily disparaging Joshua Garrett and his company as the ultimate bad guys. The legal firm that worked mostly in the background, and Clark himself, had also been the target of some unfavorable remarks.

And Silas had been livid. Still was. He hadn't spoken to Clark in months.

But Clark had been paid well, both by the firm, and with a very generous bonus from Garrett.

"But you indicated that I was a problem," Vanessa said, getting back to the origin of their conversation.

"No, I didn't," Clark replied. "I said you were more work."

He leaned forward and put his arm around her, kissing her, pulling her body against his. They were still damp from their lovemaking, but seemed ready for another go.

"It's a good thing I enjoy my work," he finished with a smile.

§

"I think this would make a good addition to my real estate portfolio," Clark said as he and Vanessa looked at the apartment building in south Denver. "I've already got houses and a few smaller complexes, but this has over a hundred units."

Henry, his real estate agent, had shown him the property a couple of days before, but Clark decided to come back with Vanessa as he was mulling it over.

"Are you sure you can handle something this big?" Vanessa asked.

"I've talked to the bank, and they've already approved me for the purchase price."

"I'm not talking about the money. I'm talking about the amount of work that would be involved in maintaining something like this."

"I wouldn't personally be involved in that. I already have a management company established for my other properties. They would manage this one for me as well."

Vanessa looked up at the ten story building. It was in a decent neighborhood and the grounds were kept up well, though they could use a little updating. Having nothing to add, she looked back at Clark, who was also looking up at the property.

"I'm going to do it," he said with a decisive nod of his head. "I'll give Henry a call when I get back home. Then we can start packing."

Vanessa smiled and shook her head as they started walking back toward Clark's car.

"I can't believe we're going to New Jersey on purpose."

"Oh, come on," Clark said. "New Jersey's not so bad."

"But a vacation spot?"

"I miss the east coast. And a lot of New Jersey is pretty nice."

"But isn't Atlantic City kind of slummy?"

They opened the doors to Clark's Porsche Carrera and got in.

"Well, yeah. But they've been doing a lot of work there. Trying to improve its image."

"Hmm," Vanessa said, but she didn't sound convinced. "I've heard about the Boardwalk. It sounds kind of interesting, but I've never been there."

Clark turned the key and the Porsche roared to life. He checked behind him and pulled out into traffic.

"The closest I've ever been was playing Monopoly with my roommate at Yale. But I'm looking forward to trying out this new casino."

Atlantic City had approved casino gambling a couple of years before. Immediately after the ruling, the Chalfonte-Haddon Hall Hotel, a century old establishment, had begun an extensive renovation. They were reopening this weekend as the first legal casino on the east coast.

"And I've been thinking," Clark continued. "Maybe while we're out there would be a good time to tie the knot."

Vanessa rolled her eyes.

"Are you still on that?" she asked.

"It's a match made in heaven," Clark said. "You won't even have to change your monograms."

"Yeah, that's a really good reason to get married. I have so many monogrammed items."

"I'm just saying that I think we're perfect together."

"I do, too. So why the hell would you want to spoil it? For God's sake, just ten years ago I was talking about free love. Now I'm considering getting married?"

"Well, what about me?" Clark said. "Before you, I never had a relationship with a woman that lasted longer than the word 'relationship.' We've actually been together for nine months."

Clark glanced over at Vanessa as he turned north onto Lincoln Street, heading toward downtown Denver.

"But you are considering it?" he asked.

Vanessa smiled.

§

Vanessa, her face haggard and drawn, carefully nipped off a couple of jagged pieces of blue opalescent glass. She picked up a piece of emery cloth and smoothed the edge along where she had cut it. Satisfied with the shape, she placed it down on the table top where she was laying out the design.

246

Her bird-themed glass art had been quite popular in the Rocky Mountain region, garnering several awards at art shows, and resulting in numerous commissions. After the depression set in, though, the quality of her work suffered, sales had dropped off and commissions were rare. She was finding it difficult to focus on her work for very long. She had started talking about having to get a regular job.

Currently, Vanessa was working on a window featuring a blue jay for a client who lived in the Denver Country Club area. She was hoping that this job wasn't a fluke, that it might generate more exposure and commissions.

She sighed as she thought about that. She didn't know if she could hold down a regular job.

Clark quietly watched her for a few moments, though Vanessa didn't realize that he was there. She lifted her head and looked out the window in front of her table, resting her chin on her hand as she considered the grey sky.

After they had gotten married in Atlantic City a year and a half before, they had been happy. They made love frequently, and took great joy in their time together. Clark actually enjoyed her company, even when they weren't in bed. The honeymoon continued for months, and Clark was sure they were in for a long and happy marriage.

As last winter approached, though, Clark began to notice that Vanessa became moody on days when the weather was dark and cloudy. The result might be that she would be irritable and they would fight, or she might be physically exhausted and spend most of the day in bed.

247

He had noticed clues now and then before they were married, when she might get a little more moody, but he had brushed it off at the time. It seemed to pass and things would be alright again. After they got married, though, it seemed to get worse. Or maybe it was just that they were with each other all the time, so it became much harder to ignore.

God, why had he been so quick to get married?

But that's not all that Clark noticed today. He did see her becoming gloomy as she looked outside, and he steeled himself for a possible fight before he left. But he also saw her bloated, misshapen body.

Okay, her body wasn't really bloated or misshapen. But it might as well have been, for the effect it had on him.

It had been a couple of months, October of 1979, since Vanessa had found that she was pregnant. Before that, Clark never could have imagined not being attracted to her. But when she started gaining weight, the effect on Clark was sweeping. He hardly wanted to look at her.

Making love to her was out of the question.

He shook his head and went back to their room where his suitcase was open on the bed. He needed to get away. He was looking forward to this "business trip." At least, that's what he told Vanessa it was.

The truth was that he just needed some time to himself. A few days in Vegas would certainly do his spirits good. And maybe the company of a beautiful woman.

He closed up the suitcase and carried it to the front door. Then he went back to Vanessa's studio. She was still staring out the *window. He walked up behind her and put his hands on her shoulders, lightly kissing the top of her head.*

It was a purely mechanical action, performed by rote. It meant nothing to him anymore.

Clark remembered when doing that would be enough to make Vanessa turn towards him instantly, kissing him in return. Their clothes would practically fall off of their bodies. They couldn't get into bed fast enough. Sometimes they hadn't even bothered with the bed.

Now, with some effort, she pulled her dull and lifeless eyes away from the window, the sadness almost sucking Clark into them. He tried not to focus too much on her face, and he glanced at the stained glass on the table, as if he was interested.

"You're leaving now?" she asked in a monotone.

"Yeah," he said. "I'll be back on Tuesday."

Vanessa nodded and tried to turn her attention back to the stained glass, as Clark turned and walked away. He had to get out of here before her sadness enveloped him.

As he got in his car and started driving east toward Stapleton International Airport, he felt a feeling of freedom wash over him. He could feel himself already getting into a better mood.

ora, having the place to herself now, sat down on the stool at the kitchen counter. There was supposed to be a couple checking in this evening, but for now, the B&B was empty except for herself. She picked up the envelope that she had gotten from her lawyer yesterday and opened it. Inside it was another envelope. She saw that it was addressed to her, in her grandmother's handwriting.

She carefully tore open the flap of the envelope and pulled out the contents. The first thing she saw was a letter, also written by Gramma.

> My dearest Dorie,
>
> This is a very difficult thing for a mother to do. But it was at your Grampa's suggestion, and that of his attorney, that I do this.
>
> My darling, I don't wish to color your judgment of your father. We didn't see very much of him in later years, except near the

end of your Grampa's life. I do hope he was a good father to you. But I'm afraid that he did some things that made us wary.

I will not burden you with details about that. But your Grampa thought it best that your father not have access to this property. So in accord with one of your Grampa's final wishes, I am signing this over to you.

These items were stored for many years at your Grampa's old cabin near Black Forest. I am signing that over to you as well. I know your father knew something about them. But they are now yours to do with as you wish.

Much love always.

Gramma

With a furrowed brow, Dora looked at the other papers in the envelope. There was another letter, a document from the lawyer, officially echoing what Gramma's letter said. Apparently, from what Dora was able to figure from the documents, Gramma had kept the papers stored for years in a safe deposit box, out of Clark's reach. Evidently, the package had only been discovered after her death.

Dora saw a photocopy of a very old deed to the Black Forest property, with the official postal address, and the exact boundaries spelled out.

Then, Dora found a photocopy of another very old piece of paper, grey where the original had probably been yellow, and deeply creased where it had been folded. The copy was of a handwritten letter, addressed to her grandfather, Silas Baskin. The handwriting was in a style that one didn't see anymore – definitely male, but with more flourishes than are used these days. Even after she had read it, she wasn't entirely sure what it was all about. But apparently it concerned a particularly sad episode involving someone named Victoria.

The letter had been signed by someone named William Joseph Stewart, apparently Victoria's father.

The next item was a copy of another old deed, this one for the Victoria Mine, and an old map showing its location. The first name on the deed was William Stewart. He had signed it over to Silas Baskin – Grampa. Finally, after his death, Gramma had signed it over to Dora, and under that was a notary's stamp and signature.

The items in the package seemed to create more questions in her mind than they answered. But they did feed the suspicions she already had about her father's real reason for being here.

She put the papers aside when she heard a knock on the front door.

§

Bridget Lindstrom sat in her car in front of Isadora's Bed and Breakfast. Looking around, she noticed that Clark's junker was not parked there. She had already turned her car off before she had worked up the nerve to go in, and the afternoon sun shining through the glass was heating up the interior quickly.

Today had been a short day for her. Her summer school class consisted of three students, two of whom lived near the Black Forest area and they had been evacuated. The third one had called in sick.

With no students to teach, Bridget was away from the school by ten o'clock. From there, she made the drive back through Manitou Springs and to the log B&B. But now, she was having a hard time determining what her objective was in making the trip here.

She opened her door and got out, climbing up to the high front porch. She wasn't sure if she should knock or just walk in. She knocked.

A beautiful, somewhat exotic-looking blonde woman opened the door.

"Yes?" she asked.

"Are you Isadora Baskin?" Bridget asked.

"Yes, I am."

Bridget still didn't know what to say. She decided that an introduction was the first order of business, so she took a deep breath and just started talking.

"Hello, Miss Baskin. It's very nice to meet you. My name is Bridget Lindstrom. I'm originally from Liverpool, in England, and I am a descendant of Beatrice Ferngood, a relative of your ancestor, Isadora Byrnes."

Dora's eyes opened wide at Bridget's mention of the familiar names.

"Please, come in!" she said. It was cool inside the B&B, and Bridget was happy to be out of the sunlight and the heat. "Would you like something to drink?" Dora asked as she invited Bridget to sit down in the living room.

"No, thank you," Bridget replied, settling down on one end of a comfortable sofa.

Dora sat down on the other end, leaning forward, looking at Bridget curiously.

"Well, I'm so happy to meet you," she said. "What brings you here?"

"Is your father here?" Bridget asked.

"My father? No, he's not. Why?"

Bridget bit her lip and took another deep breath. Rather than just jumping into the story about Clark, she figured that perhaps she should start at the beginning, lay a little groundwork.

"About twenty-seven years ago, I came to America to trace something of a family legend, this Isadora Byrnes. I followed her trail through Georgia, into Oklahoma, and finally to Manitou Springs."

Dora, remembering the excitement she had felt the year before as she was reading Isadora's account, smiled as she listened to Bridget.

"When I came here, though, to this house, I guess it was your grandmother I spoke to. She told me that her husband was sick and, not wanting to bother her, I expressed my sympathy and left."

Now came the tricky part.

255

"After that," she continued slowly, "I was down in town, and I met your father."

She hadn't meant to speak so haltingly, but that's the way it came out. The change in Dora's expression did not escape her notice.

"I'm not really sure how to say this, or how much to say," she continued. "But your father and I had a bit of a fling. I got pregnant and I had a baby girl. But being young and single, I gave her up for adoption. Something which I still regret to this day."

Dora was working out the math in her head. It was still fresh in her mind, as she had talked about that time period to Shawn just a couple of nights ago. Grampa got sick and died in 1986. Dora was about six and a half years old, her mother still alive and reasonably well, when her father was out getting this woman pregnant.

"I didn't know he was married," Bridget insisted earnestly. She had an imploring expression on her face. "But he was so good-looking, and so charming. And I was young and stupid, and very impressionable.

"I didn't see him again until sometime after I had given up my baby. And at that time, I demonstrated how young and stupid I *really* was by giving him money. He said he was having financial troubles, and since I still had some savings, I gave it to him. He insisted it was just a loan and he would pay me back. But I never saw him again."

Dora was now seething, and Bridget could see that she was agitated.

"I'm sorry, miss," Bridget said, feeling a little flustered now. "Honestly, I'm not even sure what I hoped to gain by coming here. I certainly don't expect to get my money back. I guess I just wanted to confront him. But I see that I've made you feel bad about him."

"No, you haven't," Dora said coldly. She took a breath and tried to speak in a calmer voice. "All you've done is made it just a little harder for me to feel good about him. Something I was already having trouble with."

"I'm sorry, dear. I didn't realize. Well, if he's not here, I won't bother you any more about this."

Bridget started to get up, but Dora stopped her.

"You don't have to go. My father may be a worthless piece of shit, but I try not to be. I think I can help you with at least one of your problems."

Bridget was intrigued.

§

Gash Seever, sitting in his rental car, closed his computer. He had enjoyed a drive through the Garden of the Gods, and a walk around Manitou Springs earlier this morning. He appreciated the historic charm of the little town.

After The Ancient Mariner opened, Gash went in and sat down for lunch. He was observant, watching everyone who came in. When his cheeseburger and beer arrived, he devoted some attention to that, but still discreetly watched as people came and went.

After he had finished, he inquired of the waitress, who was able to give him a little additional information. Supplemented now by some research online, he knew where he was going.

He took a couple of moments to enter the address into the GPS built into the dash, started up the car and pulled out onto Manitou Avenue. He continued westward, toward Highway 24.

§

Clark was amazed at how much shit was crammed in the little cabin. And there didn't seem to be any rhyme or reason to it. Old dusty boxes were filled with knick knacks and papers, as if whoever packed them just threw things into boxes as they came to them. Some of the papers seemed as if they might have once been important, but so far, he hadn't found what he was looking for.

It was extremely slow work, and the smoke wasn't helping. He thought about opening the window, but he figured that since the smoke was coming in from outside, that would just probably make it worse.

His eyes were burning, and he frequently had to stop what he was doing to cough. Whenever he did that, it reminded him of his father.

And of his regrets.

Clark came slowly in the door, lugging his suitcase behind him. He was feeling pretty stupid. His trips to Las Vegas and Atlantic City had varied success. Sometimes he won, sometimes he lost. The gamble and the variety were part of the appeal.

But this was the first time he had ever lost this big. It was definitely going to require some creative banking to get through this one.

He made it a point to take several trips a year, particularly during the winter months, when Vanessa was harder to deal with. Saying they were business trips just made it a little easier. It didn't require a lot of explanation.

Since little Dora was born, Vanessa seemed to stabilize a little. He didn't know if it was the hormones, or the maternal instinct, or what. She was still a mess when the weather was grey and gloomy, but at least when she had a baby to care for, she held it together a little better.

Now Dorie was four years old and, having the independence of a toddler, she didn't require quite as much from Vanessa as she had when she was a baby.

And Vanessa was slipping again.

It was the middle of the afternoon. Clark paused and listened. It was quiet. Vanessa's car was there, so he knew she was home. That meant that she and Dorie were either out back or asleep. As he walked past Dora's room, he saw Dora and Vanessa on the bed. Vanessa was asleep, but Dora was wide awake, and when she saw Clark in the doorway, she smiled at him.

Clark always felt a measure of resentment toward Vanessa, and even toward Dorie to an extent. He knew he shouldn't. But he had not wanted kids. It wasn't Dora's fault, but that's the way he felt. Against his will, though, he found himself smiling back at her.

He put his finger up to his lips, telling her to stay quiet. The longer Vanessa stayed asleep, the better.

He continued on to his room and heaved his suitcase up onto the bed. He had been sleeping in a separate bedroom for a couple of years now. He said it was because there wasn't room for both of them in the master bedroom. This way, they each had their own closet space. But that didn't explain the separate beds. It was just easier to have his own space, away from Vanessa, and her moods. If Vanessa questioned it, she never verbalized it.

He unpacked and had his things put away in just a few minutes.

Then he heard Dora giggle, and with a feeling of uneasiness, he figured that Vanessa would be awake now. In confirmation of that thought, he heard scuffing footsteps in the hall, and she was there in his doorway.

"When did you get home?" she asked as she rubbed her eyes.

"Just a few minutes ago."

260

"Was it a good trip?"

"Yeah, it was fine." His usual response.

"Good," she said, and she scuffed away toward the kitchen, to see what she could throw together for dinner.

Clark wished that she would pursue a hobby, to be interested in something again. But even her stained glass couldn't hold her attention except on the very best of days.

He sighed. Something had to change.

§

Something did indeed change, but unfortunately, it was not for the better.

Sitting in the plush office of Jake Sansom, the senior partner at the law firm, Clark was feeling small and helpless.

"I personally chose you," Sansom said. "You were one of the brightest, most promising law students I had seen in a long while. And you definitely started out on fire. But I'm afraid that fire's gone out. A law firm does not benefit from someone with an unstable record like yours, Clark."

"Unstable?" Clark tried to keep his emotions in check. He didn't want his anger to undermine his argument. "How can I be unstable? I've been working for this firm for twenty years, right out of law school."

"And where have you gone since then?"

"What do you mean?"

"You have no ambition anymore. You started out hot. You brought in some good money. But a few years ago, the partners started noticing that you seemed distracted. We heard you were

261

taking trips to Vegas and Atlantic City, which we thought was a harmless way for you to blow off steam.

"But instead, you started blowing off work. You went away more and more frequently, and when you were here, your work was shoddy.

"We gradually started assigning the higher profile corporate cases to other associates and giving you some of the more modest estate planning clients. I don't know if you even noticed the transition."

"I noticed." Clark didn't meet his eyes.

"And you didn't even have the initiative to say anything about it then!" Sansom sighed and shook his head. "And now that you're only working on estate planning accounts, you're screwing them up, too."

"Come on, Jake, there's no challenge in those," Clark said belligerently.

"You're not up to a challenge! Especially not in the afternoons when you finally come back from your long lunches smelling of bourbon."

Sansom looked down at his hands, folded on his desk. He was silent for a moment. When he looked back up, it was with a sad resolve.

"I like you, Clark. But I'm afraid I'm going to have to cut you loose. I'm sorry."

§

It had been a tough transition. A couple of clients whose accounts Clark had managed to not blunder agreed to follow him, and eventually he scrounged up a few others on his own. But for the most part, his income was now coming from his various real estate properties.

Then, there was the Tax Reform Act of 1986. It had been meant to simplify the tax code, but it had other effects as well. Among those effects, it removed numerous tax shelters, especially for real estate investments, and greatly reduced the value of these properties.

Many of Clark's properties had already lost value, simply by virtue of neglect and of his attempts to save money by cutting corners. Due to their condition, he had been forced to lower the rent on some of them, and many of them were now little more than slums and tax write-offs.

Thanks to that damn Tax Reform Act, Clark was no longer allowed to deduct as much from his gross income as he had been before. This problem was exacerbated by the fact that his gross income was nowhere near what it had been before Sansom let him go.

Now, shocked into action, Clark tried to unload several of his real estate properties, especially ones that he had missed payments on, but nobody was buying. Add the effect of the tax reform on his real estate, to his decreased income and his gambling losses, and Clark was broke.

In mid-1986, three of his houses were foreclosed on. A little later in the year, he lost a small apartment complex and the ten-story building.

Just the year before, Clark had decided to downsize his real estate portfolio. He had sold their large house in the Governor's Park area of Denver and moved into one of his houses in south

Denver. That had been a fortuitous sale, one of the few good decisions he had made in recent years.

Then Clark had to screw it all up. If he could get enough, he thought, he could pay some of his debts, and save his other properties from foreclosure. He took the money from the sale of his house, thinking he could double or even triple it with a trip to Atlantic City.

He ended up losing it all.

There were occasions when he thought that he might have a gambling problem, but he managed to submerge those thoughts. He was sure there must be a way to fix it. But each attempt only put him deeper in debt.

As desperation set in, Clark began casting about for ideas.

§

"What do you expect me to do, son?" Silas asked. He and Clark were sitting in the sunroom.

Silas, at 100 years old, was easily the oldest person Clark knew. He was also wealthy. Not nearly as wealthy as Clark had once been, but Clark was desperate now. The fact that he was here was proof of that.

"I don't know, Dad. I'm just at the end of my rope."

"I suppose those folks at the mill were at the end of their rope, too," Silas replied.

"For God's sake, Dad, that was nine years ago."

"I'm sorry. I didn't realize there was a statute of limitations for being a dick."

"Why are you still holding on to that?" Clark asked, getting to his feet, and feeling the anger rise. He looked out at the back yard for just a moment, then turned back to Silas. "I told you I was not the one responsible for those people getting fired."

"And you have never expressed any remorse whatsoever over the part you *did* play in it, either." Silas was not as mobile as Clark, but he jabbed his finger against the arm of his chair for emphasis.

"Your grandfather started that mill," Silas continued. "I started working there eighty-six years ago, when I was fourteen years old. The only thing I loved more than that company was your mother.

"Then you and that son of a bitch Joshua Garrett come in and in only a few months, you just wipe it all out and put my friends out of work."

"I'm sorry, Dad. I honestly didn't mean for that to happen. It wasn't my doing."

"You were instrumental in making it happen. And you got rich from it." Anger was strenuous for Silas and his heightened emotion left him panting a little.

"You're seriously still that angry at me about something that I unintentionally did nine years ago?"

"No, not just that," Silas answered sharply. He started ticking off a list, angrily jabbing the arm of the chair with each point he made. "I've seen how you've pissed away your money on gambling, practically taking food out of your family's mouths. I've seen you cheat on your beautiful wife with those cheap tramps. Instead of getting some help for Vanessa, you just leave her alone when things get hard and take up with your floozies. Back when you would still come around for family gatherings, I saw you ignore your wife and your darling little girl, and flirt with the wives of relatives. And since then, I've seen you keep our granddaughter away from us because you're ashamed of your shitty life and don't want to talk about it."

There was now a deep indentation in the upholstery on the arm of Silas' chair from the points he had made.

"You have been nothing but an embarrassment to the family and have brought shame on the Hodges and Baskin names."

Clark turned away, experiencing the closest thing he knew to shame. He couldn't deny anything that his father said. It was all true.

"Your mother and I have had words about you," Silas continued. "We disagree on some things, but one thing we seem to agree on is that we can't leave you our money. We know that you'd just gamble it away while your family starved to death."

Clark felt a chill grip his heart at these words. His father was his last resort. If he couldn't get any money from him, then the situation was hopeless.

His desperation began to turn into outright panic.

And it was at that moment that he had the idea.

The idea was insane, but it presented itself fully formed in his mind. And before he had time to dismiss it, he began acting on it.

"I don't blame you, Dad," he said contritely. "I know I've been an asshole. I've hurt you and Mom, and I've hurt Vanessa and Dorie. I know I've hurt a lot of people, and I am so sorry. I want to try to make it right. But I don't know how to do it."

He managed to make his voice crack a little.

§

"Your mother doesn't want me to drink," Silas said as he took the glass.

"I know, Dad," Clark replied dismissively. "But I didn't figure one little drink would hurt. Mom's not here right now. What she doesn't know won't hurt her, right? This is a toast, purely celebratory, kind of a symbolic drink.

"Last time I was here, a couple of weeks ago, you said some things that hurt. I'm not blaming you," he said quickly, shaking his head. "What you said was true. And I just wanted to thank you for the tough love. It was hard to hear, but it was what I needed."

Clark took another glass and poured a shot of bourbon in it for himself. Silas peered through his thick glasses as his son raised his bourbon to him.

"Dad," Clark said with another shake of his head, "I know that I've been a lousy son. A lousy husband, a lousy father. Hell, I've been an all around shitty person for a big chunk of my life. And now that I actually give that some thought, I find that fact amazing considering what incredible examples that I had in both you and Mom. You were wonderful parents, and wonderful role models, and I never appreciated what I had.

"I'm sorry I've let you and so many others down. So here's to me learning how to be a decent person."

Silas raised his glass a little as he looked up at Clark. He hesitated, and Clark could see that his eyes were glazed with tears. Then they both drank.

Silas closed his eyes as he swallowed the bourbon, and he smiled.

"I've missed that," he said. He opened his eyes and looked at Clark. "And I've missed you too, son."

Clark smiled and took the glass from him.

"And I hope you're sincere about what you said," Silas continued. "I'm not going to pin all my hopes on you right away. Frankly, I'm a little skeptical at this point."

"I understand, Dad," Clark said in a conciliatory tone. "I sure can't blame you. I have a long record to overcome. But I've been thinking about you a lot lately, about the example that you've set for me all my life. And I'm going to be paying much closer attention to the lessons that you've tried to teach me over the years."

"It's not going to be easy," Silas said.

"I know that. Nothing worthwhile is. But if I can do it, it'll be worth it."

Silas pulled himself out of his chair to his feet, and stepped toward Clark.

"I'll be here to help in any way I can, to give you reminders or a kick in the butt."

And he put his arms around Clark and held him. Clark was forty-six years old and couldn't remember the last time he had hugged his father.

"Thanks, Dad," Clark said. Then he pulled away and helped Silas ease back into his chair.

"I'll go wash these glasses and put them away before Mom gets home so she doesn't suspect anything," Clark said with a mischievous smile.

§

Over the next couple of weeks, Clark made it a point to visit a few more times. When he arrived one weekend shortly after stating his resolve, Silas wasn't feeling well.

"He's lying down in the den," Isadora said in a worried tone. "He didn't have the strength to climb the stairs."

Clark went to the den, opposite the living room, and knocked lightly on the door. He heard no sound from inside and he opened the door.

The room was dark, but Clark could see the form of his father lying on the plush sofa with a blanket over him. As he went inside, Silas stirred and turned his head to face him.

"Hey, Dad," Clark said softly. "Mom said you're not feeling well. What's up?"

Silas started struggling to pull himself upright, but Clark put his hand gently on his shoulder. Silas didn't have the energy to resist, and settled back down.

"I'm just so tired, son," he said. He sounded as if it was a struggle even to speak.

"I'm sorry to hear that," Clark said.

"A few days ago, I had some really bad pain in my joints. I ached all over. It hurt to move at all. Your mother called the doctor and he said it was probably just arthritis. I took a pain reliever and considered myself pretty lucky that I haven't had trouble with arthritis until now, at a hundred years old. That's what the doctor said, too."

Clark smiled.

"But the pain came back. Then, the day before yesterday, I started feeling so tired. I just can't do anything. All I want to do is sleep."

"Well, maybe that's what you should do," Clark said. "Listen to your body."

"Yeah, the doctor said that, too. He said, 'You're a hundred years old, for God's sake. You need to rest when your body tells you to.' So I've practically been sleeping ever since then."

"Well, that sounds like good advice. I can come back another time."

"Maybe that's a good idea," Silas said weakly.

"Can I get you anything before I go?" Clark asked. "A glass of water?"

"I have a glass there," Silas said, pointing to the end table. Clark picked up the glass.

"I'll go get you some fresh, cool water. I'll be back in just a minute."

Clark left the room and Silas closed his eyes. In the short time it took for Clark to refill his glass of water, Silas had dozed off.

"Here you go, Dad," Clark said, and Silas flinched as if he was startled. Clark helped Silas raise his head and take a drink, then gently put it back down. "Okay, just get some rest. I'll see how you're doing in a day or two."

Silas weakly nodded his head. He couldn't keep his eyes open.

"Thank you, son."

Clark leaned over and kissed his forehead. He pulled the blanket up over his shoulders, then left the room. He took the glass into the kitchen.

"How was he doing?" Isadora asked. Lines of worry were etched into her face.

Clark sighed and leaned against the counter.

"Not too good, I'm afraid," Clark replied quietly with a troubled expression on his face. He looked up at his mother and saw that her expression was matching his own. "I guess it's to be expected, though. He is a hundred years old."

Tears formed in Isadora's eyes. "I know. It just always seemed like he was going to last forever."

Clark smiled sadly at her as he rinsed out the glass.

"What are you doing?" Isadora asked.

"What?" Clark asked, and he looked down at the glass. "Oh, I guess my mind is elsewhere today. I should have left his water in there with him."

There was a knock at the front door. Isadora hastily wiped her eyes and went to answer it, as Clark dried the glass and put it away.

He came out of the kitchen just as his mother was finishing up with the girl at the front door. The girl was just starting to turn, to go down the steps. Before Isadora could close the door, Clark had a glimpse of a young, pretty brunette. A breeze caught her skirt, briefly lifting it and revealing her shapely buttocks. The girl quickly caught it, holding her skirt down. But there was a certain vulnerability in the unintentional exposure and her reaction that grabbed Clark's attention.

He was immediately aroused.

"I'm going to go now," he said to his mother as she came toward him. "I'll come back by in a day or two to see how Dad's doing."

"Okay, honey. Thanks for coming. I know it means a lot to your father. And to me, too."

The tears were back in her eyes and Clark gave her a hug. Thirty seconds later, he was out the door, and he saw the girl's white car driving away. He climbed into his car and started it up, waving to his mother through the windshield. He backed out onto the road and drove away.

He drove quickly at first so he wouldn't lose the girl. He caught up to her before she reached the highway. She got on Highway 24 East, to go into Manitou Springs. A few minutes later, she parked on Manitou Avenue and went into The Ancient Mariner.

Clark waited a few minutes, then he went inside.

He was suddenly feeling hungry.

§

The next day, Isadora called Clark in a panic.

"Your father's in the hospital, Clark," she said in tears.

"What's wrong?" he asked.

"I tried to wake him for lunch, but I had trouble rousing him. When he finally opened his eyes, he just lay there. He couldn't move." She paused to wipe her nose with a tissue. "His arms and legs were paralyzed, and he was having trouble breathing. The doctor's doing some tests now."

"Where are you?" Clark asked.

"I'm at the hospital. I rode with your father in the ambulance." She paused briefly. "I don't have a way home, dear." That simple statement seemed to emphasize how helpless she was feeling, and she started sobbing.

"It's okay, Mom. I'll be there soon."

§

Silas died in the hospital several hours later.

A few days after that, Isadora received a phone call from the doctor.

"Isadora," he said, "how are you doing?"

"I'm alright," she replied tiredly. In contrast to her reply, she took the wad of tissue that was now practically a permanent accessory in her hand and wiped her eyes with it.

"Well, you sound tired, so I won't keep you," the doctor said. "I just wanted to let you know that the Medical Examiner completed the autopsy on Silas. I told him I'd call you myself since I've known you both for so long."

"I appreciate that, Doctor."

"The ME was a little baffled at first, until he consulted the medical history. He found traces of cyanide in Silas' body."

"Cyanide? From the poisoning incident all those years ago?"

"That, and the fact that he used cyanide every day for so long before and after the accident," the doctor replied. "They didn't have nearly the precautions that we have nowadays. It was a very small amount that was found in Silas, certainly not a lethal dose on its own. It's pretty rare, but not unheard of. There are times when certain organs might hold onto it. The cyanide might lie dormant in the system for years.

"As he grew older and his body weakened, the effects of the poisoning began to surface. But Isadora, the man was a hundred years old. Even without the cyanide in his system, as old as he was, he wouldn't have lived much longer than he did."

"I know," Isadora said. She held the phone between her ear and her shoulder as she wiped her eyes and nose with another tissue. She eased herself onto one of the stools she kept in the kitchen, taking a deep breath and slowly letting it out.

"Really," the doctor continued, "it's not that uncommon for cyanide to exist to some extent in anybody's body, from sources such as cigarette smoke, pesticides, and even some foods like almonds.

"But if it wasn't for the cyanide, something else would have caused his old body to start breaking down. As far as I'm concerned, Silas died of natural causes."

§

Clark pulled into his garage and turned off his car. He put his head back on the headrest, closed his eyes and sighed. He was emotionally drained.

The last couple of weeks had really been a mixed bag. Clark had actually begun to feel a little spark of affection for his father. Then his father got sick and finally died. His mother's mourning for him was pitiful and heart-rending. Then there were the findings in the autopsy.

And meeting Bridget. He couldn't get that hot little number out of his mind. He had seen her once more, then she seemed to have disappeared.

He had stopped back in at The Ancient Mariner a few times, in fact every time he made it back to Manitou Springs. She wasn't there. He had also inquired at her motel, but she had checked out a few weeks before.

Clark pushed the button on the remote and the garage door began cranking back down. He unfastened his seatbelt and pulled himself out of his car.

He felt the tension rising as it usually did when he prepared to see Vanessa. It just made him so tired. Today was partly cloudy. Hopefully there was enough sunlight that she wouldn't be a total nutcase.

He closed his car door and walked around the back of his car. He was reaching for the door knob into the house when he felt something in the pocket of his jacket which was slung over his arm. Ah, yes. He remembered.

He turned around and went to the back of the garage, to his 'work area,' the section where he sometimes came to putter around if Vanessa was too hard to deal with in the house. He opened the door to the little cabinet where he kept paints and glues.

Then, from his jacket pocket, he pulled out the little canister of "Bug-Me-Not." He glanced at the label featuring a light-hearted cartoon insect juxtaposed with the ominous-looking skull and crossbones.

Worked like a charm, he thought, as he placed the canister of cyanide behind the containers in the cabinet.

§

The will had been tricky. Clark didn't know how quickly Silas had acted about disinheriting him. Or even if he had yet. But two weeks had gone by between when Silas mentioned it and when Clark had gone back to deliver the first dose of cyanide in their toast with the bourbon.

He had made it a point to be extremely careful with the poisoning. He didn't want to deliver one big, initially lethal dose. He knew that that would have been dangerous. He had recalled the insight he had as a child when he first started stealing portions of money from patrons to avoid suspicion. Delivering multiple small doses for a slower gradual poisoning, that was the way to do it.

But while the chronic poisoning was taking place, Clark had other work to do.

He was an estate lawyer, so he knew how to draw up a will. That wasn't the problem. But knowing neither the extent nor the structure of Silas' wealth made dividing it up a rather complicated project.

So he had made it a point to come back to their home at other times, when he knew his parents were gone. The times that they were both away to visit the doctor or the hospital were put to good use.

Clark scoured his father's papers. He found numerous bits of useful information in the file cabinet in his den, including bank statements. But the most helpful document was a copy of Silas' will, dated about five years before. He knew the original would be on file with his attorney, but the basic information was what he needed.

Drawing up the new will, Clark was careful to not be too generous to himself. Again, he remembered the times upstairs as a boy, when his mother was running the inn and Clark was cleaning the rooms. When Clark stole money from guests, he didn't take it all, but he minimized suspicion by taking only part of it.

He was careful to apply the same principle here. The situation required finesse.

Clark was generous to his mother, leaving her the house and the stock portfolio. Looking at the diversification, he knew that the premiums from the stocks alone would provide quite a comfortable income for her for the rest of her life.

He pondered other beneficiaries, eliminating some, reducing the payout to others. By the time he had finished, Clark would be receiving over a quarter of the liquid assets. Not a fortune by any means, especially compared to his own former wealth, but still a very respectable amount.

Using paper and an envelope that he found in Silas' desk, which he knew would likely have Silas' fingerprints on them, Clark composed the will.

> I, Silas Baskin, being now of very old age, but sound mind and memory, do make, publish and declare this to be my Last Will and Testament, hereby revoking and annulling any and all Last Will and Testaments or Codicils at any time heretofore made by me.

Upon my deathbed, having given thought to my previous will, I have reconsidered the disbursement of my estate, and do hereby direct my son, Clark Baskin, to prepare this iteration. Upon his protests of a conflict of interest, I hereby release him from blame in this action.

Clark had smiled at that final absolution. That, plus the fair and equitable distribution of the estate, should remove any possibility of suspicion.

He made certain the date on the will corresponded with one of the days that he had actually visited. Then he easily forged Silas' signature, sealed the will in an envelope marked as Last Will and Testament, and placed it in the top center drawer of Silas' desk, in full view so it could not be missed.

§

Stupid! Clark said silently to himself. Stupid! Stupid! Stupid!

He was sitting, with his mother and a lawyer, along with a court stenographer, in the judge's chambers while the judge looked at a number of papers before him. After Silas' death, his lawyer had produced the latest will that Silas had filed with him. It had been drawn up a couple of years before.

That meant that Silas hat not yet made a move to disinherit Clark. It also meant that Clark had not based his forgery upon the most recent will.

The judge looked up.

"In comparing these two wills," he said, "and the other documents in the probate, I have made my decision.

"The latest will, drawn up by Clark Baskin, does coincide for the most part with inventories included here," and he patted a short stack of papers. "Where the comparison deviates, it is not so much as to necessarily invalidate the will, and could easily be attributed to working on the document based on the decedent's memory. The decedent used percentages instead of actual dollar amounts, but those percentages can easily be applied to the current financial standings of the decedent."

That copy of the previous will, the bank statements and other documents that Clark had found in Silas' office had indeed been very helpful!

"An accusation has been made by the decedent's attorney," the judge continued, "that Clark Baskin was attempting to undermine his father's final wishes for his own gain. However, the fact that this two-year-old will names Clark Baskin as the primary beneficiary, and that Mr. Baskin would have stood to inherit well over fifty percent of the decedent's estate does not bear this out. Indeed, his inheritance, based on this most recent will, is considerably less, in fact less than half the amount of the disbursement of the previous one."

Stupid!

"Therefore, based on the information before me, I hereby declare this will, drawn up by the hand of Clark Baskin, to be a legal and binding document.

"Before adjourning, though, I would like to point out to Mr. Baskin the questionable ethics involved here.

"You, sir, are named as an heir in this will, and as such, your participation in drawing up the document may be considered a conflict of interests, as in fact your father alluded to in the opening paragraphs. He did 'release you from blame,' but the fact remains that the legal ethics involved are problematic to say the very least.

"Since you did not gain by doing this, but in fact lost a sizable amount, it does tend to remove suspicion from you in regard to your motives."

STUPID!

"However, I would advise you," the judge continued, his eyes burning a hole through Clark, "to think very carefully before agreeing to do something of this nature in the future."

Clark nodded humbly.

"Those are my findings, and I hereby declare this case closed."

Clark would go on to kick himself every day about that.

§

In the summer of 1987, Clark had returned to Manitou Springs, but by that time he had, as his father had predicted, pissed away his inheritance. He had paid a couple of debts, but had lost the bulk of it gambling.

He was a sad man when he walked into The Ancient Mariner, but he brightened up a bit when he saw Bridget walk in. She looked as beautiful as ever.

She had moved to Colorado Springs, which was why Clark hadn't been able to find her for so long. She was generally happy, though she was somewhat put out about him having gotten her pregnant. She had given the baby girl up for adoption, which was a relief to Clark.

No child support.

And he had managed to talk her into giving him some money. Oh the beautiful naiveté of the young. It wasn't a lot of money, but it would help him hold off a creditor for a bit longer.

And it was enough that he knew he would never be able to see Bridget again.

y the time I got my head together, I decided it was time to stop brooding about it and do something," Bridget said. "I decided it was time to hire a private investigator. Jack Pershing seemed to know what he was doing, but he couldn't find Clark. Of course, this was years later, after I had finished my schooling. I had just waited so long, it was my own fault really."

"That was probably after my dad had left my mom and me. He just vanished. After several years, I decided that he was probably dead. He only reappeared yesterday."

"And that's when Jack just happened to come across his charge at The Ancient Mariner."

They heard the sound of gravel crunching out front. They turned and looked out the window and saw an expensive-looking silver Lincoln pull up. Bridget's first thought, when she heard the sound, was that it might be Clark. She knew it wasn't when she saw the car.

"Are you expecting someone?" she asked.

"Not until later," Dora replied. "They must have made really good time."

But then, she realized that it was just a single man. She didn't often get walk-ins, but it happened occasionally. The women watched curiously from the sofa as the well-dressed man got out of his car, slowly, almost cautiously it seemed. He looked as if he was in his mid-thirties, his expression hard. Then he came up the steps toward the front door, and Dora got up from the sofa.

She opened the door as the man approached. He smiled.

"Hello," he said. "I'm here looking for a friend." Dora detected an east coast accent, New York or New Jersey.

"And who is your friend?" she asked.

"Clark Baskin."

"How is it everybody's suddenly looking for Clark Baskin?"

"I'm sorry, there have been others?"

"You say he's your friend?" Dora asked, ignoring his question. "How do you know him?"

"We were involved in some business back east. I was told I could find him here."

"Are you a police officer? Detective?" Dora asked.

"Police? No," he said, apparently amused. "My name is Gary Seever. I'm just looking for my friend, that's all."

"I don't think Clark Baskin is capable of having friends, Mr. Seever. But he's not here."

"Mmm. Where is he?"

"I couldn't say. He hasn't exactly been forthright with me."

"Will he be back soon?"

"I honestly don't know that either, Mr. Seever. If you'll leave your number, I can have him give you a call."

"Perhaps I can wait for him."

"I'm afraid you may be waiting a while."

"I don't mind," he said, and he started toward Dora.

Dora gripped the door, standing her ground in front of the man. She wasn't entirely sure why she distrusted him. He was polite and well-mannered, but something about him engendered a certain suspicion.

"I'm sorry," Dora said firmly, "but I'd really rather you didn't."

"I wasn't asking," he said as he pushed past her.

"Get out of my house or I'll call the police," Dora said indignantly.

"No, you won't," he said as he pulled a pistol from under his jacket. He was now inside, and he saw to the left, in the living room, Bridget sitting there, her eyes wide with fear. "Close the door," he instructed Dora, "and come in here with your friend."

Dora did as she was told, sitting back on the end of the sofa. Gash sat down in a chair facing both of them.

"Hello, ma'am," he said looking at Bridget. "My name's Gary Seever. But most people call me Gash."

"Bridget," she said quietly.

"Very nice to meet you, Bridget," Gash said. "Am I to understand that you're looking for Clark Baskin as well?"

Bridget looked at Dora, then back at Gash, but she didn't say anything.

"Don't worry, ladies. I don't want to hurt you. I just need to find Mr. Baskin."

"I already told you," Dora said, "I'm not sure where he went."

"You're not sure? Well, that's a little more promising. Where *might* he have gone?"

Dora shook her head. In response, Gash cocked the hammer of his pistol and pointed it at Bridget's head. Both women gasped and Dora put up a hand to stop him.

"Please, Mr. Seever, don't! She doesn't have anything to do with my father."

"Oh, so you're his loving daughter."

Dora made a face at that. Gash seemed to take note.

"Hmm," he said. "No love lost there. Look, all I want is information. Where might your father be?"

"I don't know where it's located."

"Where what's located?"

"An old cabin. It belonged to my grandfather."

"There must be some way you can find it."

Dora thought for a moment, keeping her eyes on the gun.

"I might be able to find it on my computer," she said.

"Well, let's get to it. Where's your computer?"

"In the kitchen."

Gash stood up, keeping the pistol trained toward them.

"Lead the way. Just don't do anything stupid."

The women stood and Dora headed back toward the kitchen. Bridget followed her, with Gash bringing up the rear. When they came into the kitchen, Dora went first to the papers she had left on the counter. Gash quickly scanned the area and saw that she wasn't going for a knife. Dora picked up the deed to the Black Forest property and went to her little cubbyhole office.

The office used to be a tiny closet, so there was only room for Dora to sit in there, in front of her computer. Gash positioned himself just outside the doorway where he could see what she was doing, but could keep the gun pointed at Bridget as well.

Dora woke up her computer and brought up Google Maps where she typed in the postal address from the deed. A few seconds later, the screen displayed the location of the cabin. Dora recognized some of the roads around it, and she shook her head.

"It's in the fire evacuation area," she said. "We can't get in there."

"And why would your father want to go there?" Gash asked.

Dora, not wanting to reveal anything about the gold mine, looked up at Gash.

"He felt like this was his last chance to see his home before he died. He's feeling nostalgic. The cabin belonged to his father."

"Well, let's go."

"I told you, it's in the evacuation area."

"If your father found a way in, we can too."

"Please, sir," Bridget pleaded shakily, "we haven't done anything. Please leave us be."

"Bridget the Brit," Gash said, imitating an English accent. "You're a long way from 'ome, aren't you love?"

A tear rolled down Bridget's cheek.

"Oh, don't worry miss. Like I told your friend here, I don't want to hurt either of you."

"Then please, just go."

"I can't do that," Gash replied. "The moment I leave, you'd just call the police and I'd have no chance at all of finding Mr. Baskin. You two ladies will be my insurance policy. If Clark Baskin is not at his ancestral manse, then maybe we can put our heads together and puzzle out where else he might be." He smiled amiably.

"But I don't know anything about him."

"Then you can just come along for the ride. It's a beautiful day, the sun's shining. Nice day for a drive." Then, the mockingly happy tone vanished, his voice becoming harder again. "So come on, let's go."

Dora quickly hit "Send" on the e-mail message that she had hastily composed while Gash had been distracted by Bridget.

§

Clark was exhausted. His discouragement was overwhelming. He had been scouring the cabin for a couple of hours and he still hadn't found anything remotely resembling a deed.

And he felt as if he were getting sick. The smoke was getting to him, as was the dry summer heat. Sweat kept pouring down his face in rivulets, burning his eyes which were already irritated from the smoke. His clothes were soaked with sweat, and he was feeling a little delirious.

Knowing that smoke rises, he had started putting boxes down on the floor as he looked through them. But that just added to his discomfort as his joints now ached from being in an uncomfortable position.

He paused, taking a moment to rest, and he leaned back against the dusty old bed. Easing his joints, he let out his breath and relaxed a little.

His life had been such a waste.

He had been selfish in so many ways – using girls, and later, women, just to satisfy his own selfish appetites; stealing and swindling money; gambling. He had been a shitty landlord, a cheating husband, a terrible father.

And a murderer.

Seventy-three years old and his whole life was a total waste. He couldn't think of anything that he had done that he could point to with pride.

Except Dora.

Dora was a truly good and beautiful person. But then, he realized that he couldn't take credit for her either. Clark had not been around much, and when he was, he wasn't a father. He certainly hadn't been an influence on her.

He remembered, again with regret, the time before they moved in late 1986, after one of his stupid losses, when little Dorie was trying to help him pack. She had been about to start unloading the cabinet in the garage that held various paints, glues and finishes.

It also held the cyanide that he had used to kill his father. Clark panicked and slapped her.

He could still see the hurt look on her little face as she ran inside crying.

Clark pulled his knees up in front of him and buried his head in his arms, as he shook his head and cried.

Even in recent years, he hadn't learned from his past mistakes. After walking out on Vanessa and Dorie, he had headed out to Atlantic City. It hadn't been a complete waste. He did win occasionally. But he had lost more than he had won.

Rather than learning his lesson, though, Clark kept it up, with the help of black market lenders – loan sharks. Looking back now with an uncharacteristic honesty, he could scarcely believe how stupid he had been.

He was in over his head, with little chance of ever being able to resurface.

A year ago, he had seen the news about Dora. Knowing that his own mother had been killed touched his heart. He had always loved Isadora. But that coin collection was what really made the national news, and grabbed his attention.

And what does Dora do with it? Sells it for millions of dollars, and then gives the money away.

Clark really couldn't fault her for that. She was a good person. He wasn't.

But then, when he saw the national news on Wednesday morning, the story about the fire, it triggered a memory. Black Forest. Clark suddenly remembered his father's old cabin. He remembered how, for so many years now, it had just been used for storage of things that the family didn't need. Including the deed for the Victoria Mine that his father hadn't been able to bring himself to work. A mine that had been producing well before being closed down. A gold mine could certainly help him out of his slump.

Without giving it a second thought, Clark got into his old beater, his smoking Datsun, and started heading west. He didn't have the money for a plane ticket, but he could manage a few tanks of gas. He knew that Jersey Joe Johnson would be pissed, to say the least, but if it all turned out the way he hoped, there would be no problem.

Clark didn't know why Jersey Joe had loaned him as much as he did. Apparently Clark had been particularly persuasive about the tip he had received. Thirty-five thousand dollars wasn't an enormous sum. In fact, he remembered, it was the amount of his first big win back when he was in college. But when Clark's "sure thing" turned out to be a bust, it was a hell of a lot more than he would be able to pay back.

Clark had been watching the news on Wednesday morning, his deadline for paying back the money in just a couple of hours. Feeling completely hopeless, he was seriously thinking about where he could get a gun, to blow his brains out.

When suddenly, the news of a destructive and devastating fire gave him hope.

§

They were in Gash's rental car, the Lincoln. Gash sat in the back seat, so he could keep his eyes on both Dora and Bridget, and keep his gun pointed at them. Dora was driving.

As they came down into Colorado Springs, they could see the smoke ahead and to the left. The sky looked overcast. There had been no rain in the weather forecast, so the smoke was obviously spreading.

Traffic was fairly heavy going through town. It was the noon hour on a Friday, and people were out and about for lunch, so their progress was slow.

Dora just wished they could get this ordeal over with.

She didn't know what was going to happen. Obviously Gash Seever was up to no good. In the back of Dora's mind was the thought that her no-good father had gotten himself – and now, Dora and Bridget as well – into this, and whatever happened to him would be well-deserved.

At the same time, he was her father. Asshole or not, she didn't want him to be gunned down by some gangland thug. And what were the chances that Gash would just let Dora and Bridget go free. The Irish thugs she had dealt with the year before weren't about to. She didn't expect that American gangsters would be any more merciful.

Once they were able to head northeast on Highway 24, their progress was faster. It had taken them nearly a half hour just to get this far, and Dora was becoming anxious. Here, there wasn't as much traffic, since they were now approaching the area that had been evacuated.

Eventually, they came to Elbert Road, but there were barricades and police cars.

"Don't try anything," Gash said quietly. Dora drove past.

Eventually, she turned onto Bradshaw Road, which initially headed straight west. The wall of smoke directly ahead of them was ominous, and even though Dora knew that, in time, they were going to get even closer to it, she was glad when Bradshaw Road curved to the north, getting the fire out of their direct line of sight.

Out here it was mostly fields, punctuated by widely scattered farm houses. Dora was being particularly observant, watching for a way into the evacuation area, and so she saw the broken and sagging barbed wire to her left, the tire tracks into the field. She filed it away as a possibility, if she couldn't find another way.

But she did. She managed to make several turns, taking lesser used back roads, doubling back at times, and finally found herself inside the evacuation zone. Here, she punched the address of the cabin into the GPS unit in the dashboard.

The directions given took them west, closer to the dense wall of smoke, and at last they pulled up at the cabin, with

Clark's junker parked in front. The miasma of smoke was hanging so densely around them that they could hardly see the structure through the dusky haze. The forest behind it was grey, all of the color filtered out by the smoke in the air.

Dora knew that, if they didn't get shot in the next few minutes, they would likely die from smoke inhalation.

§

"Well, I think that just about does it," Shawn said, relieved. Collin, his brother, smiled as he sat back in his chair.

"Remind me never to take on an estate with two executors again," he said.

The two executors were sisters, daughters of the decedent, who had started feuding over the estate a week after hiring Shawn and Colin's company. Much of the work that they had already done was in danger of being undone. With an auction scheduled for tomorrow, Saturday, Shawn and Colin had to employ a great deal of diplomacy, and had drawn up multiple documents to try to help the sisters reach an agreement.

With the signed forms in front of them now, delivered by messenger a few minutes before, Shawn and Colin were finally able to breathe easy.

Shawn smiled as he rubbed his eyes. It had been hard work, but it was a wealthy, high-profile estate. Settling it should bring good money, and more business, to their door. It was a pain in the ass, but he was glad they got the gig.

He stood up from his chair and stretched his back. It was past lunch time and he was feeling hungry.

"How does a pizza sound?" he asked. "I could call Hell's Kitchen and have one delivered."

"Sure. You buying?" Colin asked.

Shawn scoffed.

"We just settled the estate from hell, and you want to pinch pennies on lunch? Damn cheapskate."

Colin smiled but didn't refute the accusation.

Shawn pawed through the documents scattered on their work table, then he remembered that he had left his phone in his office. He found it on his desk and picked it up. He was about to pull up Hell's Kitchen's number from his list of favorites, when he saw the icon that told him he had e-mail.

But they were hungry. E-mail can wait.

§

Approaching the cabin, Dora could see flickers of light behind it, giving a sort of glittering effect. Squinting her eyes against the heat and the burning of the smoke, she tried to focus. There were flames visible through the roiling smoke.

She wasn't moving fast enough, though, and Gash Seever poked her in the back with his pistol. They continued toward the door. It didn't open. There were boxes and scattered items in front of it. Dora leaned against it and pushed it open.

As they walked in, the first thing that caught her attention was the assortment of boxes, papers and miscellaneous stuff scattered all across the floor. The cabin was full of smoke, but the air was at least a little clearer than it was outside. Then, ahead, she saw her father on the floor, leaning back against an old bed. She couldn't tell if he was breathing.

"Aw, shit," Gash said as he saw Clark on the floor. "Won't get any money out of him now."

In that moment, Dora realized that perhaps their predicament had not been quite as dire as she had originally thought. Gash wasn't necessarily here to kill her father but to collect money. But now, her father was dead.

Feeling a surge of familial love, Dora ran to his side. And he opened his eyes.

"Dorie," he said, and he struggled to sit up.

"It's okay, Dad," Dora said, putting her hand on his shoulder. He relaxed and leaned back against the bed again.

"Oh, so you *didn't* kick the bucket," Gash said, closing the door and coming forward.

His voice was somewhat muffled. The pistol was still in his right hand, and with his left hand, he held a handkerchief over his mouth and nose. He goaded Bridget ahead of him with the muzzle of the pistol.

At the sound of his voice, Clark tried to focus on him.

"Who are you?" he asked.

"Doesn't matter who I am. I'm here on behalf of your creditor, Joe Johnson. He's not too happy that you skipped out of town owing him money."

"I wasn't skipping out," Clark said, his voice little more than a croak. "I'm looking for something. If I can find it, it can help me pay back Jersey Joe."

"Come on, Baskin, you quietly slip out of town on the day your debt was due, you don't tell anyone where you're going, or even *that* you're going. Mr. Johnson wasn't very happy about that."

"I know. You're right. I shouldn't have done that. But if I *had* said anything, he wouldn't have let me go."

"So, what are you looking for? Where is it?"

Clark sighed and put his head back.

"I can't find it. I've looked in every damn box in here."

"What is it, Dad?" Dora asked softly.

Clark looked at her with shame in his eyes.

"It's the deed to a gold mine."

"The Victoria Mine?" she asked.

"Yes," he said, sitting up again. "How did you know?"

"I have it. It's at home."

"Well, you stupid bitch," Gash said. "Why the hell didn't you say anything about that when we were there?"

"What?" Dora turned on him angrily. "You mean back when you forced your way into my house, threatening us with a gun? Sorry, I was a little distracted then, trying to keep us from getting shot. Besides, you said you were looking for my father, not a mine."

"Okay, okay. Just calm yourself down."

Down low where Dora was squatting beside Clark, it was a little easier to breathe, but still the smoke was getting to Dora. She coughed and then continued.

"No, I'm not going to calm myself down. You've been bullying Bridget and me for a couple of hours now."

Hearing Bridget's name, Clark turned, looking through the smoke, trying to see her.

"You've forced us to come here," Dora continued, "and judging by the smoke and the increasing noise of the fire outside the cabin, we're probably going to die here."

She noticed that, along with the stifling heat inside the cabin, the back wall was starting to turn black.

"Well," Gash replied, "I'm not ready to die just yet. But I *will* take that gold mine. So come on. Let's go get that deed."

Dora sighed and tried to help her father to his feet.

"Forget him," Gash commanded. "The son of a bitch is half dead anyway. You ladies come with me."

"I'm not leaving my father here to die."

"You'll do as you're told or I'll put a bullet in your pretty head. We don't have time." Gash leaned over and grabbed Dora by the arm, dragging her to her feet.

She struggled and managed to hit him in the eye. Gash was startled and let go of her, but he swung his right hand, hitting her above the ear with the butt of his pistol.

Dora fell to the floor, dazed. Gash looked at her and rubbed his eye.

"Goddamn bitch!" he growled.

While Gash's attention was on Dora, Clark managed to pull himself to his feet. There was a dusty old grey axe handle on the floor and he picked it up. He raised it and started to swing it toward Gash's head. But as he was moving toward Gash, his foot bumped against one of the boxes on the floor. Hearing the sound, Gash turned and fired.

Clark fell with a bullet in his chest, blood pumping out of the wound. Bridget screamed, but the scream ended with a hacking cough. Dora pulled herself up onto her hands and knees beside Clark.

When Clark fell, Bridget, in a panic, had started pounding on Gash's back. He cowered at first under her blows, putting his hand up to shield his head and face, then he turned to push her away.

"Dorie, honey," Clark whispered, apparently oblivious to the altercation taking place just a few feet away. "I'm so sorry. For everything."

"Don't worry, Dad," she said. Tears trickled down her cheeks, leaving trails through the soot on her face. "We'll get you out of here."

Even before she finished speaking, though, his eyes seemed to lose their focus, and he was still.

Dora, seeing her father dead in front of her, was suddenly touched by emotions she hadn't felt in years. But she quickly became aware again of her surroundings.

"I've just about had it with you," she heard Gash say. He had pushed Bridget off of him and back against the door. He raised the pistol toward her.

Seeing the axe handle lying on the floor beside her father, Dora picked it up and, moving faster than Clark had, swung it hard, grunting as she hit Gash on the shoulder.

It was not a debilitating blow by any means. Gash, feeling his impatience increasing, turned toward Dora. The axe handle had bounced off of his shoulder and Dora made good use of the momentum to swing it up and around again, like a baseball bat. Increasing its force, she caught him full in the chest as he turned.

Again, while it caused Gash some pain, it would not have been a fatal blow, except that it knocked him off balance. He fell against the now fiery back wall of the tiny cabin. The wall offered little resistance as it crumbled in a cloud of ash and charred, kindling-dry wood. Gash fell through, into the blazing inferno, splinters of the dry wood erupting in sparks around him.

The fire, already climbing up the back wall of the cabin, instantly set Gash on fire. He screamed and writhed for only a moment before his body was lost among the ash and the scorched remnants of the forest.

§

"We're past the lunch rush," Shawn told Colin, "so it should only be about thirty minutes."

"Good, I'm starving," Colin replied.

Shawn now took this opportunity to check his e-mail.

There were a few inevitable pieces of junk mail. It seemed as if a lot of higher-ups in foreign countries wanted to give him large sums of money, if he would only supply them with his bank information. Shawn deleted the e-mails. Some other helpful and caring people wanted to help him enlarge his penis and be irresistible to women. He sighed as he deleted those e-mails, too.

The last one, though, looked odd. The subject line simply said, "Hostages!" It was from Dora.

Thinking it was probably one of the clever joke e-mails that she occasionally sent him, he opened it with a smile.

He stopped smiling as he read the short message.

It simply said, "Taken by armed man. Call police!"

That was followed by an address he didn't recognize.

An address in Black Forest, Colorado.

"I have to go," he yelled to Colin, as he ran out the door toward his car, already punching 911 on his phone.

§

With the back wall of the cabin open to the fire now, the flames were quickly gaining ground inside the dry and dusty structure. Dora and Bridget were blasted by the intense furnace-like heat, and it was suddenly even harder to breathe, since whatever oxygen was left in the cabin was now being depleted by the fire.

Dora struggled across the cabin toward Bridget, who had collapsed in front of the door where Gash had pushed her. Dora's eyes were constantly tearing from the smoke, and she felt as if her skin was on fire and her lungs were about to explode. She pushed boxes out of her way as she dragged her protesting body along the floor.

She reached Bridget and, inches from her face, she could see that she was unconscious but she was still alive. However, she was still partially sitting back against the door. Dora tried to push her away, so she could pull the door open, but the effort was too exhausting.

Bridget slipped to her side, and Dora fell down beside her, her face against the gaping threshold under the door.

§

"I don't know how they got there!" Shawn was yelling into his phone. "I don't know *if* they got there, but she said an armed man took her hostage to that address!"

He was driving through town, much faster than he should have, but he was afraid for Dora.

"Well, sir, as you probably know, that address is well inside the evacuation area. In fact, it's very near the fire itself."

"Yes, I'm aware of that. Isn't there anything you can do?"

"Obviously, we have police and fire units in the area. I will dispatch someone to that address. And I'll check to see if anybody has been detained at any of the roadblocks."

"Thank you!"

§

A constant current of air wafted under the door, sucked in by the vacuum the fire was creating. It was still smoky, but it revived Dora just a bit, enough that she was able to pull herself up to her hands and knees. Reaching up, she clutched at the doorknob and pulled herself a little higher. This gave her more leverage as she tried to push Bridget out of the way.

When Dora felt Bridget slipping away from the door, she tried the knob. The door suddenly swung open and Dora fell over on her back, feeling the new current of air as it was being sucked in through the open doorway toward the fire.

The new source of air inside the cabin fanned the flames, and they started rushing faster toward the door. Dora pulled herself up again and looked back.

The fire had already consumed her father's body.

Dora grabbed the back of Bridget's collar and pulled her around. Supporting herself on her knees and one hand, Dora tugged at Bridget. Free now of the obstructions littering the inside of the cabin, her body slid a little easier, and Dora pulled her toward the door. Her lungs and throat burning, she coughed with every inhalation, and pulling herself and another person required all the energy she could muster.

Down the single wooden step, once they were on the ground, it was harder to move. The rocky texture caused more resistance, and Dora's strength was quickly draining away.

Barely five feet outside the cabin door, she fell, her hand still grasping Bridget's collar.

Flames climbed the doorframe as the burning roof collapsed into what was left of the cabin. Outside the charred framework, the fire advanced across the dry pine needles and brush on the ground, toward the two unconscious women.

§

A lone police car hurtled along the empty road, pulling into a long, rutted dirt driveway. Squinting to see through the smoke, Officer Tyrone Hemmings, a big African-American, hunched over a little as he tried to see through his windshield. He could just make out a black heap that looked as if it used to be a small building of some kind. It was fully engulfed in flames.

There were two cars parked in front of the advancing fire, one a shiny new Lincoln, the other a very old Datsun. The flames were already blistering what paint was left on the Datsun, and the car was sitting at a strange angle, tilted a bit to one side, as the tires on the side of the fire had already melted.

To the left of the cars, just in front of the burnt structure, were two forms on the ground. It looked as if the flames were just inches away from them.

Hemmings got out of his car and ran to them. Both were unconscious, one of them obviously having dragged the other one out. But now, the flames were licking at the shoes of the woman closest to the cabin.

Hemmings slipped his hands under her shoulders, dislodging the hand of the other woman from her collar, and pulled her away, half carrying, half dragging her, behind his car. Then he went back for the other woman, as he struggled for breath in the stifling smoke.

Once the women were sheltered with him behind his car, he took a moment before his voice gave out to rasp into his mic a request for fire fighters and an ambulance at his location.

§

The first thing Dora noticed was the feeling of cool drops of water on her face. She opened her eyes and found herself on an ambulance gurney. The afternoon sky overhead was dark, and it was starting to rain.

She had an oxygen mask over her mouth and nose, and her throat felt as if she had swallowed a handful of hot sand but didn't have any water to wash it down. There was a bandage wrapped around her head, with a dressing over her ear where Gash had hit her with his pistol, and there was an IV snaking into her arm.

She ached with every little movement she made.

Dora turned her head a little and Shawn came into sight. His face looked worried, but he smiled when he saw that she was conscious.

In her line of sight, also, was Bridget on a similar gurney, with the EMTs still gathered around her.

Behind them, in the distance, was the black heap of the cabin among blackened skeletal trees. At this location, the forest ended at the back of the cabin. While the fire continued a little ways beyond it, feeding on the grass and brush, a couple of firefighters who had been called to assist with the rescue were easily getting it put out at this point.

Dora pointed at Bridget. Shawn followed her gesture, then he turned back to Dora.

"She's going to be alright. So are you."

A policeman, a big African-American a full head taller than Shawn, approached when he noticed that Dora was awake.

"Oh, Dora," Shawn said, turning to include the policeman in the conversation, "this is Officer Hemmings. He's the one who pulled you and your friend away from the fire."

Dora pulled the mask off her face and lifted her other hand toward Hemmings. He took her hand.

"Thank you," Dora said in barely a whisper. Hemmings nodded and smiled.

"The dispatch said you were taken hostage by an armed man?" he said hoarsely.

Dora nodded.

"He's dead, in the cabin." She looked up at Shawn. "So is my father."

Shawn looked at her, full of empathy, and squeezed her other hand.

The rain started falling harder, and two of the EMTs rushed to get Bridget in the ambulance. The other two separated from them and got Dora into hers. Shawn climbed in after her.

"It wasn't supposed to rain today," Dora whispered.

"I know, baby," Shawn said. "Maybe things are looking up."

I still don't understand why you wanted me dress up this afternoon," Bridget said. "I mean, I know you saved my life and all that, so I suppose I *am* obligated to do whatever you ask of me. But I just think it seems rather silly for me to be sitting here in me pinafore."

On a Friday in August, they sat in the sunroom at the back of Dora's B&B, sipping glasses of chardonnay, watching the rain outside. Two months after their traumatic experience at the cabin, they had become good friends.

"I didn't tell you to dress up," Dora replied, "I just said to wear something nice. Besides, I don't know what you're bitching about. I think you look adorable."

Despite her previous remarks, Bridget's face beamed at the compliment.

They each had spent a couple of days in the hospital being treated for acute smoke inhalation, before being assigned to rest at home. Shawn made it a point to be at the B&B in the mornings to help Robin with breakfast, and they each made arrangements to their schedules to help Dora at other times.

Bridget had asked a neighbor to help her out a little at first, but as she recovered, she was spending more time with Dora.

"Oh!" Bridget exclaimed, "I just remembered, I have your book in me handbag." She reached into her large shoulder bag, on the floor at her feet, pulled out a paper-wrapped bundle, and handed it to Dora.

"You finished reading Isadora's journal?"

"I did. It was fascinating. Thank you so much." Bridget spoke in such an animated manner which, combined with her accent, often made Dora smile while listening to her. "That really filled in a lot of gaps in the research I did years ago."

The bundle also contained the newspaper clippings that Dora had included, about the misadventures that she and Shawn had experienced with an old Irish criminal organization last year.

"Almost getting killed twice in one year's time," Bridget continued. "I'm not sure I should be your friend. You seem to live a dangerous life."

"I think I'm ready for a little less danger myself," Dora laughed.

They were interrupted by a knock at the front door. Dora got up from her chair with a self-satisfied smile on her face.

"I'll be right back," she said.

Bridget heard muffled voices from the front of the house, and in a minute's time, Dora returned with a pretty, well-dressed young lady who was folding up a wet umbrella.

"Bridget Lindstrom, I'd like for you to meet Geneva Parker," she said. "She lives up in Monument. She's your daughter."

Bridget gasped and was immediately on her feet, tears in her eyes. She hesitated at first, waiting to see Geneva's reaction, but the young woman spread her arms wide, her own eyes glistening as well. The women embraced, as Dora smiled behind them.

She picked up a box of tissues from the end table beside her chair and placed it on the coffee table in front of the love seat, where Bridget had been sitting. She took a tissue for herself as well.

The two women separated and, each pulling a tissue from the box, sat down on the love seat. Bridget looked at Dora with disbelief in her eyes.

"How did you do this?" she asked.

"You know I volunteer for an orphanage and adoption agency. I told you I was familiar with various methods of reconnecting."

"I know, but I remember when you helped me register with Soundex, you told me it would probably take a long time."

The International Soundex Reunion Registry is a free mutual consent service, maintained by donations, that seeks to reunite separated family members, including those separated by adoption.

"I said it *could* take a long time," Dora replied, dabbing at her eyes. "If the other person hasn't registered, a reunion can't take place. But Geneva had registered a few years ago. In that case, the results were almost immediate."

"I had all but given up on finding my birth mother," Geneva said. "Then I was contacted and told that she lives just a few miles away."

Dora heard the sound of the front door opening and closing, and she got up from her chair.

"I know you both have a lot to catch up on," she said, "so I'll leave you to that. Just relax here as long as you like."

Bridget and Geneva both gave her teary-eyed smiles as she left the room. Dora went into the kitchen where she heard Shawn moving around. His shoes and the bottom of his pant legs were wet.

"Hi sweetie," he said.

"Hi. Glad to see you didn't wash away."

"It's a wonder I didn't," he said. "It's flooding down in town."

"Flooding?"

"Yeah, the rain is running down the hill from the Waldo Canyon fire we had last year. With the vegetation gone, there's nothing to slow it down, so it's just washing all the mud and ash down Fountain Creek."

"God, why can't we just have a normal season instead of this James Taylor summer?"

"James Taylor summer?"

"Fire and rain."

Shawn smiled. Hearing voices, he nodded in the direction of the sunroom. "The reunion still going on?"

"Yes, Geneva just got here."

Shawn kissed Dora and held her in his arms.

"Little miss do-gooder," he said warmly. Dora snuggled against his chest. After a few moments, she pulled away, noticing a file folder on the countertop.

"What's this?" she asked.

"Oh, just my research on your gold mine." He opened the folder and leafed through the papers. "You have a couple of different options. Three if you want to consider working the mine yourself."

Dora wrinkled her nose and shook her head.

"You can sell it outright. The Gold Prospectors Association of America owns and operates gold mines across the country. You can contact them to see if they're interested in buying it, or you can put an ad in the *Prospecting and Mining Journal.*

"The other option is to lease the claim. You would basically rent the mine to somebody who wants to work it. They would keep whatever gold they find during the term, while you would still retain ownership of the mine and collect rent from them."

"Hmm," Dora said as she looked at the papers Shawn gave her. "I'm not sure I want to be a landlord. Seems like a lot of trouble. Finding good tenants, doing repairs, dealing with disgruntled neighbors after loud parties."

Shawn snorted at her.

"I've got enough going on here, with the B&B," Dora continued as she put the papers back in the folder. "And I do have an upcoming wedding to finance. I think I'd just like to sell the mine and be done with it."

"Sounds good to me," Shawn replied.

Dora looked at Shawn thoughtfully.

"Do you think anybody would think less of me if I kept the money this time?"

www.ingramcontent.com/pod-product-compliance
Lightning Source LLC
Chambersburg PA
CBHW050600260626
47157CB00002B/640